# AMBERWELL

Amberwell is the name of an estate on the west coast of Scotland which has been in the Ayrton family for several generations descending from father to son in an unbroken line. It was a tradition in the family that each new owner should add to the amenities of the place and in this way Amberwell grew larger and more beautiful as the years went by and was endowed with gardens and terraces and orchards.

The story is concerned with the five young Ayrtons who grew up at Amberwell and played in the gardens and then ventured forth into the world, but the " hero " of the story is Amberwell itself. To each of the children Amberwell meant something different; it influenced their thoughts and moulded their lives.

D. E. STEVENSON

# *Amberwell*

COLLINS
ST JAMES'S PLACE, LONDON
1955

PRINTED IN GREAT BRITAIN
COLLINS CLEAR-TYPE PRESS: LONDON AND GLASGOW

# PART ONE

*When the voices of children are heard on the green,*
*And laughing is heard on the hill.*

WILLIAM BLAKE

# CHAPTER ONE

WILLIAM AYRTON was born in Edinburgh in 1745. It was a stormy year in the capital of Scotland but the storms did not affect the Ayrton family, for William's father was a wine merchant with a comfortable business which was his chief concern. He was a merchant, not a politician, and as long as he could buy good wine and sell it to his customers at a profit he cared little who sat upon the throne. He steered a careful course through the angry seas and his business thrived exceedingly so he was able to give his elder children a good start in life. William was the seventh child, and an unexpected addition to the family, so by the time he grew to man's estate there was no money left to launch him on a career. He had nothing to depend upon but his own energy and capabilities—fortunately he had plenty of both.

It seemed to young William that India offered him the best chance of making his fortune (in those days India was a mysterious land, a land full of gold and jewels and fabulous riches) so to India he went, working his passage upon a trading-ship and meeting with hair-raising adventures on the way.

At first it seemed to William that India was disappointing and he realised that it offered no easy road to wealth but he was clever and very persevering, he worked hard and used his brain, and after some years of struggle he became a partner in an export firm and settled down to make his fortune in good earnest.

From his earliest days William Ayrton's ambition had

been to become a landed gentleman and to found a family. To modern ears this ambition may sound peculiar in the extreme, but in the more spacious times of William Ayrton it was a laudable ambition and not in the least unusual; in fact many respectable families were founded in the same way, by a man of parts with initiative and foresight.

Time rolled on and money rolled in until, at the age of fifty, William Ayrton had amassed sufficient capital to retire from business and carry out his plan. By now he had a wife and three children, so the family was well under way, and the only problem to be solved was where to buy his land and build his house.

After some discussion the Ayrtons decided to settle in the South West of Scotland (the Ayrton family had its roots in that part of the country) and having found a delightful site they engaged a young architect who was willing to carry out their ideas. Mr. Ayrton had very definite ideas as to what he wanted; he had thought about his house and dreamt about this house since he was a boy.

The property was situated in a fold of the hills and sloped gently down to the sea. It consisted of meadows and a little wood and some moor-land; there was a well, built of glowing yellow stone, which was fed by a spring and was always full of ice-cold water. The water itself was as clear as crystal but the reflection of the stone gave it the appearance of amber . . . it was this well which gave the property its name, Amberwell.

To William Ayrton one of the chief attractions of his new home was the water, for having spent nearly thirty years in India he valued water—and especially crystal-clear water—very highly indeed. Another attraction was the sheltered position and the mild climate which would enable him to grow sub-tropical plants. Mrs. Ayrton approved of Amberwell too, but for other reasons. It was delightfully secluded but not too isolated; just over the hill lay the little town of Westkirk—a pleasant little town with good shops and an efficient doctor. There were several charming properties in the vicinity, so they would not lack neighbours. Mrs. Ayrton could find no fault with her husband's choice. This being so the matter was settled, he bought the land and built his house.

There was nothing pretentious about Amberwell House, it was comfortable and commodious and fitted in with its surroundings; the gardens were laid out with good judgment; there was stabling for four horses, a coachhouse and several cottages. Amberwell was by no means a palace but it was definitely " a place " and its owner was well satisfied with it. Mr. Ayrton's family was equally satisfactory; six children grew up at Amberwell.

2

The gardens had been designed with a view to the future and as the years passed and Ayrton succeeded Ayrton various improvements were carried out. It became a tradition in the family that each new owner should make some definite contribution to the amenities of the place. Roger Ayrton made a walled garden for fruit and vegetables and put up greenhouses in a sheltered corner. In one of the greenhouses he planted a vine with his own hands—there was a pleasant little ceremony on this occasion. Stephen Ayrton laid out a bowling-green and surrounded it with a fine yew hedge. At one end of the broad lawn he made a raised grass platform, like a stage, with a stone balustrade and two wide steps leading up to it, so that those who were not taking part could sit there comfortably and watch the hotly contested ends. Gentlemen came from far and wide to enjoy a game of bowls with Stephen Ayrton and on summer afternoons the ladies would join the party and tea would be served on the little stage. A delightful watercolour sketch of one of these alfresco gatherings still hangs in the morning-room of Amberwell House.

After Stephen came Henry who had gone out to America in early youth and made a packet of money in land development. When he inherited Amberwell he returned with large ideas and set to work without delay to improve his property. Henry was extremely up to date (for his times); he put in gas and hot water pipes all over the house. He built a stone terrace outside the drawing-room windows; he planted an orchard; and, still not content, he built a small Episcopal Church upon a piece of his own land which adjoined Westkirk . . . and at the same time he built a rectory for the incumbent. The church was a memorial to his father and was dedicated to St. Stephen. Henry then settled down to enjoy the fruits of his labours, he died at the age of ninety-four and was succeeded by his son, William Henry.

By this time Amberwell had become old-fashioned and William the Second proceeded to modernise it completely. He installed electric light and an adequate number of bathrooms. In addition to these much-needed improvements he had the well thoroughly cleaned and repaired. In the old days all the drinking-water had been drawn from the well but for many years now the practice had been discontinued. William Ayrton had intended to revert to the practice, but when he saw the collection of strange objects which were dug up from the bottom he decided that mainwater from a tap would be more hygienic. Still he was glad the well was repaired, for even if it were not useful it was extremely ornamental.

In this way Amberwell had grown and spread and under

the cherishing care of its owners the gardens had become one of the beauty-spots of the district.

When William the Third inherited the property in 1924 one of the first things he thought of was his contribution to its amenities, but it was several years before he could decide what to do. He had been born at Amberwell and, during his childhood when his parents were abroad, he and his sisters had lived with their grandfather. They had dwelt securely in Amberwell House and had played in Amberwell gardens and to him the whole place seemed perfect. How were you to improve something which was already perfect?

The nurseries at Amberwell were on the top floor; they were large sunny rooms, somewhat shabby as regards furniture, but extremely comfortable. The nursery flat was complete in itself with its own bathroom and its own staircase leading down to the garden. Generations of Ayrtons had inhabited these rooms and from them had been promoted to the drawing-room. As they grew up in stature they came down and took their places in the adult world. Sometimes the nurseries were full (for the Ayrtons believed in large families and liked to make sure that they would have no cause to be ashamed when they met their enemies at the gate); sometimes, for a while, the nurseries were empty. Then, as another generation came into its own, the nurseries would be full again.

The third Mr. William Ayrton had five children. Roger and Thomas were the children of his first wife (who had died when Thomas was born); Constance, Elinor and Anne were the daughters of his second wife—the present Mrs. Ayrton.

When Constance was born she was welcomed with enthusiasm by both her parents—it was delightful to have a little girl—but when her second daughter arrived Mrs.

Ayrton was disappointed. Her third daughter was a disaster (there was no other word for it in Mrs. Ayrton's opinion) for not only was the child of the wrong sex but she was positively ugly; a thin puling baby with a curiously broad forehead and no hair at all. Mrs. Ayrton took one look at the new arrival and then turned her head and wept.

" She's a nice little baby," said the nurse.

" No," said Mrs. Ayrton between her sobs.

" Perhaps it will be a boy next time."

" No," said Mrs. Ayrton.

She had made up her mind there was to be no " next time." Three babies in three years was enough. If she could have been certain that the next one would be a son . . . but it might be another girl . . . she was not going to risk it.

Soon after this Mr. Ayrton's father died and the family moved to Amberwell and settled down. The children knew the place already for they had often stayed with their grand-parents. They had stayed at Amberwell for family weddings and christenings—which always took place at St. Stephen's—they had been sent to Amberwell with Nannie to recover from mumps and whooping-cough. Amberwell was HOME.

3

The William Ayrtons had been settled at Amberwell for years and still Mr. Ayrton had not made up his mind what he could do to increase the value of his property. All sorts of suggestions had been offered by various members of his family but none of them seemed right. Of course Mr. Ayrton had already spent a good deal of money upon Amberwell; he had decorated the drawing-room and modernised the kitchen premises; the avenue, which was nearly half a mile long, had been remade, but these improvements, though necessary, were not exactly spectacular. He wanted to leave his mark upon Amberwell for future generations to see.

Mrs. Ayrton understood this; she had been thinking about it seriously and although she agreed with her husband that Amberwell was very beautiful she was of the opinion that a lily-pool would enhance its attractions. Nobody had suggested a lily-pool, and the matter called for a great deal of tact. Mrs. Ayrton knew that unless her husband could be made to think that a lily-pool was his own idea he would not consider it for a moment.

It was early June. Dinner was over and dessert was on the table (a silver dish of scarlet strawberries which had been forced under glass, another dish of walnuts and a third of small russet apples—their skins a trifle wrinkled for they were last year's, of course). Mr. and Mrs. Ayrton were alone in the quiet dining-room the windows of which were opened on to the terrace. The dinner had been unusually good and Mrs. Ayrton felt the moment was propitious.

"I was wondering whether you had decided definitely what you were going to do," said Mrs. Ayrton. "You said something about a lily-pool, didn't you? But perhaps an orchid-house would be better. I had a letter from Beatrice this morning; she thinks a rose-garden would be delightful. A rose-garden with a sun-dial——"

"Beatrice has nothing to do with it!" exclaimed Mr. Ayrton.

"No, of course not."

There was a silence for a few moments, broken only by the crack of walnuts.

"I believe a lily-pool would be best," said Mr. Ayrton at last. "As a matter of fact I can't remember why we turned it down."

Mrs. Ayrton said nothing.

"We could put it in the middle of the smaller lawn," continued Mr. Ayrton thoughtfully. "It would look well there, with the grass all round it and the flowering shrubs and trees to make a background."

Fortunately this was exactly the site Mrs. Ayrton had chosen for the lily-pool. "Do you think that would be better than an orchid-house?" she asked in a doubtful tone.

"There's enough glass already," replied Mr. Ayrton.

This was exactly Mrs. Ayrton's view. "Perhaps you're right," she agreed.

"Of course I'm right. Gray has his hands full already. He would want another gardener if we had more glass."

Mrs. Ayrton nodded. "Gray has a good deal to do. He spoke to me this morning about getting another boy. I said I would ask you about it."

"Nonsense!" exclaimed Mr. Ayrton. "He's got two men and a boy. That ought to be enough for a place of this size. Sir Andrew Findlater has three gardeners—that's all—and Stark Place is twice the size of this."

"You had better speak to Gray and tell him we can't afford it," suggested Mrs. Ayrton.

Mr. Ayrton smiled and poured out his second glass of port. "I shall tell him he can't have another boy. There's no need to give any reason. Never explain," added Mr. Ayrton. "It was one of Disraeli's sayings. *Never explain.*"

Mrs. Ayrton had heard this before. Disraeli might have coined the phrase but Mr. Ayrton had made it his own; he had repeated it at least twenty times to her certain knowledge. As a matter of fact she had taken the advice to heart and found it useful. If she had occasion to dismiss a housemaid, for instance, it saved a lot of trouble to dismiss her without any explanation.

But all this had taken Mr. and Mrs. Ayrton away from

the lily-pool and Mrs. Ayrton was anxious to get the matter settled.

"What about a summer-house in the woods?" suggested Mrs. Ayrton. "We could have tea there on fine afternoons."

"We can have tea much more comfortably in the drawing-room."

"Then nothing remains but the rose-garden. Beatrice will be pleased. She has suggested it to me several times and——"

"Beatrice is too fond of offering her advice," declared Mr. Ayrton. "A rose-garden would be very pleasant no doubt but to my mind a lily-pool would be much more original."

"It *would* be more original," agreed Mrs. Ayrton thoughtfully.

"We want something original—something that other people haven't got."

"Yes, of course. Had you thought of having a little fountain in the middle, William?"

The idea of a little fountain had not occurred to William but he saw at once that a lily-pool without a fountain would be a poor sort of affair. "Of course," he said quickly. "We must certainly have a fountain—a stone dolphin, perhaps."

Mrs. Ayrton sighed for she had set her heart upon a mermaid. She could see it in her mind's eye: the graceful figure of a bronze mermaid reclining upon a rock in the centre of the pool with a shell in her hand. The crystal-clear water sprang upwards from the shell and descended in rainbow showers. Yes, it must be a mermaid.

"A stone dolphin would look quite nice," said Mrs. Ayrton, nodding. "I believe I've seen one somewhere. Perhaps it was in Princes Street Gardens. We could find out and have a copy made."

" A copy of a fountain in a public park! " exclaimed Mr. Ayrton in horrified tones. " No, no, Marion, that won't do at all. That won't do for Amberwell. We must think of something absolutely original—something really beautiful."

Mrs. Ayrton made several suggestions but none of them sounded good enough and her husband turned them down.

" We could have a mermaid," said Mrs. Ayrton at last. " But it would have to be in bronze—that's the difficulty."

" Difficulty? " asked Mr. Ayrton. " Why should it be difficult? "

" Well, I've never seen one——"

" All the better. I said we wanted something absolutely original, didn't I? "

" Yes, dear, but——"

" There's no but about it. We'll have a bronze mermaid —nothing could be better. You might write off to Edinburgh to-night and put it in hand."

This was even better than Mrs. Ayrton had expected, it was marvellous. The only trouble was she had no idea where to write. A bronze mermaid is not an article one orders every day. . . .

" Write to-night," repeated Mr. Ayrton. " I suppose you know where to get it."

" I'll ask Beatrice," said Mrs. Ayrton. " I mean we don't want an ordinary mermaid; we shall want it specially made."

Beatrice Ayrton was Mr. Ayrton's sister, she was unmarried and lived in a very comfortable flat in Edinburgh. She was a little trying at times (for she had been born and brought up at Amberwell and was inclined to interfere and to disapprove of any innovations) but Mrs. Ayrton found her useful and bore with her patiently on that account. Beatrice was always willing to undertake any commissions;

to match embroidery silks at Jenners, or to choose frocks
for the little girls. If Mrs. Ayrton had occasion to visit
Edinburgh she could stay with Beatrice for a couple of
nights and, even more convenient, Beatrice would shut up
her flat and come to Amberwell when her presence was
required. It was natural that Mrs. Ayrton should think of
her sister-in-law to help solve the problem of the mermaid.

"Yes," agreed Mr. Ayrton. "Yes, you might ask
Beatrice, but make it clear that we want no advice. As I
said before Beatrice is too ready to offer advice—she always
was. Perhaps the best thing would be for you to make a
little sketch and send it to her."

"A sketch?"

"Just a rough sketch," said Mr. Ayrton encouragingly.
"I'll help you with it. I know exactly how it should look.
A bronze mermaid sitting on a rock in the middle of the
pool . . ."

"With a shell in her hand," murmured Mrs. Ayrton
(who had already made several quite passable sketches of
her idea).

"What did you say?"

"Nothing—really——"

"I can *see* it," declared Mr. Ayrton. "It will look
enchanting."

"Yes, dear, I'm sure it will," Mrs. Ayrton agreed.
"You must show me exactly what you want."

## CHAPTER TWO

AT THE time when Mr. and Mrs. William Ayrton were discussing the lily-pool the five young Ayrtons still inhabited the nursery flat. Anne, the youngest, was now five years old; Elinor and Constance were six and seven. The two boys, Roger and Thomas, were at a preparatory school near Edinburgh so they were only at Amberwell during the holidays; strictly speaking they were too old for the nursery, but Mrs. Ayrton thought them too young to take their proper place downstairs. As a matter of fact they liked the nursery. Nannie had brought them up from babyhood and was proud of them, for they were fine strong well-grown boys. Roger and Thomas could do what they liked with Nannie, they could twist her round their fingers.

During term time, when the boys were at school, nursery life was very quiet. It was a life apart. The children lived in seclusion and knew nothing of what went on downstairs—nothing except what their eyes told them and what they could glean from an occasional chat with the underhousemaid. Miss Clarke came daily from Westkirk and taught the three little girls and although she was strict and made them work when they would rather have been out of doors they were quite fond of her. She was useful too, for the jealousy which existed between Miss Clarke and Nannie was a powerful weapon in their hands. For instance one had only to say wistfully, " Miss Clarke thinks it's too damp for us to play in the gardens," and one's object was achieved.

18

"Nonsense," Nannie would say briskly. "You're not made of sugar. Put on your wellingtons at once."

Nannie was kind and, except for her attitude to the harmless Miss Clarke, she was very sensible. She was small and thin with sandy hair; she moved quickly upon neat feet and she always wore a large, starched apron. Nannie loved babies and sometimes she so longed to hold a tiny baby in her arms—to wash it and feed it and care for its helplessness—that she was tempted to give in her notice and look for another post . . . but on the other hand she loved the Ayrton children and could not make up her mind to leave them. What would happen to them if she left? Like many another capable woman Nannie considered herself indispensable.

Under Nannie's care Anne had grown from a small puling baby into a plump little girl. She was not pretty, or at least nobody thought so. Connie and Nell had fair hair, blue eyes and pink cheeks. Anne was pale; her large grey eyes were set rather wide apart, which gave her a wondering look, her brow was broad and her brown silky hair was always untidy. She was a quiet child, serious for the most part but with an odd little humour of her own. Sometimes at meals when they were sitting round the nursery table Anne would suddenly begin to chuckle and the chuckle would develop into laughter which shook her small plump body to the core. Nannie and Connie and Nell would gaze at her in surprise and ask what was funny, but even if she were able to tell them what had tickled her they could never see anything humorous in the joke.

Every evening when the children were in bed Nannie went downstairs for a chat with Mrs. Duff. They were cronies. Mrs. Duff was about forty-five, plump and cheerful as all good cooks should be, and whereas Nannie was a mere newcomer to Amberwell—having been there only

since the present family had taken up residence—Mrs. Duff
had been born and bred on the estate. Her father had been
coachman to Mr. Ayrton's father and had inhabited the
comfortable cottage in the stableyard. There had been
several years of absence from Amberwell of course when
young Kate Fraser had gone off to service in Edinburgh.
Presumably, she had met Mr. Duff and married him, but
Mrs. Duff was somewhat secretive about this episode in her
career and even Nannie was not sure what actually had
happened. Enough to say Kate returned to Amberwell
with a wedding ring but with no other evidence of her
changed status, she went into the kitchen as kitchen-maid
and in due course became cook.

Nannie and Mrs. Duff sat by the fire in Mrs. Duff's
comfortable sitting-room and drank innumerable cups of
tea and discussed all sorts of things but principally the
affairs of Amberwell. Nannie told Mrs. Duff all that
happened in the nursery—what the children had said and
done and the latest grievance against Miss Clarke—and
Mrs. Duff told Nannie all that had happened in the kitchen
and detailed the delinquencies of the new kitchen-maid.
Sometimes the table-maid and the head-housemaid joined
the party and brought the latest news from the dining-room
and the house, and sometimes Mr. Gray would look in for
a few minutes to drink a cup of tea and report what was
happening in the gardens. It was all very cosy and a great
deal more interesting than the wireless programmes.

Mr. and Mrs. Ayrton would have been surprised if they
could have listened in and heard what was said about their
affairs in Mrs. Duff's comfortable little sitting-room.
Nothing unpleasant was said (Nannie and Mrs. Duff and
Mr. Gray were far too loyal to say anything unpleasant
about their employers), but they knew all that was going
on; everything that was said and done was noted and

reported and discussed. If Mrs. Ayrton bought a new hat
they knew what she had paid for it; if Mr. Ayrton " had
words " with his sister Beatrice (a not infrequent occurrence) they knew the ins and outs of the matter; and they
knew (goodness' knows how) when Mrs. Ayrton's youngest
brother, who was the black sheep of the family, got himself
into trouble with a married woman and had to be extricated
and sent off to Australia at Mr. Ayrton's expense.

Of course they knew all about the lily-pool and the
fountain. Janet, the head-housemaid found several torn-up
sketches in the waste-paper basket and fitting them together
brought them into Mrs. Duff's room. Mr. Gray happened
to be there at the time.

" So it's to be a fountain! " he said. " Well, it's a pity.
I'd have liked an orchid-house——"

" Oh, maircy, it's a naked woman! " exclaimed Mrs.
Duff.

" It's a mermaid," said Nannie. " See, she's got a fish's
tail! There's no need to be shocked about a mermaid."

" That's as may be," declared Mrs. Duff, pursing her
lips. " To my mind a naked woman is a naked woman
whether she's got feet or not."

" I think it's awful pretty," said Janet.

" I wonder where they'll put it," said Mr. Gray thoughtfully. " It'll need pipes and what not. They'll be wanting
to dig up my flower-beds to lay the pipes. . . ."

" You and your gardens! " exclaimed Janet scornfully.

2

The gardens at Amberwell were beautiful at all times of
the year but perhaps at their most beautiful in early June.
There was such a blossoming then, such a pouring out of

colour that it almost took one's breath away. There was laburnum (a whole grove of graceful trees with their golden rain of flowers), there was lilac, white and purple and mauve; there were great bushes of pink and white rhododendrons; there were azaleas and lupins and snow-white may. Beneath the birch trees on the hill was a sea of wild hyacinths (which the English call bluebells) and masses of golden gorse.

But there was beauty in the gardens at all times of the year, even in winter they had their charm. There was always something to be seen: the Christmas roses were scarcely over before the first snowdrop was peeping shyly through the grass.

The show part of the garden was near the house. Outside the drawing-room windows there was a sweep of velvety lawn and a long border which was a blaze of colour from May until October. It was here that Mr. and Mrs. Ayrton liked to walk . . . not so the children. The children avoided this part of the garden like the plague. They preferred to wander in ways untrodden by grown-up feet. The Ayrton children were haunted by a curious feeling of guilt which was apt to make them deceitful. For instance if their parents happened to encounter them and asked what they had been doing Connie and Nell and Anne usually remained dumb or else said, " Nothing—really," for an occupation which seemed perfectly harmless might easily turn out to be a crime. It was very much easier to keep out of the way and their instinct was to hide if they saw their parents coming.

Sometimes the children played on the bowling-green where the tall yew hedges sheltered them from the wind; sometimes they played in the woods; they liked the walled garden with its orderly rows of vegetables and fruit. Mr. Gray was a friend and they spent a good deal of time in his

company, pursuing him into the greenhouses or sitting
upon a little bench in the potting-shed, watching him at
work. Beyond the walled garden the land sloped down to
the shore where they could paddle or bathe or search for
crabs amongst the rocks. There was a tiny cave here,
paved with golden sand, which was a delightful place for
a picnic. The view was superb. Westwards was the coast-
line of Ireland; north-westwards lay Arran and the Mull
of Kintyre. Sometimes the mountains were to be seen
clearly across the sparkling waves of the summer sea, at
other times they were wreathed in mist as if they were
lands in a dream ... and there were days of low cloud
and fog when they disappeared completely and the
waves which lapped upon the yellow sand were languid
and grey.

Just outside the east door of the walled garden, near
the path which led to the woods, there was a huge clump of
mauve rhododendrons. Mr. Gray did not prune it for it
was outwith the gardens proper and being a " common "
rhododendron it was not worth bothering about. Nobody
had bothered about it for years and years so it had spread
to an immense jungle of gnarled old branches and shiny
green leaves.

One day when the children were playing at Indians Tom
had crept into this jungle through a little gap beside the
wall and had discovered a secret hiding-place in the middle
of it. The space was quite large, it was like a tent of green
leaves with an earthen floor. Tom was enchanted with his
find and at first he had decided to keep it a secret from the
other children ... but Tom was kind-hearted and impulsive
and in a few days all five children had been shown the
secret hiding-place. They were all delighted with the
retreat for it was so safe; once inside the jungle nobody
could molest you, not even Mr. Gray. The dim light was

extraordinarily peaceful and the curious smell of damp earth and rotting leaves was enchanting.

Roger had learned from Mr. Gray that this particular kind of rhododendron was called Ponticum, so the secret hiding-place was called Ponticum House. It was used for all sorts of activities and gradually it was furnished with odds and ends of furniture: a couple of wooden stools which Tom found in the attic; a large wooden box which did duty as a table and a receptacle for treasures; a kitchen chair with a broken leg and two square biscuit tins. Roger, who was something of a carpenter, found a board in the potting-shed and nailed it between two gnarled branches to serve as a shelf.

When the boys were away at school Ponticum House became a kind of dolls' house and was used for dolls' tea-parties and such-like feminine ploys, but it was never used for this purpose in the holidays. It was really the boys' place and the boys would have been disgusted to find it cluttered up with dolls.

There was so much to do in Amberwell gardens that the three little girls never wanted to go outside the gates and this was fortunate because they never were taken outside the gates except for an occasional visit to Westkirk to see the dentist or to buy clothes.

Westkirk had not changed much since the first Mrs. William Ayrton had seen it and approved of it. There were no industries to make it grow. The little town consisted of one broad street, where all the best shops had their premises, and several smaller streets which sloped down to the harbour where the fishing-boats lay. Southwards from the harbour there was a sweep of sands and grass-covered hillocks and a row of pleasant residential houses with gardens. Westkirk boasted two churches, the Scottish Presbyterian Church in the High Street and St. Stephen's

Episcopal Church which had been built by Henry Ayrton
on the outskirts of the town.

### 3

Mr. Orme was the present incumbent of St. Stephen's.
He was a very tall man, big-boned, with a thin face and
greying hair. He had come to Westkirk from a parish in
the East End of London where he had nearly worked himself to death. Mr. Orme's intention had been to come to
Westkirk for a rest and then return to the battle, but as
time went by he realised that he was unfit for the front line
and had better remain where he was. If he took things
fairly easily his heart gave him very little trouble, but if he
did more than usual the messenger of Satan gave him a
buffet and laid him out. In Westkirk there was just enough
work to keep him busy; his congregation was small (for
most of the people in the district were Presbyterians) but
he read a good deal and presently began to collect material
for a book. He was never lonely for he walked with God,
but sometimes he became worried because he was far too
comfortable; the Rectory was a delightful little house and
he had an extremely competent housekeeper called Mrs.
Green who looked after him like a mother, bullied him a
little when necessary, prepared the most appetising dishes
imaginable and mended all his clothes. Mr. Orme was
convinced that no man ought to live in such luxury, but
what could he do? It was unthinkable to dismiss Mrs.
Green simply because she was too kind.

One night in June Mr. Orme was called to the bedside
of a ploughman on Sir Andrew Findlater's estate. The
man died very early in the morning and when Mr. Orme
had done what he could to comfort the family he came out

of the little cottage and walked slowly down the hill. He was very tired so he decided to take a short-cut home through the Amberwell gardens. There was no reason why he should not, for he had the Ayrtons' permission to walk in the gardens whenever he pleased.

It was a beautiful morning, cloudless and still, the woods were carpeted with wild hyacinths as blue as the sky. The sun, shining through the pale-green leaves of early summer, patterned the path with gold. Here and there a rhododendron in full flower blazed like a coloured light. What a lovely world it was! So fresh and sweet, so peaceful.

As Mr. Orme came out of the woods he paused for a few minutes beside a mossy stone and looked down at Amberwell House lying amongst its gardens. He wondered what it would feel like to own a place like this, to have so many responsibilities. He did not envy the Ayrtons for it seemed to him that people with heavy responsibilities got more worry than pleasure out of life. For instance he got a great deal of pleasure from the Amberwell gardens; he enjoyed their beauty far more than the Ayrtons and without any worries at all. The Ayrtons took their responsibilities very seriously, they were extraordinarily generous; Mr. Ayrton was always ready to head the list of any subscriptions to the church or to help a deserving case when it was brought to his notice. They were generous not only with money but with fruit and flowers and vegetables from the gardens. They attended church with unfailing regularity and invited Mr. Orme to dine at Amberwell once a month . . . and yet with all this there was something wanting.

Mr. Orme had been here for ten years—yes, it was ten years this month since he had left his London parish and come to St. Stephen's—but he had never got close to Mr. and Mrs. Ayrton, never for one moment had he felt any sort of bond.

Perhaps it is my fault, thought Mr. Orme sadly.

He was still standing there and looking down. It was so early that Amberwell had not awakened; no smoke rose from its chimneys, and even Mr. Gray—who was always out early—had not made his appearance upon the scene. Mr. Orme had the whole world of Amberwell to himself ... but wait! There was a small figure on the bowling-green. It was a fairy!

Mr. Orme was a trifle dazed for he had been awake all night so he rubbed his eyes and looked again. It was not a fairy of course, it was a child—a little girl in a pale grey overall. She was dancing lightly on the emerald-green sward, bending and turning, lifting her arms in a delightful natural pose, hesitating for a moment and then running a few steps and jumping in the air.

Mr. Orme was enchanted. He had been feeling sad and discouraged but the sight of the child's joy and the free-flowing movements of her rounded limbs lifted his heart. After watching her for a few minutes he went down the path and pushed open the gate in the yew hedge.

When the child saw him she turned to run away but he called to her and she stopped obediently and came towards him across the grass. He noticed that her feet were bare and wet with dew and her silky brown hair was in a tangle.

" I thought at first you were a fairy," said Mr. Orme gravely.

" But I'm too fat," she replied, looking up at him with wide, grey eyes.

" Not fat," objected Mr. Orme. " Just right, I think." He hesitated and then added with a surprised inflexion in his voice, " You must be Anne."

The surprised inflexion was due to the fact that he had not seen Anne since she was a baby (he had christened her in St. Stephen's) and that did not seem very long ago to

Mr. Orme. It was amazing to think that this person had developed from that baby . . . and in so short a time. He sat down upon a teak seat and Anne stood in front of him. They looked at each other for a few moments in silence.

" Do you often dance like that? " asked Mr. Orme at last.

" I wake up early. The sun shines in at the window, you see. It makes me not want to stay in bed. Nannie doesn't know. I don't think she'd mind very much—really."

Mr. Orme did not feel qualified to give an opinion on the matter. " Do you know who I am? " he asked.

Anne nodded her head. The soft hair fell over her eyes and she pushed it back. She knew who Mr. Orme was because Nannie had taken all three little girls to a special Children's Service and Mr. Orme had been there, standing up in front of everybody in a white night-gown and talking about God. Mr. Orme knew all about God; he was a very important person.

" Who am I? " asked Mr. Orme.

" You live in church," replied Anne after a moment's hesitation.

" Not all the time. My house is next door to the church. Your great-grandfather built it."

Anne made no comment. She stood and gazed at him and wondered.

Anne's world was very small. All children begin with a very small world: with the faces of people around them, with the carpet on the nursery floor and the legs of the nursery table. Gradually their world expands to more faces and to other rooms in the house; later it expands to the garden. At five years old Anne's world was still very restricted. She knew vaguely that there were other places in the world besides Westkirk—Nannie occasionally went to see her sister at a place called Edinburgh, sometimes Father and Mother went " abroad."

Anne's inquiring gaze did not embarrass Mr. Orme at all for although he was a bachelor he understood children and loved them dearly . . . and this child was so sweet and innocent. She was as sweet and innocent as the June morning.

" Why are you out so early? " asked Anne after a long silence.

" I've been to see a man who was very ill. I'm on my way home."

" You're not a doctor."

" No, not a doctor—but sometimes when people are very ill they like to see me."

" You can tell them about Heaven," nodded Anne understandingly.

" I try to tell them," he agreed.

There was another silence. A blackbird was singing on a tree. The sunshine was warm and pleasant.

" God likes boys better than girls, doesn't He? " asked Anne suddenly.

" No," replied Mr. Orme. The question startled him —in fact it horrified him—but he answered it quite quietly. " No," he repeated. " Certainly not."

" I thought He did," said Anne. " Boys are more important, aren't they? "

" No, we are all of equal importance in the sight of God. He loves us all."

" When we're good," agreed Anne.

" He loves us just as much when we're bad. If I take the wings of the morning and dwell in the uttermost parts of the sea, even there Thy hand shall guide me and Thy right hand shall hold me."

This was queer sort of talk. Nobody in Anne's small

circle of people ever talked like this. As a matter of fact
no grown-up person had ever talked to Anne before—not
really *talked*. In Anne's experience grown-up people told
you to change your shoes or sit still and not fidget, or run
along and play. Her religious education had consisted of
Bible stories read by Miss Clarke and singing hymns accom-
panied by Miss Clarke on the nursery piano ... and
Nannie had taught her to say, " Gentle Jesus meek and mild,
Look upon a little child." Anne did not understand what
it meant (nobody had thought of explaining it to her),
but she said it every night at bedtime. Then there was the
large engraving which hung upon the wall in Mrs. Duff's
sitting-room. The picture was intended to represent
Elijah being taken up to Heaven in a cloud; but Anne and
Nell and Connie thought it was a picture of God: God
with a long white beard and a stern expression upon His
countenance. It was for this reason that Anne was surprised
to hear He would bother about an unimportant little girl.

Mr. Orme saw incredulity upon the expressive little face
and he began to talk to her and to question her gently and
he discovered that she was, to all intents and purposes, a
heathen. It was dreadful. Something must be done about
it at once. The other children belonging to his congregation came to Sunday School and he taught them himself
but he had imagined that the Ayrton children were receiving religious instruction at home.

" Will you come to Sunday School ? " he asked.

Anne did not reply. For one thing she did not know
what Sunday School was, and for another it was not in her
power to say whether or not she would go. If she were
washed and dressed and taken to Sunday School she would
go, and if not she would stay at home—it was as simple as
that.

" Will you come ? " repeated Mr. Orme earnestly.

Anne remained silent.

Mr. Orme sighed. He said, "I'll ask your mother."

There was a long silence after that. The blackbird was still singing and the sun was still warm but Mr. Orme was not so happy. It seemed ridiculous that he should feel this child was neglected, that she was "a lost lamb," but that was what he felt. He would have liked to pick her up and take her home and care for her and teach her about God's goodness and love.

## 4

The next time Mr. Orme dined at Amberwell House he broached the subject of Sunday School to his hostess.

"I think not," said Mrs. Ayrton. "There's chicken-pox in Westkirk just now."

"They receive religious instruction from Miss Clarke," added Mr. Ayrton.

"I should like them to come," said Mr. Orme. "There are about twenty children. I teach them myself."

"Perhaps later on," said Mrs. Ayrton. "They're quite small, you know. Anne is only five. Miss Clarke is quite capable of teaching them."

Mr. Orme had evidence that she was not, but he could not produce the evidence.

"Try one of these apples, Mr. Orme," said Mr. Ayrton. "They don't look up to much but they have a particularly sweet flavour. If you like them we could send you a basket."

Mr. Orme accepted the apple and began to peel it. He felt angry and frustrated—there was nothing he could do— he saw quite clearly that it was no use saying any more. Sometimes he wondered if it were any use going to Amberwell House once a month and dining with the Ayrtons. They were very kind but the conversation was always trivial and he always came away feeling that the evening had been wasted. The time would have been better spent in his study or in visiting people who had need of him. But the Ayrtons were his responsibility—just as much as the poorest member of his flock—and perhaps some day they would need him.

After dinner they strolled into the garden and Mr. Orme was shown the site that had been chosen for the lily-pool. It was a stretch of green lawn at the south side of the house. All round the lawn there were flowering shrubs and trees.

" It will be here," said Mr. Ayrton. " It will be a round basin about fifteen feet in diameter with a stone rim. In the middle of the pool we intend to have a rock with a bronze mermaid reclining on it. Marion, my dear, we must show Mr. Orme the sketches. Of course it will take time. Pipes will have to be laid for the water and that can't be done in a day. I think we shall be lucky if the fountain is in working order a year from now."

Mr. Orme tried to simulate interest in the fountain but it was very difficult and presently he made his excuses and came away.

As has been said before Mr. Orme had permission to walk in Amberwell gardens whenever he pleased. He often took advantage of the privilege but hitherto he had walked there in the evening so he had never seen the children. Now he altered his routine and began to take his walk in the afternoon. If the children were not to be allowed to come to him for religious instruction he must go to them. He knew they played in the gardens and was sure he would find them . . . but he was disappointed.

The children saw him, of course, but they avoided him —as they avoided all grown-ups—and they melted into the bushes or curled up in a convenient ditch until he had passed. It was a game, really, and quite an amusing game. Mr. Orme gave them a great deal of excitement and pleasure. They had no idea he was looking for them (*that* never occurred to them for a moment) but if it had occurred to them they would have avoided him just the same.

" 'Ware Mr. Orme! " Connie would cry. " He's coming through the gate! "

Immediately the others would leave whatever they were doing and take cover behind the raspberry-canes or rush into the potting-shed and close the door. They would remain there, trembling with delicious excitement, until the danger was past.

# CHAPTER THREE

On a warm afternoon towards the end of July there was a flitting taking place at Ponticum House. A doll's pram had been brought to the south gate of the walled garden and was being loaded with all sorts of odds and ends which had accumulated since the Easter holidays. The three little girls were as busy as ants, running to and fro, but unlike ants they were chattering as they worked.

"We'll have to make another journey," said Nell. "The pram won't hold everything."

"I think we'll manage," said Anne. "If one of us wheels the pram and the others hold the things on——"

"I don't know how we collect so much stuff," declared Connie with a sigh.

There was certainly a lot of stuff. Most people would have said "a lot of rubbish" but to Connie and Nell and Anne it was very valuable indeed. There were two wooden boxes with some hay in the bottom which had done duty as dolls' beds. There was a tin tea-set, somewhat battered, and two small enamel mugs. There was a blue glass vase with dandelions in it and a shabby little chest full of dolls' clothes. . . . All this in addition to the dolls themselves, a varied collection but all rather the worse for wear. A doll dressed as a sailor, with a square collar and bell-bottomed trousers, was the smartest of the collection though not the most loved. He belonged to Nell (Aunt Beatrice had given him to her for her birthday). He had a super-cilious smile and his clothes would not "take off." Even

34

his round sailor cap was fixed securely to his fair curly hair.
How could you love a creature that you could neither
cuddle nor undress? Jack was the bane of Nell's existence
for he made her feel guilty of hard-heartedness. One day
she slipped him into a drawer and tried to forget about him;
she almost succeeded . . . and then, when she was going to
bed, she saw him sitting upon her pillow, sneering at her.

" Look! " said Nannie cheerfully. " There's Jack. I
found him in the drawer with your winter woollies. Had
you forgotten about him? "

" Nearly," said Nell with a sigh.

After that it was no use trying to forget Jack so he was
taken about with the other dolls.

The pram had been loaded and Connie was giving a last
look round in Ponticum House to make sure that nothing
had been left.

" Oh! " she cried. " Look at this! " and she pounced
upon a tiny glass feeding-bottle with a rubber teat which
had fallen down behind the shelf.

The others looked at it in horror.

" It's a good thing you found it! " exclaimed Nell.

Anne leant over the seat and poked about to see if there
was anything else which might offend masculine sensi-
bilities. She poked amongst the pile of withered leaves
and came up with something in her hand. It was a china
saucer with little flowers on it.

" I've never seen that before," declared Nell.

None of them had ever seen it before. The three heads
were close together as they looked at it.

" Isn't it pretty? " said Anne.

" How can it have got here? " wondered Nell.

" Somebody must have left it here——" began Connie.

" But nobody knows about Ponticum House except us! "
cried Anne.

"Long ago, perhaps——"

They all looked round their secret hiding-place with widely-open eyes. It was very curious to think that somebody else had played here long ago.

"It's like Robinson Crusoe," said Anne vaguely.

"What *do* you mean?" asked Connie in surprise.

"I mean when he found Friday's footprint in the sand."

"Friday's footprint!" echoed Connie in bewilderment. "But it's a doll's saucer!"

Anne could not explain. It was always difficult for Anne to explain things even when they were clear to herself, and in this case she scarcely knew what she meant.

"Well, anyway, we can keep it, can't we?" said Nell. "It will be lovely when we have tea-parties for the dolls."

They had so few toys that the little saucer was a treasure. It really was beautiful. The pattern of tiny flowers was delightful, and it was so delicate that when you held it up to the light you could almost see through it.

Nell began to dig in the heap of leaves to see if there was another saucer—or better still a cup—but the only thing she found was a lead soldier about three inches tall dressed in a sort of uniform. The paint had flaked off him in parts but there was enough left to show that he had once been clad in a gay scarlet jacket and white breeches.

"Funny!" said Anne, looking at him curiously.

"We'll put him in the treasure-box," said Nell. "The boys would like him."

It was now nearly tea-time so they set off home through the walled garden, Connie wheeling the pram and Nell and Anne walking beside it and steadying the load. They were hurrying along, intent upon their task, so unfortunately they did not notice the little group of people at the door of the greenhouse until it was too late.

Mrs. Ayrton had been showing Sir Andrew and Lady

Findlater the vine. Mr. Gray was there too; he had been explaining his method of pruning.

When Mrs. Ayrton looked round and saw the cavalcade she was aghast. The girls were dirty and untidy; the dolls' pram, laden with rubbish, was disreputable in the extreme. In fact her three little daughters looked for all the world like tinkers. The effect was considerably worsened by a confusion of ideas on the part of the children: Connie tried to stop and turn back and the other two tried to push on quickly. The pram overturned and everything fell off in a heap.

" Goodness, what *have* you been doing! " exclaimed Mrs. Ayrton angrily.

" Nothing," said Anne, replying to the usual question in the traditional manner.

" Nothing! " cried Mrs. Ayrton. " You look as if you had been digging in the rubbish heap. You're absolutely filthy! Where did you find all those broken boxes? "

Lady Findlater had thought at first that these were the gardener's children but now she realised that they must be Ayrtons. " Are these your three little girls? " she inquired sweetly.

" Yes—I don't know what they've been doing," replied Mrs. Ayrton, trying to control her rage.

" It looks like a flitting to me," said Sir Andrew smiling.

The children said nothing. They began to collect their treasures off the path.

" Leave it," said Mrs. Ayrton. " Leave all that rubbish where it is. Mr. Gray will burn it. Run straight home to Nannie and get washed; you're not fit to be seen. Do you hear what I say? "

They heard and obeyed. They left everything and ran off as fast as they could.

" It's all right," gasped Nell as they climbed the nursery

stairs. "I've got the saucer—and Mr. Gray—winked at me——"

2

As has been said before, the nursery-flat at Amberwell was self-contained; it could be reached by two staircases, one of these led to the house, and was shut off by a green baize door, the other led directly to the gardens. Nursery meals came up from the kitchen in a small service-lift which had been put in by Mr. Ayrton's father. Before that everything had to be carried up three flights of stairs from the kitchen. The nursery itself was a large square room with a cork carpet and a few shabby old mats on the floor; there were several cupboards and basket chairs, a large solid table and an ancient rocking-horse. The two boys shared a large room at the end of the passage; Nell and Anne shared a smaller room; Nannie and Connie each had a room to herself. In addition there was a bathroom, a small pantry and a cupboard for drying clothes.

Nell and Anne had shared a room since they were babies. In those days their cots had been close together so that they could chatter to each other quietly before they dropped off to sleep. Now that they were older and the wooden cots had been replaced by two small beds they still slept side by side and still chatted quietly after the light had been put out. Nannie knew this of course but she saw no harm in it. Sometimes she listened at the door and heard the two little voices getting lower and more drowsy until they died away into silence. Connie was different; she went straight off to sleep the moment her head touched the pillow and no more was heard of her until she was wakened in the morning.

In term time the nursery-flat was very quiet and moved

in an orderly routine, but when the boys came back from school it was suddenly transformed and life became exciting. Roger and Tom (who were now twelve and eleven years old respectively) were full of fun and high spirits. Although they were so much older than their half-sisters the little girls amused them and, after three months of boys and nothing but boys, they were not averse to a spell of feminine society. Sometimes the five children played together in the gardens; the boys decided what was to be the order of the day and the girls did as they were told with admirable submission. As a matter of fact they would have done anything the boys told them for they realised it was a great privilege to be allowed to join in the games. They did not enjoy it quite so much when other children came to play. The two Findlater boys were older than Roger and Tom, and were apt to take charge and to order the others about, Mary Findlater was the same age as Connie. There were Dr. Maddon's two children, Arnold and Harriet, and there was Gerald Lambert.

Gerald went to the same school as the Ayrton boys and was Tom's particular friend. He was a large ungainly boy and had the habit of saying the rudest things in a quite unconscious manner. The Ayrton children (trained by Nannie in the time-honoured tradition that " personal remarks " were bad form) disliked Gerald's derogatory comments upon their appearance. Gerald referred to Nell and Anne as " Skinny " and " Fatty "—in fact he never called them anything else. They thought it most extraordinary that Tom should like Gerald.

Gerald's father was a director of a Glasgow firm of shipbuilders and travelled to Glasgow several times a week. The Lamberts had bought a piece of land adjoining Amberwell, they had built a fine house upon it and laid out a pleasant garden.

In addition to the Findlaters, the Maddons and Gerald Lambert there were several other families of children in and around Westkirk . . . all these children were at home in the holidays and occasionally came and played in the gardens. They played hide-and-seek, they tracked Indians in the woods and sometimes they played stump-cricket in the meadow. If they grew tired of these activities they went down to the shore and paddled or bathed. There was no end to the joys and the variety of entertainment at Amberwell.

On wet days Roger and Tom got out their clockwork trains and spread the rails all over the nursery floor. They built stations and goods yards and tunnels with bricks. It took a long time to get everything in running order and Connie and Nell and Anne were allowed to help if they did not offer too many suggestions. The boys found them quite useful (sometimes they were allowed to wind up the engines under careful supervision) and more often than not it was left to Connie and Nell and Anne to tidy up the mess when the game was over and the boys remembered that they had other important business to attend to.

Connie and Nell and Anne did not mind at all, they rather enjoyed putting everything away neatly in the proper boxes; they would have undertaken far less pleasant work for the privilege of playing with the boys.

The dolls were always banished during the holidays but one day when Tom was rummaging in the nursery cupboard he discovered the sailor doll.

" Oh, my dear paws! Oh my fur and whiskers! What a horrible-looking thing! " exclaimed Tom, holding it up by one arm and laughing derisively.

Certainly Jack was not prepossessing. His sojourn in the nursery cupboard had not improved his appearance. His blonde hair was tashy and his round sailor cap had slipped over one ear.

" Who does it belong to? " asked Tom. " Who's the owner of this pretty thing? Don't all speak at once."

" He belongs to Nell but she doesn't like him," said Anne.

" I do like him," said Nell, but without conviction.

" You don't! " cried Connie and Anne with one voice.

" Give him to me, Nellie," suggested Tom. " I mean if you don't like him——"

Nell gazed at Tom in amazement.

" If you don't like him give him to me," repeated Tom. " I'd like to have him."

" But you said he was horrible! "

" Perhaps I've changed my mind," said Tom smiling. " At any rate I want him—very badly."

" Tom's going to be a sailor," said Connie, reminding them of a fact they all knew. " That's why he wants Jack."

Somehow this did not seem reasonable to Nell and she still hesitated. She was only too willing to give the doll to Tom—but was it right? Was she justified in handing over Jack to the tender mercies of Thomas?

" Please Nellie," said Tom wheedlingly. " Be a sport. I want him—honestly."

Thus adjured Nell had no option. " All right," she said in a doubtful sort of voice. " But what are you going to do with him? "

" Play with him, of course," replied Tom.

3

This curious transaction had just been completed when the nursery door opened and Mr. Ayrton appeared. As a matter of fact he had been up on to the roof of Amberwell House with the plumber to examine some lead piping and

arrange to have it renewed (he believed in a personal in-
spection of such-like important details) and coming down
through the skylight into the nursery flat he had heard his
children talking and decided to pay them a visit. It was
perfectly simple—and perfectly natural—but, as he had
never visited the nursery before in the memory of child,
his sudden appearance alarmed them and they gazed at
him blankly.

"What have you been doing?" asked Mr. Ayrton in a
friendly manner.

It was the usual question and Anne answered it instinctively.

"Nothing," she said.

"Nothing?" asked Mr. Ayrton in surprise. "That
doesn't sound very interesting." He looked round the circle
of faces and mistook alarm for guilt. It was obvious that
they had been up to some mischief. "What are you doing
with that doll, Thomas?" he inquired. "It belongs to
one of your sisters, I suppose?"

"Yes," said Tom. "At least——"

"Give it back to her at once," said Mr. Ayrton.

"I've given him to Tom," said Nell hastily, anxious to
clear Tom of all blame. "Tom wants him, you see."

Mr. Ayrton did not see. He was convinced there was some
mystery. "Why does Thomas want the doll?" he asked.

This was what everybody had been wondering.

"Because he's a sailor," suggested Connie. "I mean
Tom is going to be a sailor, so that's why he wants Jack."

This was Connie's theory and she put it forward confidently, but the result was unfortunate for this was the first
intimation Mr. Ayrton had received upon the subject of
his son's future career.

"Thomas wants to be a sailor!" he exclaimed in surprise.

"Yes," said Tom simply.

" Why do you want to be a sailor? "

There were all sorts of reasons why Tom wanted to make the Navy his career: he loved the sea—it was a great big beautiful mystery, clean and free; he was fond of ships they fascinated him; he wanted to travel and see foreign countries; he wanted adventure and the companionship of his own kind. Ever since Tom could remember he had wanted to go down to the sea in ships, but now, standing before his father with the stupid doll in his hand, he found it impossible to give his reasons.

" Why? " repeated Mr. Ayrton.

" I think it would be nice," mumbled Tom.

" Gerald is going to be a sailor," put in Anne, trying to be helpful.

" That's no reason at all," declared Mr. Ayrton irritably He was annoyed because he had other ideas about his younger son's future. Roger was going into the Army—that was already decided—but Thomas was different. Thomas was extremely clever, his reports from school were more than satisfactory, and Mr. Ayrton had made up his mind that Thomas must go to Oxford and read medicine—or perhaps law. There had been several eminent physicians and barristers in the Ayrton family. Mr. Ayrton's uncle, Lawrence Ayrton, had been a famous judge, his picture hung in the hall of Amberwell House and several people had remarked that Thomas resembled him. All things considered there seemed no reason why Thomas should not rise to the same dizzy height. Mr. Ayrton's intentions were excellent, his reasoning was perfectly sensible, he opened his mouth to explain . . . and then he remembered Disraeli's words.

" Well, you can put the idea out of your head," said Mr. Ayrton. " I have no intention of allowing you to go into the Navy. I have other plans."

" But Father——"

" Let's hear no more about it," said Mr. Ayrton kindly but firmly, and he went away.

Tom rushed out of the nursery; he left the door open and they heard him clattering down the stairs to the garden. Roger followed him. The three girls were left alone.

There were several mysteries here. Why had their father visited the nursery? Why had he said Tom was not to be a sailor? Why had Tom wanted Jack? The first two mysteries were insoluble—they were the sort of strange vagaries to be expected from grown-up people—but the third mystery was at least arguable.

" I told you——" began Connie.

" Yes, but it isn't," declared Nell earnestly. " It's something else—and I shouldn't have let Tom have him."

" But you couldn't say no when Tom wanted him so badly," objected Anne.

This was true, of course, and it was a comforting thought. She could not have said no to Tom.

" I'll tell you what it is," continued Anne. " He wants to take Jack to school and have a joke with the other boys. You know how Tom loves jokes."

Nell was still dubious. " Perhaps," she agreed. " I'd just like to know what he's going to do with Jack—that's all."

## CHAPTER FOUR

WHEN MR. AYRTON said it would take a year before the fountain was in working order he was just about right. Meantime the construction was a source of unfailing interest to the children. They watched the masons laying the stones, they watched the trenches being dug for the pipes and they listened sympathetically when Mr. Gray bewailed the mess in his precious gardens. It certainly was a mess. Heavy-footed men clumped all over the flower-beds, rolled their wheelbarrows over the grass and mixed cement upon the crazy pavement. There were heaps of rubble piled up against the rose trellis and the roots of the magnolia tree were disturbed, so that it sickened and died. These interesting though somewhat upsetting activities went on all winter and spring; it was not until the following July that the mermaid was put into her appointed place and the men packed up and departed.

Mrs. Ayrton had decided to have a garden-party for the Opening of the Fountain, but naturally this could not be held until the mess had been cleared up and everything put right, so the party was arranged for the end of August, and meanwhile the fountain stood idle. Obviously it would be ridiculous (said Mrs. Ayrton) to invite guests to see the Opening of the Fountain when it had been playing for weeks. Mr. Ayrton agreed with her and the order was given that the fountain was not to play. Nobody was to see it playing until the great day arrived.

Meanwhile the little bronze mermaid sat upon her rock

in the middle of the lily-pool with the shell in her hand. She looked hot and dusty. The sun shone down upon her bronze head and her naked, bronze shoulders. Her tail was coiled round the rock. Just below her was the pool of clear, cold water but the mermaid could not bathe.

The afternoon before the party was warm and misty and although the sun shone it was veiled in cloud. It was reflected in the water of the lily-pool, pale and hazy like the moon. Nell and Anne were leaning over the low wall which surrounded the pool, whispering together.

" She looks sad," said Anne.

" She hasn't got long to wait now," replied Nell comfortingly.

" To-morrow night," agreed Anne. She hesitated and then added, " You know I sort of feel as if I was her."

" Why? " asked Nell in surprise.

" Well, she's the same size as me—exactly—only not so fat."

" I love her," said Nell with a sigh. " I love her dear little tail."

" Won't it be exciting to see the water beginning? She'll be so pleased. She'll wake up when she feels the water beginning because mermaids love water—I mean they're half fishes, aren't they? "

The children were still talking about it when they went in to tea and took their places at the nursery table. They had talked about it for weeks but the subject was inexhaustible. Their lives were so quiet and monotonous that it was no wonder they were excited about to-morrow night.

" But you won't see it," said Nannie suddenly.

There was a moment of incredulous silence.

" Not see it? " asked Anne in amazement.

" No," said Nannie. " The boys are to stay up for it, but you're all to go to bed at the proper time."

" Oh Nannie! " exclaimed Nell in horrified tones.

" Oh Nannie! " cried Connie. " Surely I am old
enough——"

" We all are," declared Nell earnestly. " We're all old
enough to stay up. We all want to see the beginning of the
fountain—in the moonlight. Oh, Nannie, please——"

" Your mother says——"

" Did you ask her? " demanded Connie. " Did you tell
her we wanted to see it? Did you? "

Nannie pursed up her mouth and remained dumb . . . so
of course they knew she had. Also it was quite obvious
that Nannie was not pleased.

(Most certainly Nannie was not pleased. She had been
looking forward to appearing on the terrace with the three
little girls all dressed in their best frocks to see the Opening
of the Fountain. Now she would have to see it from the
garden in company with Mrs. Duff and the rest of the staff,
which was not the same thing at all. Nannie was almost
as disappointed as the children if the truth be told.)

" It's beastly unfair! " exclaimed Tom. " Why shouldn't
they stay up and see it? They've been looking forward to
it frightfully."

" Their mother says they're too young," said Nannie.

" Nannie, listen——" began Roger.

" It's no use asking me," declared Nannie. " It's not
for me to say."

Anne had remained silent but her mouth drooped pathe-
tically and her eyes filled with tears.

Nannie's heart was softened. " Never mind," she said
comfortingly. " You can see it next day. I'll ask Mr. Gray
to turn it on specially, and once it's been opened you'll be
able to see it playing quite often."

" But it won't be the same," wailed Anne. " It won't
be the beginning. We want to see it begin."

It was no use of course. They all knew that. Roger had a wild idea of going to his father and trying to explain what the little girls were feeling about it but on second thoughts he abandoned the project. Roger realised that he would be putting his head into the lion's mouth for nothing. Mr. Ayrton never interfered with the children's upbringing and he certainly would not interfere with this. An order was an order in the Ayrton household.

It's a shame, thought Roger, as he looked round the table at the miserable little faces. They're such decent little kids. . . .

2

By bedtime the little girls had recovered some of their spirits and seemed resigned to their fate. Connie minded least, for she was the least imaginative, and Nannie's promise that Mr. Gray would turn it on the next morning for the children's benefit pacified her completely. It would be more important to have it turned on specially, Connie thought.

At half-past six the three girls went off to bed as usual while Roger and Thomas, who had been promoted to dinner in the dining-room, got ready for the meal.

No more was said until Nell and Anne were in bed and Nannie had turned out the light.

" It's no good minding," said Nell softly. " I mean the mermaid will enjoy it just the same whether we're there or not."

" But I do mind," returned Anne in a thoughtful voice. " I mind all those people seeing it before us—when we love her and they don't."

Nell felt exactly the same but she was always the comforter. " I know—but we can think about her. She won't be sad any more when the water begins."

"D'you know what I think?" said Anne eagerly. "I think she climbs down at night and splashes in the pool—specially when the moon shines."

"But only when nobody's there," returned Nell. "She won't climb down to-morrow night when all those people are watching her."

Anne sighed. "It's a lovely moon for her to-night."

"Yes," agreed Nell. A sword of moonlight was streaming in through the open window of their room. "Yes, it's a lovely moon."

"D'you think——" began Anne, and then suddenly was silent.

The door opened very softly and Roger peeped in. Tom was just behind him.

"Hallo, what is it?" whispered Nell.

"They're not asleep," said Tom in conspiratorial tones.

The two boys stood at the door and looked across the room at their sisters.

"Perhaps we'd better not," said Roger doubtfully.

"What?" asked Nell. She sat up and stared at him.

"Can you keep a secret?" Roger asked.

"You know we can!" cried Anne indignantly. "We've kept Ponticum a secret for years. What is the secret *about*?"

"We thought we'd turn on the fountain."

The two little girls were speechless with amazement.

"It's pretty safe, really," added Roger. "The parents have gone to the Lamberts' to play bridge."

"I know how to do it," explained Tom. "I watched Mr. Gray after tea. He was turning it on and off and oiling the handle to make sure it would be all right for to-morrow night. We thought it would be a lark to turn it on."

Tom was always daring, but this was the most daring

thing the little girls had ever heard of. It was positively breath-taking.

" If you'd like to come," said Roger doubtfully. " Connie is asleep, but——"

" Oh Roger, of course! " cried Anne, bounding out of bed.

" You'll have to keep it dark. There'd be an awful row——"

" Of course we'll keep it dark! "

" They're all right," said Tom. " They won't let on . . . and it's such a stinking shame they can't see it to-morrow. Come on, kids, put on your dressing-gowns."

The boys had chosen a good hour for the expedition; Mr. and Mrs. Ayrton had driven off in the car and Nannie had gone downstairs to have her usual chat with Mrs. Duff. The table-maid had finished clearing the dinner and the housemaid had turned down the beds and drawn the curtains. The house was perfectly quiet.

The four children crept down the nursery stairs into the garden. It was quiet here too, the moonlight poured down in a silver flood. The night was warm and there was not a breath of wind, the leaves of the trees hung down in a tired sort of way as if they were resting after the day of sunshine. The scent of the night-stock in the border was almost overpowering.

Nell was a little frightened as she pattered along the path after the others. It was such a huge adventure, it was so dreadfully naughty. Supposing somebody found out? But Roger waited for her and took her small hand in his and they went on together. Tom had run ahead. Although he was younger than Roger it was usually he who took the lead in any escapade . . . and this was his " special thing " for it was he who had watched Mr. Gray oiling the mechanism of the fountain. It was he who knew how to turn it on.

The lily-pool lay still in the moonlight, it was like a big round mirror. In the middle was the black rock with the mermaid sitting upon it. Tom took off his coat and rolled up his sleeves, he went round the pool and leaning over the edge of the stone rim, plunged his arm into the water.

"It's a sort of handle," he said, looking up. His face was very earnest and a lock of dark hair had fallen over his brow. "You had better stand back," he added. "We don't want the kids to get wet."

Roger and the two little girls retreated to the steps . . . the next moment a jet of silver water shot up from the shell in the mermaid's hand. It shot up in a stream which curved at the top and fell in a shower of rain over the mermaid and into the quiet pool.

It was lovely. It was the prettiest sight imaginable. A pale opalescent rainbow formed amongst the silvery drops as they fell. The mermaid, half hidden by the veil, seemed to stir, seemed to come to life and relax her position as she felt her own element of water falling upon her head and shoulders.

"She's happy," murmured Anne.

Nobody else said anything. The gentle sound of drops pattering into the pool was the only sound.

For a little while they stood and watched in ecstasy and then Tom crept to the edge of the pool and turned it off. The jet of water faltered and died, the rainbow vanished, the pattering ceased and all was still . . . but the mermaid was bedewed with drops which glistened like diamonds in the moonlight.

Nell drew a long breath. It had been even more beautiful than she had imagined. There were no words to describe how marvellous it had been.

"Off with you!" cried Roger, shooing them along the

path. " Cut along back to bed as quick as you can. Nannie may be up any minute. . . ."

The two little girls picked up their long nighties and scampered away—along the path and up the stairs as fast as they could go—they were breathless when they reached the nursery floor and crept into bed and pulled up the bedclothes.

" Wasn't it fun! " whispered Anne.

" It was lovely," breathed Nell. " Oh, it was lovely."

" Were you frightened? "

" Just a wee bit——"

" I was terrified. It was heavenly," declared Anne and she began to chuckle.

" Anne, you're not to laugh," said Nell earnestly. She knew only too well that when Anne began to laugh there was no stopping her.

" I can't help it," chuckled Anne. " It was—so funny ——"

" Stop laughing at once—or—or I'll hit you. Listen! I can hear Nannie coming along the passage! "

Anne managed to stop. They lay and listened, holding their breath.

" It isn't," said Anne. " There isn't anybody. You imagined it."

" Well, anyhow, I made you stop," replied Nell. She turned over and snuggled down.

Later, when Nannie came in to look at them, as she always did before she went to bed, they were both fast asleep. She smiled as she looked at them: they were so sweet and good. She had brought them up from babies and she knew everything that went on in their dear little heads. It was a shame that they were not to be allowed to see the fountain—it really was.

As Nannie turned to come away she was a little surprised

to see some damp foot-marks on the linoleum but it did not worry her unduly for she was no Sherlock Holmes. She just made a note in her mind to remember to tell the under-housemaid about it to-morrow morning.

### 3

Perhaps Nannie would have taken more interest in the damp foot-marks if her mind had not been full of the interesting conversation which had taken place that evening in Mrs. Duff's room. All the usual habitués had been there and the talk had been about the party to-morrow night.

"It'll be a grand show," declared Mr. Gray. "We've got wee fairy-lights to string up in the trees—all different colours they are—but if the moon's as bright as to-night we'll scarcely need them."

"I'm sick of the whole thing," declared Janet, the head housemaid. "Mrs. Ayrton's been after me all day telling me to polish this and polish that . . . and Miss Ayrton's coming to-morrow."

"I thought she'd be coming," said Nannie with a sigh.

The others said nothing. None of them was fond of Beatrice Ayrton.

"Poking her nose into everything," continued Janet. "Every time Miss Ayrton comes her room has to be spring cleaned—and that on the top of everything else, mind you."

"Well, ye get paid for yer work," said Mrs. Duff.

Janet laughed scornfully. "I'd get better pay in a shop and half the work . . . and I'd not have Her nosing after me."

"That's no way to talk," reproved Mrs. Duff.

"Ye should boo tae the bush that bields ye," added Mr. Gray.

"That's an old-fashioned notion," retorted Janet. "I'll not boo to any bush. I'm as good as her any day. I'll not demean myself."

Mr. Gray leaned forward and shook his finger at her. "That's foolish talk," he said. "There's nothing demeaning in showing a proper respect for yer employer—if you respect him he'll respect you. And there's nothing demeaning in an honest day's work. Ye can stand up and look the whole wurrld in the face. It's the shirkers that need to look sideways."

"I'd as lief be my own master," declared Janet, somewhat taken aback.

"And how would you be that?" asked Mrs. Duff tartly. "If ye worked in a shop ye'd have a master, wouldn't ye?"

"And maybe a less considerate one," put in Nannie.

"That's a true word," nodded Mr. Gray. "Ye're looked after in a place like Amberwell. Ye get yer pay regular and ye've no cause to worry. My brother's got a wee cycle shop in Dumfries. He's doing well but there's a deal of worry in it and I wouldn't change with him. My father was in the South Lodge for forty years—and now I've got it. That makes ye feel safe—if ye see what I mean."

"Och, you've no ambition!" exclaimed Janet.

"That's no way to speak to Mr. Gray," said Nannie.

"I'm not worrying," said Mr. Gray smiling. "It's true I'm a contented man and I've no desire to better myself, but I've got a few wee ambitions all the same. I like to see the gardens well kept. I've done my best to have everything in apple-pie order for to-morrow. And then there's the Show . . . the roses are nice this year and I've a marrow that'll be hard to beat. Och, yes, I've got ambitions."

Mrs. Duff changed the subject tactfully. "Well, ye'll be glad the fountain's finished anyway," she said.

"I am that," he agreed. "It's been enough to turn my hair grey, what with one thing and another."

"Ye've been gray all your life," replied Mrs. Duff seriously.

Appreciative smiles greeted this sally. "That's a good one," admitted the victim. "I'll need to mind that, and tell Jean."

"She'll be coming to-morrow night?" asked Mrs. Duff. "We're all to be there and see the fountain. It'll be a grand show——"

"We're all to be there except the children," said Nannie.

"The children!" exclaimed Mr. Gray. "But they've been talking of little else for months. Are they not to be there? Could ye not allow them to stay up and see the fun?"

"It's not for me to say," declared Nannie, setting her mouth grimly.

"Well, I call it a shame!" cried Janet. "It's Her, of course. She's nothing but a hard-hearted old wretch."

"Wheesht!" said Mrs. Duff in scandalised tones.

"I'll not wheesht! Those children get no fun at all, they're shut up in the attics from one year's end to another —it's a wonder to me if their mother knows them by sight. I wouldn't be them for a good deal." Janet rose as she spoke and flounced out of the room, adding as a parting shot, "The dog has a better life; he's allowed to lie on the hearth-rug anyway."

An uncomfortable silence followed Janet's departure for there was too much truth in what she said for her audience to treat it lightly. Mrs. Duff and Nannie and Mr. Gray had all thought the same—in their inmost hearts—though they were too loyal to breathe a word of it.

"Och well," said Mr. Gray at last. "They'll not be neglected as long as they have Nannie—that's certain." He rose and went away, for it was obvious that there could be no more comfortable talk that evening. Janet's bomb-shell had effectually burst up the party.

Mr. Gray wandered round to the lily-pool. He had made certain that everything was all right for to-morrow but his mind was disturbed and he thought he would have another look at the fountain before going home to bed. He approached it through the trees—and suddenly stood still, petrified with amazement. The fountain was playing. The bright water was leaping up and falling in rainbow showers . . . my, it's pretty! thought Mr. Gray regarding it in awestruck admiration.

His first idea was that Mr. and Mrs. Ayrton were trying it out, and then as he approached near he saw the little group of children on the steps. At that moment Tom turned off the water and the children dispersed and vanished. The two little girls ran away up the steps and into the house, the boys followed more slowly. The fountain slept.

"Well, what d'ye think of that!" exclaimed Mr. Gray. Possibly he was addressing his remark to a tree, for no human being was present.

Still half dazed Mr. Gray went forward and kneeling down made sure that the handle had been properly turned off and no damage had been done. Then he rose and considered the matter.

"Maybe I dreamed it," murmured Mr. Gray (though as a matter of fact the drops of water glistening upon the mermaid's shoulders proved that he had not). "Maybe it was a dream—and anyway it's none of my business."

He went home chuckling.

# CHAPTER FIVE

THE GARDENS at Amberwell had never looked better than upon the August day when the mermaid fountain was to be displayed for the first time. Mrs. Ayrton had banked on a fine day and the weather had not disappointed her; the sun was shining with golden warmth and the skies were cloudless. The guests had been invited for five o'clock so that they might see the gardens while it was still light. When the light began to fade they were to come in and have a meal and listen to some music . . . and then, when it was dark and the moon had risen, they were to go out and see the fountain. A great many people had been invited, people from far and wide all over the south of Scotland, and nearly all had accepted for this was no ordinary party, this was an Occasion.

Mrs. Ayrton had decreed that the children were to appear for the first part of the entertainment so they were scrubbed and polished and dressed in their best clothes. They were ready far too soon and Nannie shepherded them out to the bowling-green, spread rugs for them to sit on and gave them picture-books. She herself took a chair and her knitting and sat down beside them. They looked nice, grouped upon the rugs, and Nannie was proud of them.

" When are the people going to arrive? " Anne inquired.

" Will we have to speak to them? " asked Nell in anxious tones—" speaking to people " was a dreadful ordeal to Nell.

" They'll arrive soon," replied Nannie. " And, if they speak to you, you'll rise and answer politely."

57

The boys were restive. They were much too hot, dressed up in their kilts, and there were all sorts of things they wanted to do.

" What a waste of a good afternoon! " growled Tom under his breath.

" We might have bathed," said Roger wistfully.

The mere idea of bathing in the cool green sea made Roger feel hotter than before. It was almost unbearable. He asked Nannie if he could go and get a drink of water, but she refused. " It won't be long now," she assured him.

" Nannie, my nose is bleeding! " exclaimed Tom.

" It can't be! "

" Yes it is," declared Tom and held out his handkerchief to prove the truth of his words.

" Oh, poor Tom," said Nell—but she said it instinctively and without consternation for she was aware that Tom's nose only bled when its owner wished it to do so.

" Oh dear! " cried Nannie in anguished tones. " Don't let it bleed on your shirt! " but she spoke too late for already there were three large crimson drops upon Tom's carefully laundered falls.

Tom rose. " It's a pity, isn't it? " he said. " I had better go and change before they come."

" Lie down on your bed," advised Nannie. To lie upon your bed was Nannie's cure for every ill that flesh is heir to and it never occurred to her that it was not good treatment for nose-bleeding.

Tom did not reply. He walked away slowly with his handkerchief held to his nose. The other children watched the pathetic sight with envy.

" I'd better go, just to see that he's all right," said Roger, leaping to his feet and following his suffering brother.

Nannie did not know what to do. She supposed she

ought to go after them, but that would mean leaving the little girls who were really her responsibility. The boys were out of her hands now; they were not " hers " any longer. Nannie sighed and remained where she was.

Aunt Beatrice was the first person to speak to the children; she had arrived at Amberwell that morning to stay for a few days and join in the festivities. She often came to Amberwell (in fact she came whenever she was asked) and she did her best to please but unfortunately she had a hasty temper. Miss Ayrton had wanted a rose garden for Amberwell—a rose garden with a sun-dial—and in her opinion the fountain was a ridiculous piece of extravagance, no use to anybody. She had arrived at Amberwell with the firm intention of concealing her feelings upon the subject, and she had managed to conceal them more or less, but the strain had told upon her and she was not feeling very amiable.

Miss Ayrton kissed her three nieces and asked how they were and then without waiting for an answer she turned to Nannie.

" Why are you sitting here? " she inquired.

" Mrs. Ayrton wished them to be here," replied Nannie in the ultra-refined voice which she always put on for Miss Ayrton's benefit.

" It's a foolish place to sit—much too hot," declared Miss Ayrton. " You should use your discretion, Nannie."

Nannie boiled, but not with the heat of the sun. She was about to reply but at this moment the guests began to arrive and Miss Ayrton went to meet them.

" What's a discreshon, Nannie? " asked Connie with interest.

" It's a parasol, silly," said Nell.

2

The guests had been received by their host and hostess in the drawing-room and invited to walk round the gardens. They strolled out in twos and threes or in little groups; the ladies attired in silken frocks and wide-brimmed hats trimmed with flowers, the gentlemen in more sober garb. They were like birds or butterflies, thought Nell as she watched them drift across the lawn, but they made more noise of course; such a chatter filled the air as had not been heard for years in the quiet gardens. Some of the guests came and spoke to the children who, prompted by Nannie's stern eye, rose and replied politely.

" They're like flowers themselves, the little dears," commented one of the ladies.

" Sweetly pretty; especially the eldest," agreed her elderly companion in a low voice.

Connie was delighted with the compliment but Nannie was annoyed for she was of the old school and disapproved of children being praised to their face.

" All girls! " said another lady in slightly disappointed accents.

" We've got two brothers," declared Connie. " They don't like parties so they've gone to bathe." This was a *faux pas* on Connie's part but she was slightly flown.

" Lucky little devils! " exclaimed a gentleman who was standing by.

" Where do you bathe? " asked the first lady.

" In the sea," replied Connie. " It's quite near."

The gentleman seemed anxious to visit the sea but the ladies were determined to walk round the gardens and a slight argument ensued.

"You can do both quite easily," Connie told them. "I'll show you the way."

"A guide would be most welcome," said the gentleman smiling.

Nannie was shaking her head reprovingly but Connie took no notice; she thought it would be amusing to walk round the gardens with her new friends. She went off with the party and disappeared.

"Look at that!" exclaimed Nannie who had now lost three of her five chickens and could do nothing about it. "I'll sort Connie when I get her . . . and what in the name of goodness made her say the boys had gone to bathe!"

Nell and Anne looked at one another and were silent.

People came and went. Most of them were strangers to the children and even the people they knew looked strange in their party clothes. They saw the Findlaters in the distance, they saw nice Dr. Maddon and his family, and they saw Mr. Orme. Presently Mr. and Mrs. Lambert appeared with Gerald in tow.

The children knew the Lamberts of course and rose politely as they approached. Mr. Lambert was large and hearty with a red face and a flourishing moustache; Mrs. Lambert was very small and dainty. She was always beautifully dressed but to-day she was even more exquisite than usual in a sprigged muslin frock and a hat with a little veil. Gerald, who was usually very untidy, was extremely smart in a new grey flannel suit.

"I say, where are Roger and Tom?" demanded Gerald. "I bet they're bathing. It's just the sort of afternoon for a bathe. I think I'll——"

"No, Gerald," said Mrs. Lambert.

"Oh, but look here!"

"No Gerald, you must stay with us. You'll get dirty,"

declared Mrs. Lambert who knew her son and was aware that the only way to keep him reasonably clean was not to let him out of her sight. "It will soon be time to go in to supper," she added craftily.

Gerald was about to disobey his mother but now hesitated uncertainly.

"It's a lovely supper," said Nell. "There's lobster mayonnaise and cold chicken and ham and cold grouse and jellies and trifles."

"Sounds good," said Gerald approvingly.

Mrs. Lambert looked at Nell and smiled; she was amused, and grateful. Although she lived next door, so to speak, she scarcely ever saw the little Ayrton girls; nobody ever saw them, they were kept in the background as if they were something to be ashamed of.

"You're Constance, aren't you?" asked Mrs. Lambert.

"Great Scott!" exclaimed Gerald roaring with laughter. "Fancy you not knowing that's Nell!"

Nell and Anne expected the skies to fall but Mrs. Lambert did not seem to mind . . . all the same Nell was sorry for her.

"I've grown a lot," Nell explained. "I've grown so fast that I can wear Connie's last year's dresses and of course we've both got yellow hair."

"But you're not *like* Connie," said Gerald looking at her critically. "You're horribly skinny and your hair is quite straight."

"What nonsense, Gerald!" exclaimed Mrs. Lambert.

"It isn't nonsense. Connie is much prettier than Nell."

"In that case Connie must be very pretty indeed."

"Come on, Poppet," said Mr. Lambert impatiently. "I want to speak to Gray about the fuchsias."

"Well, I never," murmured Nannie under her breath as they walked away.

Gerald only stayed long enough to make a long nose at Nell and then he lumbered off after his parents in his usual ungainly fashion.

"Poppet!" said Nell. "That's a funny name, isn't it? I do think she's sweet, don't you?"

Anne had begun to laugh. "I can't help it," she gurgled. "They look so—so funny. She's like a fairy—and Gerald —Gerald's like—a bear."

"Come along," said Nannie firmly. "It's time for bed."


3


Nannie had expected trouble at bedtime and was surprised when Nell and Anne ate their bread-and-milk quite cheerfully and went off to bed like lambs. They were actually in their beds when Connie rushed in, breathless and excited, and announced that she was to stay up after all.

"That lady was Lady Annan," declared Connie. "I mean that lady who said I was the prettiest. She's very important. I took her all round and showed her everything and she liked me so much that she asked Mother specially if I could stay up and see the fountain and Mother said I could, so I'm going to have supper downstairs and I'm going to see the fountain."

Even this—which Nannie thought most unfair—did not disturb the younger children.

"That's lovely," said Nell, snuggling down in bed. "I'm so glad you're going to see it after all. It's a lovely, lovely fountain; the moon makes the water look like rainbows and the drops patter down like rain."

"The mermaid wakes up when the water begins," added Anne dreamily.

It was just as well that Nannie and Connie were both too full of their own affairs to listen intelligently. Nannie had intended to punish Connie for her disobedience (and lo and behold she had received unmerited reward) and Connie was far too excited at her good fortune to notice what anybody said.

There was no trouble here—except that Nannie was cross—but there was trouble and to spare in another quarter. Roger and Tom had indeed gone to bathe, as their sisters had surmised, and most unluckily were seen by Mr. Ayrton returning to the house with their hair wet and straggling, and sand all over their clothes. He caught them as they were skulking in by the side door which led to the nursery stairs.

"What does this mean?" demanded their father in stentorian tones.

This was a variant of the usual question and neither of the boys could find an answer to it.

"Have you no proper feeling at all?" continued Mr. Ayrton, working himself up into a rage. "Don't you realise that we are offering hospitality to our friends? Amberwell is offering hospitality, and you belong to Amberwell. You ought to be mixing with our guests—they're your guests as well as mine—you ought to be helping to entertain them, acting as hosts, making yourselves useful. You can bathe any other afternoon. To-day you should be on duty."

Roger and Tom were speechless. They had never thought of the party in this light. The idea that they were in any way responsible—that they were on duty—had never occurred to them for a moment.

"You will both go straight to bed," stormed Mr. Ayrton "If you can't behave like reasonable people you must be treated like children."

" We didn't know," began Roger. " Nobody told us——"

" You were told to be present in your best clothes."

" Yes, but——"

" Nonsense! " exclaimed Mr. Ayrton. " Perfect nonsense. There's no excuse. You ought to be ashamed of yourselves."

Strangely enough they were. It was two very chastened boys who crept up the nursery stairs and went obediently to bed.

" Lobster mayonnaise," said Tom with a heavy sigh as he turned out the light.

" I know," agreed Roger. " But it isn't that so much. I mean—I mean if Father had told us before about being on duty——"

4

It was probably Mr. Gray who enjoyed the party more whole-heartedly than anybody else at Amberwell. The host and hostess were slightly anxious (slightly worried in case something should go wrong) and the household staff were busy with all manner of tasks, but Mr. Gray was free. He and his assistants had been working for weeks to put the gardens into order and it was all finished now. If anybody could find a weed in his borders Mr. Gray was willing to give that person sixpence—so he had said.

In appearance Mr. Gray was like a Border Terrier; he was small and neat; his hair and moustache were sandy, and beneath his thick sandy eyebrows his brown eyes peered out alert and intelligent. To-day he was a very smart Border Terrier, attired in a new navy blue suit, a spotless white collar and a maroon tie. He walked about

C

the gardens, alone amongst the crowd, looking at all the people and listening to their admiring comments.

Very few people knew Mr. Gray personally but practically everybody knew who he was the moment they laid eyes upon him. If Mr. Gray had been labelled like his own rarer plants they could not have been more sure of his status. (It is difficult to explain the matter except by saying that there is a sort of sixth sense which operates only in a land like Scotland where people have held their position —high or low—for centuries; where people know their own position to a hair's-breadth and are satisfied to keep it.)

" Hallo, there's the head gardener! " exclaimed one of Mr. Ayrton's guests. " I must just ask him about his delphiniums. Never saw anything so fine! "

Of course Mr. Gray was delighted to explain his method of cultivation. He explained about the tomatoes too; they were growing out-of-doors in pots in a sheltered corner of the walled garden.

By this time quite a number of guests had assembled to seek Mr. Gray's advice: the hydrangeas were simply marvellous, especially the lovely white one. Did Mr. Gray think it would grow in a garden near Peebles? What was the name of the huge plants—rather like rhubarb—with pretty blue flowers which seemed to be growing wild near the burn? Could Mr. Gray recommend something as a hedge—something unusual? What sort of manure was used for the leeks? When did Mr. Gray prune his peach-trees?

To all these questions Mr. Gray answered not only with patience but with pleasure and at length. He was afraid hydrangeas would not do well at Peebles; he was not sure, of course, but he rather thought the situation was too high. The huge plants near the burn were a kind of forget-me-not. They liked lots of seaweed. Yes, it seemed queer, admitted

Mr. Gray, but seaweed was the thing. Of course seaweed was easy enough to get at Amberwell, you could barrow it up from the shore.

" Do you grow endives here? " asked one gentleman. " I can't think what Scott does with the endives. They're always so bitter."

" It's the light makes endives bitter," replied Mr. Gray. " September's the month for blanching them. You should put a big flower-pot over them and a stone on top to keep out the light."

Some of the gentlemen cracked jokes with Mr. Gray and Mr. Gray laughed heartily and replied in kind and enjoyed himself tremendously.

When the guests went in to supper Mr. Gray went home to have his meal, but he was ready and waiting at the lily-pool half an hour later, for although Mr. Ayrton intended to turn on the fountain with his own hands it was essential for Mr. Gray to be there.

The light had faded now and the stars were bright. There was the sound of music drifting into the garden through the open windows of the drawing-room. Mr. Gray sat down on the teak seat which had been put near the lily-pool and waited. He felt happy. He felt quite young and romantic. It was many years since he had courted Jean Macdonald and won her; Jean was now middle-aged (as he was) and had a double chin, but to-night, sitting alone in the garden and listening to the distant strains of " The Chocolate Soldier," he remembered her as she used to be. So pretty she was with her smooth pink cheeks and her smooth dark hair!

Time was passing and the moon had not yet risen above the trees. Supposing it did not rise! thought Mr. Gray in sudden anxiety. Supposing that to-night it failed to keep tryst! Fortunately Mr. Gray's anxiety did not last long

for after a few minutes he saw a radiance in the proper airt.
In a few minutes more there was visible a pale golden disc
which looked for all the world as if it were hanging in the
branches of the chestnut tree; it hung there for a while and
then sailed into the clear sky and flooded the garden with
light.

Perhaps Mr. Ayrton had been watching it too (he too
may have been a trifle anxious) for no sooner had the moon
risen than the french windows of the drawing-room were
thrown open and the company streamed out on to the terrace.
This was Mr. Gray's signal to switch on the fairy-lights
and he did so.  The tiny bulbs of all colours suspended
in the branches of the surrounding trees were extremely
effective.

" Oh, how lovely! " exclaimed the ladies.  " Oh, what
a beautiful night!  Not a bit cold!  Look at the moon!
Look at the fairy-lights! "

They were all talking at once and laughing as they came
along the terrace and down the steps into the lily-pool
garden.

Connie was one of the first to appear, with Lady Annan
by the hand; they were followed by Mrs. Lambert and
Sir Andrew Findlater.  Then came a group including
Dr. Maddon and Miss Ayrton, Lady Findlater and Mr.
Orme . . . and after that such a crush of people that it
was difficult to see who was who.  The two Findlater boys
and Gerald Lambert, finding themselves hemmed in,
climbed over the stone balustrade and ran down the slope.
Mr. Ayrton was there too, of course, he pushed his way
through the crowd and came over to where Mr. Gray was
standing.  To-night even Mr. Ayrton seemed excited.

" You'll have to stand back a bit! " he shouted, waving
his arms.  " Make a circle round the edge of the lawn.
You don't want to get wet."

The guests obeyed cheerfully. Some stood round the lawn, others on the steps, a few had remained upon the terrace and were looking down at the scene.

What a scene it was, thought Mr. Gray. It reminded him of a scene in the theatre; it was too gay and beautiful to be real! The ladies looked like flowers in their lovely dresses (thought Mr. Gray who had gone all poetical with excitement). The silver moon, the fairy-lights, the velvet shadows on the grass . . . but there was no time to dream for Mr. Ayrton was taking off his jacket.

Mr. Gray went forward and took the jacket and watched while Mr. Ayrton rolled up his sleeves.

" It's here isn't it, Gray? " asked Mr. Ayrton, stooping down.

" Just a wee bit to your right, sir."

Everybody had stopped talking and there was a strange hush. Then suddenly the silvery fountain sprang up and opened like a flower and the drops came pattering down.

Somehow to Mr. Gray it was an anti-climax and just a trifle disappointing, for Mr. Gray had already seen it playing. Last night the fountain had enchanted him, it had seemed magical and other-wordly, it had filled him with awe. To-night it was beautiful of course but the crowds of people and the fairy-lights detracted from the enchantment and made it seem (as he had thought before) like a scene in the theatre—a transformation scene. But Mr. Gray was probably the only person present who was disappointed; on all sides there were murmurs of applause and expressions of astonishment and admiration at the lovely sight.

It was late when the guests decided to leave. Mr. Gray waited until the last guest had gone before he turned off the fountain. Then he and Mrs. Gray walked home through the gardens together.

"What a grand day it's been!" said Mr. Gray with a sigh.

"It's been your day, Jamie," said Mrs. Gray, taking his arm and pressing it gently. "The fountain was all very well in its way, but the gardens are the real thing. You'd get tired of the fountain but you'd never get tired of the gardens—that's what I've been thinking."

Mr. Gray had been thinking the same thing himself.

# CHAPTER SIX

MR. AND MRS. AYRTON usually went to the Riviera in March; but one year, when Anne was twelve years old, they decided to spend the winter in South Africa. The children were not told of their parents' plans and the first they knew of it was when several large new trunks arrived and were placed upon the landing.

" Is Mother going away? " said Nell to the under-housemaid.

" They're both going to South Africa," replied Agnes. " They'll be away three months. Miss Ayrton's coming to stay."

" For three months? " asked Nell in horrified tones.

Agnes nodded.

When the other children heard the news they were equally horrified, for to have Aunt Beatrice at Amberwell for three whole months would be frightful. Aunt Beatrice would not leave them alone; she was always appearing in the nursery at odd hours (sometimes she even invited herself to tea in the nursery) and Nannie did not like her. Nannie was terribly polite to Aunt Beatrice but the moment she had left the room Nannie seized a duster and flew round like a whirlwind, polishing everything she could lay her hands on (it was just as well to keep out of Nannie's way on these occasions, the children had found); and it was not only Nannie whose equilibrium was upset by Aunt Beatrice; the whole house seethed in an uncomfortable manner. In fact it was rather like living upon the slopes of a volcanic mountain. Nothing really happened, there was no eruption, but one had a feeling that at any moment the volcano might burst into flames.

On this occasion however Aunt Beatrice was on her best behaviour and managed to refrain from criticism of the way the house was run. She had a friend to stay with her part of the time and that kept her busy. The two ladies walked together in the gardens and went for drives in the car. Quite often they went out to tea (for Beatrice Ayrton, having been born and brought up at Amberwell, knew a great many people in the district).

When Miss Cannan left Miss Ayrton felt a little dull and began to bestir herself. The three girls were still having their meals in the nursery, surely it was time that they came downstairs to lunch. She suggested to Nannie that they should do so.

" Perhaps their mother should be consulted," suggested Nannie in the ultra-refined voice which the children disliked so much.

" But that would take weeks," objected Miss Ayrton.

" Well, it's for you to say, Miss Ayrton."

" Yes, I should like them to come down to lunch—they can have their other meals in the nursery of course—and I shall take them to church on Sunday mornings. It's ridiculous that they're never taken to church. Please have them ready at the proper time."

Nannie swallowed hard. She was quite pleased for the girls to go to church but she was furious at being told to have them ready at the proper time—as if she had to be told! Naturally she would have them ready at the proper time.

Having settled the matter satisfactorily Miss Ayrton went downstairs quite oblivious of the fact that she had given mortal offence. Poor woman, she did not mean to be offensive but she had been born with the knack of saying the wrong thing.

Connie and Nell and Anne were somewhat dismayed when they heard of the new arrangements—especially as regarded their midday meal—but it was not nearly as bad as they had expected. Aunt Beatrice was quite pleasant and chatted to them about her various activities in Edinburgh and her annual visit to Rome. Every May Aunt Beatrice went to Rome and stayed in a " Pensione " near the Spanish Steps which was run by a Frenchwoman, Madame Le Brun. It was a very select Pensione and one met very interesting people there; people who knew what was what and appreciated good cooking. Aunt Beatrice liked talking and she found her nieces exceedingly good listeners so all went well. Connie and Nell and Anne learned a great deal about Rome, about St. Peter's and the Catacombs and the pictures in the Vatican, but they heard even more about Madame Le Brun and the Pensione Valetta and Aunt Beatrice's fellow guests . . . for as a matter of fact Aunt Beatrice was really more interested in present-day people than in ancient history.

Just occasionally Aunt Beatrice startled her young companions by a cutting remark—her tongue had always been an unruly member—but they realised she was doing her best to be " nice " and were suitably grateful.

The boys came home as usual for the Christmas Holidays and as usual the house woke up on their arrival and was full of bustle and excitement. Roger was now at Sandhurst, he was tall and slender and fair—a very grown-up young man in his own opinion and in the opinion of his sisters. Tom was still at school but was going to Oxford shortly.

Aunt Beatrice was in her element when the boys came home, she was gay and happy and allowed them to do exactly as they liked—which was a pleasant change from the strict rule of their parents. She agreed immediately when Tom suggested they might have a Christmas Party at Amberwell and entered into the preparations with zest. Invitations were sent out to all the young people in the neighbourhood and Mr. Gray was instructed to dig up a young conifer and bring it up to the house ... and the fairy-lights, which had been bought when the fountain was opened, came in very useful.

The two boys had a delightful time climbing upon ladders and decorating the branches, sprinkling them with boracic crystals and hanging up the lights, while Connie and Nell and Anne looked on and admired and ran to get coloured string and pieces of wire and tied labels on to the little parcels which were to be given to their guests. It was all tremendous fun and, if the truth were told, Nell and Anne enjoyed the preparations very much more than the party itself. Nell and Anne were so shy, and so unused to the society of their kind, that they found parties an ordeal.

The others enjoyed it of course for it was a good party with games and country dancing and an excellent supper —Aunt Beatrice had seen to that—and last of all the surprise of the evening when the Christmas Tree was revealed in all its glory and the gifts were distributed to the guests.

Tom was the most social member of the Ayrton family; it was he who had wanted the party and it was he who enjoyed it most of all. It was he who had discovered a little piece of mistletoe in the woods and had hung it upon the chandelier in the hall without telling anybody about it. Aunt Beatrice was his first victim, he caught her coming out of the dining-room and kissed her soundly before all the guests, and Aunt Beatrice laughed and blushed like a girl and was tremendously pleased with her nephew's attention. After that Tom caught quite a lot of people, some old and some young, but it was not until the party was over and the guests were on the point of departure that he managed to catch Mary Findlater, for whose especial benefit the trap had been set.

2

Mr. and Mrs. Ayrton returned to Amberwell in March. They had enjoyed their trip, but they were glad to get home and to settle down in their own comfortable quarters. It was now time for Aunt Beatrice to pack her boxes and go back to Edinburgh. She had held the fort nobly in their absence and had made friends with her nephews and nieces—and if she had gone at once without opening her mouth she would have left pleasant memories behind. Unfortunately Beatrice Ayrton had a complex nature; when she was happy she was kind and agreeable, but when she was upset or her temper was roused she was by no means so pleasant.

" It was very good of you to stay here while we were away," said Mrs. Ayrton at breakfast the morning after their return. " I hope you were comfortable, Beatrice."

" Of course she was comfortable," said Mr. Ayrton smugly. " Amberwell is a very comfortable house."

Beatrice had been comfortable—and happy—but her brother's attitude annoyed her. " It would be a much more comfortable house if the servants were more amenable," she declared. " It's Nannie of course! "

" Nannie! " exclaimed Mrs. Ayrton in surprise.

" She's very impertinent."

" Oh no, Beatrice. I don't think so. I've had Nannie for years and she's never been impertinent to me."

" It's her manner," Beatrice declared. " She puts on a

very strange sort of voice when I speak to her, and she has a bad influence in the house. You ought to get rid of Nannie. In any case you don't need her now that the children are older. It would be better to get a French maid. And then there's Mrs. Duff," continued Beatrice, getting into her stride. " Mrs. Duff is ridiculously extravagant and her cooking leaves much to be desired. She has been here far too long and she's careless. Janet is lazy and underhand. The fact is they all need to be watched and kept up to the mark—but Nannie is much the most troublesome."

Mrs. Ayrton bore this with patience. She did not intend to take her sister-in-law's advice, but Beatrice could not help being tiresome so it was foolish to quarrel with her. Mr. Ayrton's temper was not so mild and when Beatrice turned her attention to the gardens and their management he rounded upon her fiercely.

" Gray has been here for years! His father was here before him! " exclaimed Mr. Ayrton.

" He doesn't plan ahead sufficiently."

" I have every confidence in Gray."

" More confidence in Gray than in me, I suppose."

" Yes. Gray knows about the gardens and you don't."

" That's what you think! As a matter of fact I know much more than he does. The waste that goes on in the garden is deplorable."

" I don't believe it," shouted Mr. Ayrton. " There's no more waste in Amberwell gardens than there is anywhere else."

" And the manure," continued Beatrice raising her voice. " Cartloads of manure! Gray ought to make compost."

" He does! " bellowed Mr. Ayrton. " There's a compost heap near the potting-shed."

" It isn't properly prepared; he should——"

Mr. Ayrton struck the table with his fist. " I don't want

your half-baked advice," he shouted. " Gray knows what he's doing and I'm perfectly satisfied with him."

There had been rows before of course, for William Ayrton and his sister were too alike to get on well together (both had easily-roused tempers and undisciplined tongues, both were as stubborn as mules); but this was a worse row than usual and it took all Mrs. Ayrton's diplomacy to avert an open breach. Beatrice had intended to leave at the end of the week but now announced that she would go to-morrow instead. Perhaps it was just as well, thought Mrs. Ayrton, who felt a little tired.

The row had taken place at breakfast-time and by midday everybody in the house knew about it, for Agnes the under-housemaid (who had been dusting the hall during the breakfast hour) had heard every word. It was a great pleasure to disseminate the news and it lost nothing in the telling. Mrs. Duff was informed of Miss Ayrton's opinion of her cooking; Nannie heard that she was impertinent and ought to be sacked; Janet was told that she was lazy and underhand. Mr. Gray had looked in at eleven for a pleasant cup of tea and found everyone in an extremely bad temper and was given an exaggerated account of what had been said about *him* in the dining-room.

If Miss Ayrton could have heard what was said about her in the kitchen she would have been surprised.

3

The only human beings in Amberwell who did not know about the row were Connie and Nell and Anne. They knew something was wrong for Nannie had been polishing madly all the afternoon and when they sat down to nursery-tea her face was like thunder. Nobody spoke and nobody ate very much; the atmosphere was so charged with electricity that you could almost hear it crackle.

At last Nell could bear it no longer. " Why are you cross with us! " she cried, and suddenly burst into tears.

" Cross? " asked Nannie, glaring at her.

" Yes—cross——" sobbed Nell. " We haven't—done anything——" She threw out her hands in a gesture of despair and knocked over the milk jug. She had done something now, of course. The clean cloth was flooded and milk poured over the edge of the table on to Nannie's apron.

" You'll go straight off to bed, Nell," said Nannie rising. " That's the best place for you. I'm sure I don't know what's the matter with you—sickening for measles, I wouldn't wonder."

" It's you! " wailed Nell. " It's not me at all! "

" Off to bed," said Nannie firmly.

Nell went off to bed without another word—she was not sorry to go—but Anne was appalled at the injustice. Nannie was usually so kind; she was usually so sensible. What had happened to Nannie? Anne left her tea half finished and fled from the scene of disaster, down the stairs and out into the garden. Her one idea was to escape, to find a place where she could hide from the world—and weep. Ponticum, of course! Ponticum was a sure refuge.

Anne sped through the walled garden and out at the gate and dived through the little gap between the rhododendron bushes . . . then suddenly she halted with a heaving chest; somebody was here before her! It was Aunt Beatrice.

Anne was petrified with astonishment.

" Come here," Aunt Beatrice said.

Anne hesitated. Her instinct was to fly.

" Come here, Anne," repeated Aunt Beatrice in a curiously rough voice.

Anne went and stood before her. She was sitting on a box—the box where they kept their treasures. Anne had always been a little frightened of Aunt Beatrice and she was much more frightened now for Aunt Beatrice looked so queer. Her eyes were red and her cheeks were wet and her hair was hanging in wisps over her forehead. Anne gazed at her in horror—it had never occurred to Anne that grown-up people cried.

" You needn't stare like that," said Aunt Beatrice with a little catch in her voice.

Anne gazed at the ground.

" Why are you frightened? I'm not going to eat you," Aunt Beatrice added.

Anne said nothing.

" I'm going away to-morrow. You'll be glad, won't you? Everybody will be glad to see the last of me." She drew a sobbing breath and continued, " You think I'm mad, don't you? But that's because you don't understand; you don't know what it's like to be miserable. I was like you—once—long ago—running about Amberwell, happy and carefree. I never thought of the future and I don't suppose you do. Perhaps some day you'll be like me."

She paused for a moment to mop her eyes with her soaking wet handkerchief.

Anne was so frightened that she was shaking all over.

" Some day," continued the harsh unsteady voice. " Some day, sooner or later, you'll be turned out of Amberwell. It will belong to Roger. It won't be your home any more. You'll have no right to walk in Amberwell gardens. You'll have no right to pick a flower. Perhaps you'll be asked to come when Roger and his wife want your help, but you'll be thrown out when they have no further use for you—that's very certain. You'll be expected to smile and look pleasant. If you don't, you won't be asked again."

"But Aunt Beatrice——" began Anne in a very small voice.

Aunt Beatrice laughed hysterically. "It's true!" she cried. "It's all true—every word. You won't marry. You aren't like Connie—a pretty, empty-headed doll! You aren't the type to marry."

"I don't want to—to marry—anybody——" gasped Anne.

"Then you're a fool. Marriage is the only thing that could save you!" cried Aunt Beatrice wildly. "Marriage while you're young—before you lose the freshness of youth—that's your only hope. Long ago there was a man who wanted to marry me—yes, me—that surprises you, doesn't it? I wasn't pretty but I was young—and we loved each other. But they said he wasn't good enough—not good enough for a Miss Ayrton—so they sent him away. There was nobody else—ever. Nobody else ever looked at me. Why should anybody look at me when the other girls were prettier and more attractive?"

Anne was speechless. This was the most terrible thing that had ever happened to her.

"That was my only chance," said Aunt Beatrice, her voice hardening. "If I had married I would have had a life of my own—a place in the world—somebody to care for. At least I would have been necessary to somebody, not utterly unloved and unwanted."

Anne felt she could not bear it a moment longer, she looked round desperately.

"All right, you can go," said Aunt Beatrice sitting up and blowing her nose.

"I'm—sorry," said Anne. She knew it was inadequate but what else could she say?

"I believe you are," said Aunt Beatrice, looking at her curiously. "Well, never mind; it isn't your fault anyway.

I wouldn't have been such a fool if you hadn't taken me by surprise. I thought I was safe in the wigwam."

This seemed to end the interview so Anne came away. For a little while she sat in the potting-shed, not exactly thinking—she was too shattered—but musing in a dazed sort of way about all that Aunt Beatrice had said. The awful part was it was true. Every word was true . . . unloved and unwanted, thought Anne.

After a bit she got up and went back to the nursery and, although she had probably been out less than half an hour, so much had happened that she forgot there had been a row. But the storm was over and the skies were blue; Nannie, regretting her bad temper, was all smiles and Nell was quite happy sitting up in bed and reading Count Hannibal with absorbtion.

Anne went in and sat on the end of her bed.

" Hallo! " said Nell looking up and smiling.

" Hallo! " replied Anne listlessly.

" What's the matter? "

" Nothing—really. I saw Aunt Beatrice."

" Where did you see her? "

" In Ponticum."

" In Ponticum! " exclaimed Nell, her voice going up in a squeak. " Do you mean she knows about Ponticum? "

Anne pushed back her unruly hair. " I suppose she must."

" But didn't you ask her? Perhaps she played there when she was little."

" I don't know," said Anne flatly.

" What did she say? " asked Nell.

Anne could tell nobody—not even Nell—what Aunt Beatrice had said.

" Surely she must have said something," urged Nell.

"She called it the wigwam," said Anne who had just remembered.

"How funny! The wigwam! It's rather like a wigwam, isn't it? I wonder if the little saucer belonged to her. Did you ask her about it?"

"No."

"Anne, what's the matter? Was she beastly to you?" asked Nell anxiously.

"N'no," replied Anne in a doubtful tone.

"Well, never mind," said Nell comfortingly. "We don't need to worry about her. She's going away to-morrow and I don't expect she'll be back for ages."

Anne was silent.

# PART TWO

*Standing with reluctant feet*
*Where the brook and river meet;*
*Womanhood and childhood fleet.*

HENRY WADSWORTH LONGFELLOW

## CHAPTER SEVEN

TEN YEARS had passed since the opening of the fountain but Amberwell had changed very little. Some of the trees had grown larger and a few had been cut down. An alpine garden had been made at the end of the lawn outside the drawing-room windows; it was rather attractive with its black boulders and the rock plants nestling in the crevices. There were little paths and steps, so that you could walk round and look at all the plants . . . but to the children this little garden was completely spoilt by the labels. Each plant had a label attached with its name printed clearly upon it, and the smaller the plant the larger the label. For instance there was a tiny plant with soft grey leaves and a sweet little blue flower which was labelled Meritoriana Cannabilis Alpiniensis—or some such nonsense. The children felt certain that Zobji the hobgoblin must haunt the alpine garden. Nothing enrages Zobji so much as swank latin names, and the person who calls a foxglove Digitalis Purpurea may be taken suddenly with night cramps—and well he deserves it.

In addition to these alterations some rhododendrons in the spring garden had been cleared to make room for a grove of wild cherries, and four small palm trees had been planted in a sheltered glade beside the avenue.

Mr. Ayrton was very proud of his palms, and took his guests to admire them—especially if the guest happened to come from south of the Border.

" Palm trees in Scotland! " the guest would exclaim in-

85

credulously, which of course gave Mr. Ayrton the right opening.

" Chamaerops excelsa," he would say and would continue with a dissertation upon the delightful soft mild climate of Amberwell, due to its sheltered position and the proximity of the Gulf Stream.

If the guest were not very careful he would find he had let himself in for a comprehensive tour of the estate, which might have been pleasant enough if he had been allowed to admire the flowers and bushes in peace but which most people found extremely tiring in the company of Mr. Ayrton. They were hurried past beds of roses and halted before a small bush of purple flowers. " Olearia Semidentata," their host would say. " It's wonderful, isn't it? But wait until you see my Passiflora coerulia."

There were very few who emerged from the odreal with flying colours.

Mr. Ayrton was usually the worse for these personally conducted tours, they brought on his lumbago. He put it down to the unwonted exercise and to standing about too long. The children knew better of course, they knew it was Zobji getting his own back.

The gardens had changed very little with the passing years but the children had changed a good deal. Roger was a subaltern in the Guards, Tom was reading medicine at Oxford. The three girls were not at school—they had remained at Amberwell—and Miss Clarke still came in daily to give them lessons.

To do her justice Miss Clarke had tried to persuade Mrs. Ayrton to send them to school (she thought it would do them good and she felt they deserved a better education than she was able to give them) but Mrs. Ayrton had never been to school herself and saw no reason why her daughters should be highly educated. They would marry—that went without saying—and the money spent upon teaching them Latin and Geometry and such-like nonsense would be wasted. Connie was very pretty. She could sing quite nicely and play the piano—and of course she could dance. Nell was less attractive, but no doubt she would improve. Anne's future was a matter of indifference to her mother. Mrs. Ayrton had never forgiven Anne for not being a boy.

The three girls had been given a half-holiday and had decided to have a picnic on the moor. It was the first picnic of the season, the first day of Spring. There was a smell of Spring rising from the moist brown earth and the grass in the meadow. The hedges had a dim green mist upon them, a promise of leaves which would soon clothe them in emerald brilliance; soon there would be primroses in the banks, hiding amongst their soft leaves, and the birds would begin to collect moss and sticks and fragments of wool and feathers to build their nests.

Connie had walked on ahead but Nell and Anne lingered for they had decided to make a Nature Book of Amberwell. It was to be a diary of the weather and the birds and the flowers and the trees. The project, still fresh in their minds, was fascinating.

" It's the right day to begin," said Nell eagerly. " It's the day of beginnings . . . all the trees are budding. Look at this chestnut! I love chestnut buds; they're so brown and sticky."

" Just like glue," agreed Anne. She laid her hand upon the bole of the chestnut tree gently (almost as if it were alive, thought Nell, as if it were a dog or a pony and could feel her caress) and looked up at the budding branches with a strange light in her face. " It's a part of Amberwell," she continued in a soft dreamy voice. " Its roots are in Amberwell ground and its leaves breathe Amberwell air."

" Like us," agreed Nell, nodding to show that she understood.

Anne did not answer for a few moments and then she said, " But it will die here. Nobody will pull it up by the roots and move it to another place."

Nell was about to ask her what on earth she meant but they heard Connie's voice calling to them impatiently so they hurried on.

" Whatever were you doing? " asked Connie. " I've carried the basket all the way."

" I'll take it! " exclaimed Anne, seizing it from her.

They went on together through the woods and over the stile on to the open moor for they had decided to have tea in a little quarry by the side of a burn. This moor really belonged to Sir Andrew Findlater and he had let it to the Lamberts for the shooting but the Ayrton girls knew that nobody would mind if they had their picnic there.

When they reached the quarry they saw somebody sitting on a rock; a young man in a grey flannel suit and a blue shirt, open at the neck.

" It's Gerald," said Anne in a low voice. " What a nuisance! Let's go back."

But Gerald had seen them. He rose and waved to them and came towards them smiling.

" Hallo! " he cried. " Is this really you? I haven't seen you for ages."

Anne and Nell hung back, for they were shy (and this pleasantly-smiling young man seemed quite different from the Gerald they remembered) but Connie was equal to the occasion and went forward to meet him.

" Hallo, Gerald, we didn't know you were home," said Connie.

" Only for a few days," he said ruefully. " I'm one of the world's workers, you know."

" You're in your father's firm, aren't you? "

He nodded. " Yes, and I like it immensely, it's a very interesting job, but you needn't think that because I'm the boss's son I have an easy time. I work as hard as the last-joined apprentice—and for longer hours."

" Tell us about it," suggested Connie. " Come and sit down and have tea. There's sure to be lots of food."

" The basket weighs a ton," murmured Anne.

Gerald accepted the invitation with alacrity and soon they were sitting on a bank in the quarry eating scones and jam and talking cheerfully together—Nell and Anne as well—for although this young man seemed quite unlike Gerald he was a friendly young man.

2

" It's funny how we're all scattered," said Anne. " I mean we used to be all here together in the holidays and now there are no proper holidays at all. You're in Glasgow, Roger is at Caterham and Tom is at Oxford."

" Tom gets long holidays, doesn't he? " Gerald inquired.

" Not really," replied Anne. " He seems to do most of his work in the vacations. He's going to be a doctor, you know."

" I know," said Gerald, accepting another scone. " At one time Tom and I were crazy about the Navy but Dad was frightfully keen for me to go into the firm and of course I saw the idea. Building ships is just as good as sailing them, and as a matter of fact I get quite a lot of the sea because I often go out for trials."

" To see how the engines work," suggested Connie.

Gerald smiled. " That's the idea, really."

" It's a pity Tom can't do that," said Anne with a sigh.

" Tom loves the sea. He was frightfully disappointed about it."

" But why? " asked Gerald. " Why didn't he go into the Navy? "

" Father said he was to go to Oxford," explained Anne.

" Goodness! " exclaimed Gerald incredulously. " I can hardly believe it. D'you really mean he wasn't allowed to choose his own career? "

None of the girls could find an answer to that. They were aware that Gerald had always been allowed to do as he wanted.

" Oh well," said Gerald after a short but rather uncomfortable silence. " It seems a bit odd to me, but I expect Tom will make a very good doctor."

" Of course he will! " cried Anne. " He's getting on splendidly. Tom can always do anything he sets his mind to; he always could."

" And he's quite happy," added Connie who liked to think that everything was for the best.

Anne had been talking a lot—she was not as shy as Nell—and Connie had a feeling that it was now her turn to carry on the conversation so she asked politely about Gerald's life in Glasgow and whether he had made many new friends:

" Oh, it's all right," said Gerald. " I know a few people of course. I play tennis occasionally, but more for exercise than anything else."

" It doesn't sound as if you enjoyed it much," said Connie sympathetically.

By this time Gerald had been able to have a good look at his companions and size them up. He smiled at them and said, " You don't know how funny it is to see you. I always thought of you as tiny little girls and now you're all grown-up."

"We're not grown-up," said Anne seriously. "Connie is *nearly* grown-up. She's going to London with Mother to buy clothes."

"I'm sure she'll look charming in them," said Gerald.

It was so funny to hear Gerald being polite that Anne began to giggle.

"Shut up!" whispered Connie, frowning and shaking her head.

It was no use of course. When Anne began to giggle it was hopeless trying to stop her. Anne shook with internal convulsions; she was seized with uncontrollable mirth and flung herself upon the bank writhing helplessly.

The others caught the infection and laughed too.

"What are we laughing at?" asked Gerald at last in a trembling voice. He took out his handkerchief and wiped his eyes. "Come on, Anne. Tell us the joke."

"Anne can never tell you," said Nell hastily (for Nell had a pretty shrewd idea of what had amused her young sister). "Anne never can tell you the joke, and even if she does it isn't a bit funny."

Gerald could hardly believe this. It certainly was difficult to believe that a joke which had thrown a young woman into such a passion of mirth would not be worth hearing. "Do try, Anne," he said earnestly.

At this Anne laughed the more.

"It's no good," said Connie. "Honestly, Gerald. We'll just have to talk about something else."

"Have some more cake," suggested Nell, offering him the last piece.

Gerald accepted it and they talked of something else.

"This is a nice place for tea," he said looking round the little quarry. "I haven't been here for years and years— not since Roger and Tom and I had a shooting-match with a sailor doll."

There was a dead silence. Six round eyes fixed themselves upon Gerald's face.

"A sailor doll with a cap and bell-bottomed trousers," continued Gerald cheerfully. "It made a fascinating target. Tom stuck it up against a rock and we all had shots at it with Roger's rook-rifle. There wasn't much left of it by the time we'd finished. Funny how you remember things, isn't it?"

"Very funny," agreed Nell in a shaky voice. She had not thought of the sailor doll for nearly ten years but now, all of a sudden, she remembered him so clearly that she could almost see him with his blond curly hair and his supercilious smile. Of course she was now too old to mind (and when she saw Anne looking at her anxiously she managed to smile back in a reassuring manner) but all the same she felt a trifle queer.

## CHAPTER EIGHT

CONNIE HAD always been pretty, she had blue eyes and golden hair which was naturally wavy. When she was eighteen she was very pretty indeed. Her mother took her to London and they had a delightful time buying clothes and visiting some of Mrs. Ayrton's relations. Everybody without exception said how pretty Connie was and naturally her mother was very proud of her. They had intended to be away from Amberwell for a fortnight, but they stayed a month, and when they returned Connie was well and truly grown-up. There was no doubt about it.

Mrs. Ayrton discovered that it was very pleasant to have a daughter in the house—a charming little daughter who was always ready to go out with her in the car and to accompany her to parties. She discovered too that Connie was a " draw." Young people in the neighbourhood (who had never thought of calling at Amberwell House before) dropped in at tea-time and accepted invitations to see the gardens. They asked Connie to small dances or to meet them at the Club for tennis. Mrs. Ayrton liked the stir; she liked to see young people about the place. Mr. Ayrton was not so pleased, but he could always retire to his library if he wanted peace.

It seemed to her sisters that Connie had grown up with startling suddenness. They could not understand it. They had talked about it often (in fact they had discussed the matter off and on ever since Connie had returned from London) and they were still discussing it one fine bright

day in October, sitting on the rocks near the Smugglers'
Cave.

" It happens when you're eighteen," said Anne thoughtfully. " You'll be eighteen next year."

" But I don't want it to happen! " cried Nell in alarm.
" I couldn't go out to parties and—and talk to people—
and go downstairs to dinner and all that."

" Perhaps when you're eighteen——"

" Not when I'm eighty! I'd rather things went on just
as they are for ever."

Anne sighed. She knew things could not go on for ever.

" I don't want it," repeated Nell earnestly. " We're
much happier as we are."

" I know," agreed Anne. " But you get older every day
whether you want to or not. Someday we shall be as old
as Aunt Beatrice." Her voice died away into silence.

Anne had never forgotten her meeting with Aunt Beatrice
in Ponticum House. She had never spoken of it—not even
to Nell—and she did her best not to think about it, but
the impression it had made upon her mind was deep and
lasting; every word Aunt Beatrice had said was imprinted
clearly upon her memory. Since that dreadful day Anne
had never felt secure; the time would come when she
would grow old and nobody would want her. The time
would come when she would be turned out of Amberwell
—like Adam and Eve from the Garden of Eden—and she
would be homeless. Even when Anne was not actually
thinking about it the thoughts lay at the back of her mind;
they coloured her whole life and upset her balance. Sometimes she was unnaturally gay and at other times she was
dreamy.

" Do you think Connie is really grown-up inside, or
just pretending? " asked Nell suddenly.

Anne had wondered the same thing; it seemed strange

that a person could change so quickly.    Before she went to
London Connie had been one of themselves and now she
had moved to another sphere.    She had moved downstairs
to a bedroom on the second floor; she spent her leisure in
the drawing-room; she lived and moved and had her being
in the adult world.    Occasionally they saw Connie walking
round the garden with her friends, and once they had seen
her tripping lightly across the hall in her smart new high-
heeled shoes.    On that memorable occasion Connie had
stopped to speak to them.

" Hallo! " she exclaimed.    " What have you been doing?"

They were so astonished at hearing the well-known
question fall from Connie's lips that they were struck dumb,
unable to answer.

Certainly Connie had changed.    She was not the Connie
who had played stump-cricket in the paddock and had gone
for picnics with Nell and Anne on the moor.    They did
not mind, because they still had each other . . . but what
would happen when Nell became eighteen?

" Did you hear what I said? " asked Nell.    She asked
quite amiably for she was used to Anne's vague moods.
Sometimes Anne got lost in thought and did not hear a
word.

" About Connie——" began Anne, coming back to earth.

" No, that was ages ago.    You've been dreaming.    I was
telling you what Miss Clarke said this morning.    She said
Mother wanted to talk to us about something very important."

Anne turned and looked at her sister in surprise.    " About
what? "

" Clarkie wouldn't say.    She just said it was something
nice."

" We might not think it was nice," said Anne appre-
hensively.

Nell nodded. Grown-up people often had the strangest ideas about what was nice.

It was now getting on for tea-time and Nannie would be waiting for them so they rose and brushed the sand from their skirts and went up the slope together; and as they went they tried to guess what it could be. It might be a party (neither Nell nor Anne liked parties but they were aware that parties were supposed to be nice) or it might be something even worse than a party.

" Perhaps one of us is to move into Connie's old room," suggested Anne.

" Oh no! " cried Nell in horrified tones. " They couldn't do that! It would be dreadful not to sleep together. I couldn't bear it."

Anne pushed open the door of the walled garden and they went in (closing the door carefully behind them to keep out the rabbits which were the bane of Mr. Gray's existence). They walked on towards the sheltered corner where the greenhouses had been built. As they passed the vinery they heard voices . . . and by one accord they tiptoed to the door and peeped in.

There were two people in the vinery, Connie and Gerald; they were standing very close together holding each other's hands. Then Connie looked up and smiled at Gerald—and he bent down and kissed her.

Nell and Anne turned and hurried away. They were both so startled that they were speechless. Nell was quite shocked. One had read about love in books of course, but this was Connie . . . and Gerald! They hurried up the nursery stairs and into the bathroom. It was not until they had washed their hands and were drying them on the same towel that Anne found her voice.

" It's begun," she said.

" What's begun? "

" Growing-up has begun."

" But not for us! "

" Yes—for everybody.  Things won't ever be the same again.  You'll see."

Nannie was waiting for them in the nursery.  " Tea's ready," she said smiling.  " Goodness, you do look hot! Have you been hurrying? "

" No," said Nell.  " At least—yes, we did hurry a bit."

" I've got a nice surprise for you," said Nannie.  " You're both to go down to dinner to-night; it's a very special occasion."

2

Meanwhile Gerald had kissed Connie gently on her soft rosy cheek and she had let him kiss her—for they were engaged.  Gerald was not very experienced in matters of this sort but he had a feeling that there was something missing.  He stood back and held her hands and looked at her earnestly.

" You *do* love me, darling? " he asked.

" Of course," replied Connie in surprise.

" I mean——" said Gerald.  " I mean you do *really* love me?  It's not just because—because——"

" Because what? "

" Well," said Gerald, trying to explain.  " Well, sup-posing your father and mother and my father and mother all said we weren't to get married—what then? "

" But Gerald, they're all delighted! "

" I know; but supposing they weren't delighted?  Sup-posing they all said no?  What would you do? "

" It would be horrid," declared Connie.  " But we needn't worry, need we?  It's silly to worry about some-thing that hasn't happened."

Gerald sighed. He said, "You always do what they tell you."

"Yes," agreed Connie. "It's because everything is so much nicer, that's why. It saves such a lot of bother if you do what you're told—and I like people to be pleased with me. That's not wrong, is it?"

"No, of course not, darling. I just mean . . . I mean you aren't marrying me because it will please everybody, are you?"

"How silly you are!" Connie exclaimed.

"Darling, I know I'm silly," said Gerald. "I love you so frightfully. I wish all the parents were furious with us for getting engaged. I wish your parents would forbid you to speak to me—then I would know whether you really loved me."

Connie laughed. "How would you know if I wasn't allowed to speak to you?"

"Because you *would* speak to me—you'd tell them to go to hell—then I'd know for certain."

"It would be awfully uncomfortable," said Connie looking up at him. "It's ever so much nicer as it is, with everybody pleased and happy. At least I think so."

Gerald sighed. He did not really want the Ayrtons and the Lamberts to be upon Montague and Capulet terms but he was a romantic at heart and it all seemed too suitable, too easy. If there had been snags in the course of true love Gerald would have felt more comfortable, but there were no snags at all; as Connie had said everybody was pleased. Already the two mothers were putting their heads together and talking about the wedding. It would take place at St. Stephen's of course and Nell and Anne would be bridesmaids. Mrs. Ayrton thought a Christmas wedding would be delightful, and Mrs. Lambert agreed with the greatest amiability, so it was to be two days after Christmas. The

two fathers were putting their heads together and talking
about settlements. They had always been cronies but now
they were even more matey than before. When they met
Mr. Ayrton would slap his friend on the back and exclaim,
" Ha, ha, my boy! " and Mr. Lambert would reply, " What
ho! " and they would both laugh.

The first time Gerald saw and heard this inane performance his blood boiled; his hands itched to take the
two grey heads and knock them together . . . Ha, ha and
what ho! It was a sort of desecration, Gerald felt. But
of course he had to bear it and being a kindly-natured
person he bore it with outward good humour.


3


Anne had been right when she said growing-up had
begun and nothing would ever be the same again. Connie's
marriage was the first break in the family. It was a magni-
ficent affair and was arranged and managed by Mrs. Ayrton
with her usual efficiency. The church was beautifully
decorated, the bride was a dream in white satin and lace,
and the reception at Amberwell House went off with tremendous éclat. Nothing occurred to mar the perfection of
Connie's wedding—even the weather was propitious.

When it was all over Mrs. Ayrton felt extremely flat.
She missed Connie dreadfully and she missed the youthful
company which had flocked round Connie and livened up
the house . . . but of course Mrs. Ayrton had two more
daughters. They were not so pretty as Connie—or at least
Mrs. Ayrton did not think they were—Nell was too thin
and Anne was too plump. In addition they were both very
shy and awkward. But Mrs. Ayrton thought she could
make something of them. Of course Nell was not yet quite

eighteen and Anne was a year younger but she could begin
to get them into shape.

The first thing to do was to get rid of Miss Clarke, so
Mrs. Ayrton summoned her and told her very kindly that
her services were no longer required.

" Are the girls going to school? " asked Miss Clarke.

" No," replied Mrs. Ayrton. " I'm going to have them
with me."

" You can't mean that they are going to stop having
lessons? "

" They've learnt quite enough."

" Oh no! " cried Miss Clarke. " Oh, Mrs. Ayrton—
they're so young! Anne is only sixteen——"

" Their father and I think it best," said Mrs. Ayrton
sweetly. " We're very grateful to you for all you've done
for the girls and of course we shall be glad to give you an
excellent testimonial."

Miss Clarke was not thinking of testimonials. " Oh
Mrs. Ayrton, please reconsider the matter! " she exclaimed.
" Nell has a very good brain—I had hoped she might go to
Oxford—and Anne is so very young—just a child! I don't
ask you to keep me on, but I do beg you to get someone
else, or better still to send them to school. A year at school
would——"

" No, I think not," said Mrs. Ayrton. She was a little
uncomfortable and it was a relief when she remembered
Disraeli. Never explain, thought Mrs. Ayrton, looking dis-
tastefully at Miss Clarke's anguished face.

So Mrs. Ayrton gave no explanation but merely smiled
sweetly and vaguely and Miss Clarke was powerless.

Miss Clarke had been coming to Amberwell daily for
over twelve years so it was a frightful wrench to tear herself
away. She had no cause to complain of her treatment
for she was presented with a handsome honorarium—in

addition to the excellent testimonial—but she was very miserable all the same. Nell and Anne were unhappy too; they liked Miss Clarke, and her departure put an end to their childhood. They were to be promoted to the place left vacant by Connie, and they did not want promotion.

"Good-bye," said Miss Clarke, kissing them fondly. "You'll read, won't you? Go on reading whatever happens . . . and go on with your Nature Book."

"Of course," agreed Anne. "We will have lots of time——"

"Even if you have no time," said Miss Clarke wildly. "People can always read—if they want to—whether they have time or not."

Nannie was sorry to see Miss Clarke go. She had never liked Miss Clarke but now she realised that Miss Clarke might have been a lot worse, so she shook hands cordially with her one-time enemy and wished her well. Nannie was staying on at Amberwell for Mrs. Ayrton had decided that although the girls would not be in the nursery any more it would be useful to have Nannie there. Nannie could mend the linen and look after the girls' clothes, and later on, when grandchildren began to arrive, Nannie would be very useful indeed.

Mrs. Ayrton toyed with the idea of moving Nell and Anne downstairs to two single bedrooms on the second floor, but Amberwell House was not so very large and the two single bedrooms were convenient for guests, so she decided to leave the girls where they were for the time being.

All these arrangements were easy to a woman of Mrs. Ayrton's ability, and were carried out successfully. The house settled down into the new routine. Unfortunately Mrs. Ayrton was not so successful with her daughters. She had hoped that Nell and Anne would be pleased with their promotion; she had hoped that when they had no lessons to keep them busy they would enjoy going to parties with her and get into the swim and bring young people to the house. She was disappointed. Certainly they did what they were told; they went out with her when she asked them to come, and when she spoke to them they replied politely, but they were not companionable. Mrs. Ayrton came to the conclusion that they never talked at all—and then one day she happened to overhear them chatting to each other and laughing. When she went in and asked what had amused them Anne pointed to a shabby old book which lay upon the table; it was a very old edition of *Measure for Measure* by one, William Shakespeare.

" But Shakespeare isn't funny," said Mrs. Ayrton in surprise.

Anne and Nell did not contradict their mother. They were too polite.

" I suppose you found it in the library? " asked Mrs. Ayrton.

" Yes," replied Anne. " We used to read Shakespeare with Miss Clarke, but we never read this play. It's rather difficult to understand—at least bits of it are."

" Perhaps I could help you," suggested Mrs. Ayrton smiling sweetly. She remembered " doing " *A Midsummer Night's Dream* with her governess (or at least she remembered she had " done " it). She had a vague recollection of fairies and a man with a donkey's head.

" What's a bawd? " asked Nell.

" It's a sort of committee," replied Mrs. Ayrton promptly. " Your father was on the Board of Directors of a big Insurance Company at one time."

Her daughters gazed at her in bewilderment.

" But Pompey was put in prison! " exclaimed Anne.

" He was an unlawful bawd," Nell reminded her.

Mrs. Ayrton was equally bewildered. She picked up

the book and began to turn over the pages and in a very few moments her idea that Shakespeare's Plays were suitable reading for the young received a severe shock. She replaced the book in her husband's library and informed her daughters that they were not to read Shakespeare's Plays.

" Oh well, there are lots of other books," said Anne.

There were lots of books in the library and the girls browsed amongst them very happily, and in addition they continued to collect wild flowers. It was now April and plants were beginning to wake up after their winter sleep. Most plants had country names, which were much more fun than their ordinary everyday names, and many plants had little stories attached to them. Dog violets were called Blue Mice; wood-rush was Chimney-Sweeper, because of its spiky brush; nettles—less obviously—were Adam and Eve in the Bower.

One afternoon when they were returning from an expedition they met Mr. Gray in the gardens and showed him their treasures.

" Och, they're just weeds," he said in disgust.

" But so interesting," said Nell. " We're finding out stories about them. For instance the Red Indians call the plantain White Man's Foot, because when the white men went over to America they took some seeds of it with them and it seeded itself everywhere."

Mr. Gray was heard to say in his deep, rumbling tones that he also had a name for the plantain.

" Oh, what? " asked Nell eagerly. " Do tell us and we'll put it in the book."

But Mr. Gray refused to tell them and offered the feeble excuse that he did not know how to spell it . . . " And that's just mugwort, no more no less," he added, pointing so the feathery flower with its green and silvery leaves.

"It's magic," Nell told him. "Long ago people in China thought it was a magic plant."

"I wouldn't wonder," said Mr. Gray. "It grows like Jack and the Beanstalk. One day it's not there, and a week later it's thriving like mad. See here, Miss Nell, there's no need for you to go seeking for that sort of rubbish; I'll pick you a nice bunch of pretty flowers for your room whenever you like."

# CHAPTER NINE

MR. GRAY did not understand the fascination of collecting wild plants and making a book about them, and Mrs. Ayrton had even less patience with her daughters' hobby. There was nothing wrong in it, of course, but it seemed so "queer." She wanted Nell and Anne to be like other girls—like Connie for instance—and to take their proper place in Society. She wanted them to play tennis and make friends with other girls, and possibly with young men.

Mrs. Ayrton did her best with them; she had their hair waved, she bought them pretty clothes and she kept on urging them to make an effort.

"What sort of effort, Mother?" asked Anne.

"You must smile at people and talk," said Mrs. Ayrton. "You must be friendly. You must meet people half-way."

Unfortunately Nell and Anne were so unused to meeting people that they could not meet them half-way; they could not manufacture polite conversation, it was difficult even to smile. At parties they stood close together all the time and if anybody spoke to them they blushed and trembled. Their behaviour was all the more annoying to their mother because, now that they had been smartened up, they were really very nice-looking (even Anne, the ugly duckling, had a curiously appealing charm). They were young and fresh, their figures had improved, and their complexions were beautiful, but people found them dull. Mrs. Ayrton could not blame people for finding her daughters dull; she found them dull herself.

Perhaps it would have been better, thought Mrs. Ayrton, if she had tried one at a time; if she had taken Nell and left Anne in the schoolroom for another year. Then they could not have clung to one another in that ridiculous fashion.

Mrs. Ayrton was at her wits' end when she received a letter from her sister-in-law asking Anne to go and stay with her for a month. Perhaps it will help, thought Mrs. Ayrton. Beatrice knows a lot of people in Edinburgh . . . but it must be Nell, of course. Nell is the elder. She wrote back at once thanking her sister-in-law and suggesting that Nell should come. Miss Ayrton replied that it was Anne she wanted. Oh well, thought Mrs. Ayrton, Anne had better go; perhaps when Anne is not here I shall be able to do something with Nell.

She explained the matter to her husband.

" Well, I don't know," he said doubtfully. " Beatrice is rather a fool—but it's for you to say, of course."

" It will do Anne a lot of good," declared Mrs. Ayrton. " And it will be good for Nell, too. They've never been separated and they cling to each other like limpets."

Nell and Anne were horrified when they heard the news. It was an absolute bomb-shell. They discussed it together in private.

" Why should I go? " said Anne. " I don't want to go. It's frightful. Fancy being separated for a whole month! And I'm terrified of Aunt Beatrice! I shall tell Mother I don't want to go."

" It's no use," replied Nell miserably. " Mother has made up her mind. She thinks it will improve you."

" It won't," said Anne in a hopeless voice. " Nothing will improve me. I just can't make polite conversation. I can't think of anything to say—especially when Mother is watching me."

" Mother won't be watching you," Nell pointed out.

This was true of course but it did not do much to relieve the gloom.

" It's worse for me, really," continued Nell. " I shan't have you to help me."

" But you'll be here, at Amberwell," said Anne with a sigh.

" Perhaps you needn't stay a whole month," suggested Nell. " Aunt Beatrice may get tired of having you or something."

" I can't think why she wants me at all," declared Anne. She heaved another sigh and added, " You'll write to me, won't you? "

" Yes, and you'll write to me. I tell you what, Anne, I'll get up early and meet the postman. Then you can tell me everything that happens and I won't have to show your letters to Mother."

Oddly enough Nannie was on their side. She was dismayed at the news that Anne was to spend a month in Edinburgh with Miss Ayrton. She said nothing to the girls, of course, nor did she broach the subject to their mother, but Mrs. Duff heard her views in private session.

" It's ridiculous," declared Nannie. " Anne's far too young to go off to Edinburgh on her own."

" But she'll be staying with her aunt," objected Mrs. Duff.

Nannie snorted scornfully. " Her! " she said.

" Anne's nearly eighteen now—that's not so very young. I mind when I was eighteen I was airning my living and——"

" And so was I," interrupted Nannie. " But you and me were brought up very different, Katie. Anne's just a bairn and Nell's not much better. I wouldn't say this to anybody but you, but the fact is they've not been properly brought up. There's been no notice taken of them; they've not been anywhere or seen anything all their lives; they've not even been to the pantomime. That's the truth and you know it as well as me."

This was plain speaking indeed.

2

It was very dull at Amberwell House when Anne had gone. Nell was miserable and far from being better company for her mother she was worse. She mooned about the gardens and went for long walks over the moor and she spent hours sitting in Ponticum House where nobody could find her. Every morning she got up early and met the postman in the avenue and in the first week she received three long letters.

The letters were quite cheerful. Anne said she missed Nell very much but on the whole it was not as bad as she had expected; Aunt Beatrice was very kind. They had been to the Zoo and to the Botanical Gardens and to the theatre together. Aunt Beatrice had bought Anne a new hat and taken her to tea with some friends and she had met several people who were quite easy to talk to.

The second week there were only two letters, and they were much shorter; the third week there was only one.

Nell had met the postman every day and had been disappointed so often that she was thrilled when he handed her a bulky envelope; she could hardly wait until his back was turned before tearing it open to devour its contents.

DARLING NELL,

I am so sorry I have not written to you before but such a lot has been happening that I have had very little time. We have been going about all over the place and I am really getting quite good at talking to people. I can see now what Mother meant when she said we ought to meet people half-way—so I am doing it. Of course Aunt Beatrice does not watch me like Mother which makes it easier. Aunt Beatrice took me to a dance on Thursday night. It was given by some friends of hers who have a lovely country house at Barnton. I had nothing nice to wear so she took me to Jenners and bought me a real evening dress. It is pale pink with little frills—and very pretty. I was rather frightened at first because I did not think I would know anybody to dance with, but oddly enough Aunt Beatrice understood. She said she used to feel the same and then she made up her mind not to care, but just to enjoy herself. Also she gave me a glass of champagne before we started! I don't know whether it was the champagne or the new dress or Aunt Beatrice's advice but I felt on top of the world and enjoyed myself tremendously and I had plenty of partners. Martin was there—he dances beautifully—and there were several other men that I had met before. Aunt Beatrice played bridge most of the evening and did not bother about me at all. Aunt Beatrice is very keen on bridge, she belongs to a club which meets twice a week. She asked me if I minded being left alone while she went out, and of course I said no. The first time it seemed a bit queer being all alone in the flat but now I don't mind a bit. There are plenty of books to read and I can have the wireless. To-night is one of her club nights but I shall not be here alone because Martin is coming to take me to the theatre. It will be fun. I can't make up my mind whether to wear my bridesmaid's dress or my old blue silk. It is difficult to know. I miss you very much and I miss Amberwell. Sometimes when I am alone

I long to be home—especially at night. I miss our talks in bed and everything. All the same I really am enjoying myself and I feel as if I were beginning to grow up and become more like other people. Aunt Beatrice wants me to stay on a little bit longer so I have written to ask Mother if I can.

Lots of love, darling Nell. I wish you were here.

Your loving

Anne

P.S. Aunt Beatrice says my bridesmaid's dress is too smart so I must just wear my blue. I hope Martin will not think it very shabby. I wish you could meet Martin because I am sure you would like him.

P.P.S. I see I have not explained who Martin is. He is Martin Selby and he teaches mathematics in a big school in London. Of course he is very clever but he is amusing too, and not a bit alarming. Aunt Beatrice got to know Martin last year when she was staying in Rome at the Pensione Valetta. Do you remember how she used to talk about her visits to Rome? Martin talks about Rome too, but of course he is much more interesting and knows more about ancient history. Martin has been ill and is staying in Edinburgh for a holiday but he will have to go back to London soon.

A. A.

It was fortunate that Nell had got this letter from the postman because if she had received it at breakfast-time her mother would have insisted upon reading it and somehow she felt that her mother would not have approved of it at all. There was nothing very private about it but it gave Nell a feeling of unease. She read it several times and became more and more worried. Why did Anne want to stay on with Aunt Beatrice and not come home? It seemed so queer. Nell was not very experienced in worldly matters but she was a year older than Anne. Anne was just a child. She was adorable of course, dear and sweet and funny, but she knew nothing about life. Now, here she was, suddenly whirled into a gay round of parties with nobody but Aunt Beatrice to look after her—and apparently Aunt Beatrice was not looking after her at all.

Another thing that worried Nell was the way in which "Martin" kept cropping up in the letter. A schoolmaster —who taught mathematics—seemed a most unlikely sort of man to appeal to Anne. Nell felt certain she would not like Martin; she was even more certain that her parents would not approve of him.

Oh dear! thought Nell . . . but perhaps Mother will say she has got to come home.

Mrs. Ayrton did not share Nell's apprehension; she had received a letter from Anne and one from her sister-in-law as well, and from these she gathered that Anne was emerging from her shell and behaving more like a reasonable human being, so she replied very graciously that Anne might stay a little longer and added that it was very kind of Aunt Beatrice to give her such a good time.

Nell wrote too of course, but she found it difficult to put her feelings into words. She wanted Anne to come home immediately but it seemed selfish to try to persuade her to come home when she was enjoying herself so much. Nell could not help feeling a trifle hurt for it was obvious that she missed Anne much more than Anne missed her. It was even more difficult to find the right thing to say about "Martin" so she left the subject alone. Her letter was mostly about a Garden Party at the Lamberts, which she had been forced to attend and which she had not enjoyed at all. When she re-read her letter it seemed terribly dreary but there was no time to rewrite it so she let it go.

After that Anne's letters were very short and, even worse, there was no mention of her coming home to Amberwell.

### 3

One morning when Nell went down to breakfast she saw a letter in Anne's writing lying upon the table. She looked at it eagerly and then she saw it was addressed to her father.

Nell suffered a qualm of anxiety when he took up the letter and looked at it. (Mr. Ayrton's habit was to examine the outside of his letters carefully and then slit them open very neatly with a paper-knife. Nell had watched this performance often but never with such impatience as to-day.)

" I thought this was from Anne—it looks like her writing —but the postmark is London," Mr. Ayrton remarked.

" London! " gasped Nell.

He took no notice. He was unfolding the letter now . . . Nell watched him as he read it and saw his face change and his brow darken with rage.

" Good heavens! " he exclaimed. " The girl has gone mad! "

" What's happened? " asked Mrs. Ayrton in alarm.

" She's married—that's what's happened."

" Who is married? " asked Mrs. Ayrton.

" Anne, of course."

" Anne—married! It can't be true! "

" It's true," declared Mr. Ayrton furiously. " She says so herself——"

" But William——"

" There you are! " he cried, throwing the letter across the table to his wife. " Read it! She's married a school-

master without a penny to his name—a schoolmaster!
She's done it without as much as a ' by your leave,' without
telling us a thing about it! "

" But she couldn't! " exclaimed Mrs. Ayrton, seizing the
letter.

" She has, I tell you," raged Mr. Ayrton. " She's
married the man and gone to London with him. That's
what she's done. She's schemed and plotted behind our
backs——"

" But Beatrice! What was Beatrice thinking of to allow
it! "

" Beatrice! She's fixed up the whole thing of course!
The woman is crazy. I said at the beginning we shouldn't
allow Anne to go—but you insisted. Well, I hope you're
satisfied."

" Perhaps it isn't so bad——" began Mrs. Ayrton.

" Bad! It's as bad as can be," stormed her husband.
" How could it be worse? If the man had the slightest
sense of decency he would have asked my consent. It's
obvious he's an absolute blackguard. For all we know he
has a wife already and half a dozen brats! "

" Nell, you had better go upstairs," said Mrs. Ayrton
hastily.

" But I want to know——" began Nell in a trembling
voice.

" You know all that's necessary," declared her father.
" Your sister has gone mad and married an out-and-out
blackguard. That's quite enough, isn't it? "

# CHAPTER TEN

AFTER THAT one terrible row Anne's name was not mentioned by either of her parents—or at least not in Nell's hearing. A dark silence descended upon the house. Nell bore it for two days and then she could bear it no longer and plucking up courage she went to her mother and asked for news of Anne.

"We know nothing," said Mrs. Ayrton shortly.

"But you *must* know something."

Mrs. Ayrton hesitated for a moment, looking at Nell's miserable face, and then she said, "I know it's hard for you, Nell, but you must be brave. Anne has behaved disgracefully; I couldn't have believed any daughter of mine could have behaved like that. Your father is furious—as you know. We can't do anything about it because she is married; she has chosen her own path; she must go her own way."

"I'd like her address," said Nell.

"Your father doesn't wish you to write to her."

"But Mother——"

"That's enough," said Mrs. Ayrton and she turned her back and continued to arrange the flowers.

Nell realised that the interview was supposed to have ended, but anguish gave her courage. "I must know," she said in a shaky voice. "She's not—ill or anything, is she?"

"She seems perfectly well, and not in the least ashamed of her extraordinary behaviour." Mrs. Ayrton hesitated and then added, "If anybody outside the family asks about

Anne you can say she has married a friend of your aunt's and that we are not very pleased about it; there is no need to say more."

" Aunt Beatrice must have liked him, so perhaps——"

" Aunt Beatrice must have gone off her head. There is no other explanation. Your father has written to her—and to Anne as well. The matter is closed."

" Closed! " echoed Nell in dismay.

" Yes, closed. It's no use talking about it any more."

Of course Nell expected a letter from Anne—surely Anne would write and tell her all about it—and when no letter came she disobeyed her mother's injunction and wrote to Anne, care of Aunt Beatrice, beseeching her to reply . . . but she heard nothing. Anne seemed to have vanished completely—more completely than if she had died.

Even Nannie knew very little about it, and for once Mr. and Mrs. Ayrton had been able to keep a secret from their staff. The matter was discussed in Mrs. Duff's sitting-room and commented upon, but all that was known was that Miss Anne had married a Mr. Selby of whom her parents disapproved.

Nell moved in an unhappy dream. She was like two people in one skin. One of these people walked and talked, dressed in the morning and undressed at night, the other person suffered. A dozen times a day she thought, I must tell Anne about that when she comes home . . . and a dozen times she remembered that Anne was not coming home.

Meals were the worst time for Nell. She sat at the table and listened to her parents' conversation. They talked about all sorts of matters but they never mentioned Anne. Nell wondered if Anne was in their minds or whether they had been able to banish her completely.

Nell's thoughts went round and round. It's a dreadful thing for her to have done, thought Nell. It's no wonder they're angry . . . but it isn't really her fault. Nobody could understand unless they knew Anne as I do. She's just a child. She hasn't had a chance to grow up properly. I'm the same, thought Nell wretchedly. I'm not properly grown-up. We can't talk to people; we don't enjoy things that other girls enjoy. Perhaps we're not normal!

This dreadful idea that she and Anne were not normal —not quite right in the head—took root in Nell's mind and haunted her persistently. As a matter of fact she was so distraught by her sufferings, borne alone and in silence, that she found herself doing all sorts of stupid things. She would go upstairs to fetch something and forget what it was she had come for; she lost her comb and discovered it put away in a drawer where it had no right to be; she went up to dress for dinner and knew no more until she discovered herself getting into bed . . . and one day when she was sent to Mr. Gray with a message she found Mr. Gray and could not remember what she had been told to say.

" Maybe it would be about the peas? " suggested Mr. Gray.

" It's all right," said Nell, trying to speak casually. " It isn't anything important."

She was turning to go away when Mr. Gray stopped her. " I'm hoping you've got good news of Mrs. Selby? " he inquired.

For a moment Nell did not know whom he meant.

" She'll always be Miss Anne to me," added Mr. Gray. " But it's the right thing to give folks their proper titles. You've good news of her, I hope? "

" Oh—yes—at least—I haven't heard—lately," stammered Nell.

"You'll be hearing," said Mr. Gray nodding. "I wouldn't worry too much, Miss Nell. Maybe it'll all come right sooner than you're expecting."

Nell gazed at him. She wondered how much he knew —but there was no time to say any more for Mrs. Ayrton was coming down the path.

"There you are, Nell!" she exclaimed. "Have you asked Mr. Gray about the raspberries?"

"There's none left," replied Mr. Gray. "I was just telling Miss Nell they're finished."

"Oh, what a bother! Mr. and Mrs. Lambert are coming to dinner."

"There's peaches, m'm. Mrs. Lambert likes peaches. I'll send up a nice dish of peaches for dessert."

Mr. Gray did not wink at Nell (as he had done long ago when he had saved the children's treasures from the bonfire); Nell was too old to be winked at now, but he gave her an understanding look which comforted her a little.

2

There was nothing unusual in the Lamberts coming to dinner at Amberwell; they came often, and Mr. and Mrs. Ayrton just as frequently dined at Merlewood. They were "nearest neighbours" and they all four liked a game of bridge. When Nell heard the Lamberts were coming she was pleased in a mild sort of way for anything was preferable to the usual family dinner, when the three of them sat round the table talking about everything except Anne. Besides Nell liked Mrs. Lambert; she was so small and gay. Admittedly Mrs. Lambert was mischievous and made somewhat startling remarks in her pretty tinkling voice, but her remarks did not hurt, for they were not malicious, they

merely made you sit up and blink. Of course Mrs. Lambert
had aged since the day of the Fountain Party but she was
still very pretty and still like a fairy—like a middle-aged
fairy if such a creature were possible.

When Nell went downstairs the Lamberts had arrived
and the four friends were having sherry in the drawing-
room. The conversation ceased suddenly as Nell appeared,
so of course they had been talking about Anne. Naturally
the Lamberts would have to be told something about the
affairs of their son's sister-in-law. She wondered how much
they had been told.

"Hallo, here's Nell!" exclaimed Mr. Lambert cheerfully. "Why don't you lend us Nell for a bit. I've always
wanted a nice little daughter, and Poppet produced a great
big clumsy son."

"It was very clever of me," said Mrs. Lambert smiling.

Everybody called her Poppet and (although she was not
silly but quite the reverse) the silly name seemed to suit
her.

At dinner Nell sat next to Mrs. Lambert and listened to
the conversation in silence; she was "the odd man out"
of the party but it did not worry her. They talked about
Connie and Gerald and about the baby which was expected
in November; there was a good deal of laughter upon the
subject of Grandpas and Grandmas and Mr. Lambert
offered to buy little lace caps for the two ladies the next
time he was in Glasgow . . . and then quite suddenly they
were grave and were talking about Hitler.

Everybody was talking about Hitler in that summer of
1939.

"It's nonsense to think of another war," declared Mr.
Ayrton. "Hitler doesn't want war—he's bluffing, that's
all—he'll climb down pretty quickly if we take a firm line."

"Have you read *Mein Kampf*?" asked Mr. Lambert.

" Well, I have. Hitler's all out for war. Besides I happen to know . . ." He hesitated.

" What ? " asked Mrs. Ayrton.

" Oh well, it's our job to build ships. I don't suppose it matters telling you that we're working like blacks to finish two destroyers for the Admiralty."

" You mean—they want them—quickly ? " asked Mrs. Ayrton in alarm.

" Mh'm," said Mr. Lambert nodding significantly.

" Rubbish ! " exclaimed Mr. Ayrton. " That only means we can bluff too. Mark my words, Johnnie, there will be no war. This tension will blow over in a few months' time."

All this was new to Nell. She had been so wrapped up in her own misery that she had not read the papers nor listened to the news on the wireless. The whole thing seemed unreal.

The argument continued and became so heated that Mrs. Ayrton was obliged to intervene and she did so with her usual tact by asking about the shooting prospects. Had the grouse come on well, and what was " Johnnie " doing about pheasants ? When this comfortable subject was well under way she sat back and allowed it to continue.

" You can play Bridge instead of me, to-night," said Mrs. Lambert to Nell.

" Oh no ! " exclaimed Nell.

" Nell can't play Bridge," said Mrs. Ayrton. " Connie plays but——"

" Since when ? " asked Mrs. Lambert raising her eyebrows. " Nell often played when she came to Merlewood and she played a very good game."

" It was just nursery-bridge," said Nell hastily. " The boys liked playing—so they taught us—so that they could have a four——"

" The boys were lucky," declared Mr. Lambert smiling.

" Oh, we liked it," Nell said. She remembered as she spoke what fun they used to have, sitting round the nursery table playing Bridge. There were five of them of course so one of the girls had to cut out. Naturally the boys both played—nobody ever thought of anything else. They had played for pennies (which would have horrified Nannie if she had known) and sometimes when they had been playing for hours on a wet afternoon as much as three pennies changed hands. Nell could remember those pennies now. If they came out of the boys' pockets they were warm when you touched them . . . and somehow you hated taking them from the boys.

" A penny for them, Nell," whispered Mrs. Lambert.

Nell looked at her in astonishment. Was she really a fairy ?

" A penny for your thoughts; or are they worth more ? "

" Not as much," replied Nell, trying to smile.

" Oh well, perhaps I can guess," nodded Mrs. Lambert; then she abandoned the subject and leaning forward addressed her host. " William, I want to see the fountain."

" What? Now ? "

" Yes, if you've finished your port. Nell wants to see it too, don't you, Nell ? "

" It's too cold to stand about outside, and there's no moon," objected Mrs. Ayrton.

" Oh, Marion, you are a spoil-sport! "cried Mrs. Lambert. " I want to see it. I can't think why you don't have it on more often. If I had a pretty toy like that I should play with it all day long."

" Come along, Poppet, you shall have your toy," said Mr. Ayrton smiling indulgently. He rose as he spoke and they went out together.

### 3

Nell loved the fountain and agreed with Mrs. Lambert that nowadays it played all too seldom. It was Mr. Ayrton's privilege to turn it on and he never seemed to want it. To-night it was to play at Mrs. Lambert's special request but Nell felt that she had been invited to attend the private view so after a moment's hesitation she followed her father and Mrs. Lambert out of the room.

The night was still—which was all to the good—and although there was no moon it was not very dark. The sky was ablaze with myriads of bright stars, like diamonds. By this time Mrs. Lambert and Mr. Ayrton were in the garden beside the lily-pool . . . Nell leant upon the stone balustrade of the terrace and looked down.

The fountain had not yet been turned on. Mrs. Lambert and Mr. Ayrton were standing beside it talking.

" What nonsense, Will," Mrs. Lambert was saying in her light clear voice with a suggestion of mischief in it. " If your heart was broken it mended very quickly. You consoled yourself—twice! "

" Wicked Poppet! "

" Oh, I know. But it's fun to be wicked . . . and I've always wondered, why twice? "

" For safety, of course."

" The door was bolted already! "

" Safer to be bolted on both sides."

Nell was astonished. She was so astonished that she was rooted to the spot. She ought not to be listening, but the conversation did not seem to be private for they were both speaking quite loudly and if they had looked up they would have seen her standing there. It crossed her mind that they were talking like people in a novel—saying serious things in an amusing manner—but whether it was just banter or they were really in earnest she could not tell. Mrs. Lambert was often amusing, but Nell had never heard her father talk like this before. She could hardly believe it was her father talking.

" I suppose you really want that thing, Poppet? " said Mr. Ayrton, looking at the fountain.

" Don't you? " asked Mrs. Lambert. " Don't you like it, Will? "

" I'm rather bored with it," said Mr. Ayrton frankly. " It's rather a silly toy, Poppet. Don't you think so? "

" I think it's fascinating," she declared.

" Do you mean you really want to see it playing? "

" Of course I want it. Why do you suppose I asked for it? "

He did not answer that. " I shall get wet," he complained.

" Only a very little wet," she told him in a wheedling tone. " Surely you're not afraid of a few drops of water."

" What will you give me to turn it on for you? "

Mrs. Lambert laughed. " All right," she said. " But you'd better hurry up or Johnnie and Marion will come out to see what we're doing."

Mr. Ayrton put his arms round her and kissed her. The kiss was by no means a casual embrace and it lasted several moments.

Then Mrs. Lambert disengaged herself and sighed; " You always were good at it," she said gently.

It was now quite obvious to Nell that she should not be there—she should have gone away before—but it had happened so quickly that there had been no time to think and it had happened quite naturally. In fact it had seemed so natural that Nell was not shocked. She left her vantage point and hurried back to the house thinking how strange it was that you could live all your life with a person, under the same roof, and never know him; wondering what had happened all those long years ago, and what it would have been like to have Mrs. Lambert as one's mother.

Before Nell got to the french windows of the drawing-room she heard the splashing sound of the fountain.

4

A few days later when Nell was returning from the town she met Mr. Orme outside the gate of the Rectory. Nell would have smiled at him and passed on, but Mr. Orme stopped her.

" If you have a few minutes to spare I'd like to speak to you," he said.

There was nothing for it but to go in.

Nell had been to the Rectory before (she and Anne had attended Confirmation classes in Mr. Orme's study) but the morning was so fine and sunny that instead of taking her into the house he led her to a seat in the little garden.

He was going to talk about Anne. Nell was sure of this. She felt she could not bear it. She did not look at Mr. Orme as he sat down beside her on the seat, but stared across the garden to a little platform, raised upon a post, with a coconut dangling from it.

" You're looking at my bird-table," said Mr. Orme. " I made it myself and although it isn't a very good job from a carpenter's point of view I'm rather proud of it. The birds appreciate it, which is the main thing. It's amazing how many birds come to dine at my table. I love to watch them. Perhaps the robin is my favourite—he's so friendly and cheeky—but he isn't very kind to his fellows."

Nell was beginning to feel better. There was something

about Mr. Orme that made you feel better. It was not so much what he said. There was a warmth in his deep voice which radiated comfort.

" Mr. Orme," said Nell suddenly. " People aren't always kind, are they? "

" Not always," he agreed rather sadly.

" You know about Anne, don't you? "

" I know a little. I should like to know more if you feel able to tell me."

" You probably know more than I do," said Nell, trying to control her voice. " I hoped—perhaps—you knew. Of course Anne has been—very silly—but—but I love her so much."

" Of course you do, my dear. It would be dreadful if we stopped loving people because they were silly."

There was a little silence in the garden and then Mr. Orme added, " I should like to write to Anne if you will give me her address."

" But I don't know it! " cried Nell. " I want to write to her too—I don't know where she is—I don't know what she's doing—I don't know anything."

There was quite a long silence after that. Nell, glancing at Mr. Orme's face, saw that it was very grave and stern. She had a feeling that he was angry and was trying to control himself before he spoke . . . and when he did speak it seemed as if he were talking to himself rather than to her.

" How helpless one is," he said, gazing across the garden at a tit which was hanging upside down upon a coconut and eating voraciously. " I should have done something before—but what could I do? "

" Before what? " asked Nell.

" Long ago, when you were children. I did try to get in touch with you, but I failed. Perhaps I should have tried harder—taking a strong line—but at the time it seemed to me that I should be doing more harm than good."

"I don't understand," said Nell in puzzled tones.

"No," he agreed. "It's just that I feel I could have helped if I had been allowed to." He hesitated and then added, "The Good Shepherd knew His sheep, so when one of them strayed and was lost upon the hills He was able to find it."

"You mean—you don't know—us?"

"Not as well as I should like to," replied Mr. Orme turning his head and smiling at her. "And you don't know me very well, do you? Perhaps if you knew me better you would trust me."

"I'm beginning to know you," said Nell in a low voice. "I thought you would be angry with Anne—but you're not, are you?"

"No, just very sorry."

"And yet you don't know Anne—like I do," continued Nell thoughtfully. "I mean I know her so well that I can understand in a vague sort of way how it happened. It was because—because she didn't feel—safe."

"Safe," he repeated nodding. "Yes, so few people feel safe. When the storm blows up they get frightened and yet all the time the Pilot is there, ready to guide them into the harbour."

Mr. Orme said no more about that and Nell, reminded of the Lamberts by mention of ships, asked him if he thought there was going to be another war. He replied sadly that he thought it was inevitable.

"Oh, Mr. Orme!" cried Nell. "Surely not! It seems so dreadfully wicked. It seems as if we were going back instead of forward—it seems as if we were no better than savages."

"Yes, it does seem like that, but as long as there are bad people in the world we must have policemen . . . and we're not going back," declared Mr. Orme earnestly. "Never think that. It's a terrible thought. If you read history you can see that we're improving—or at least trying to improve. It's the trying that matters. R. L. S. put it like this: 'Let it be enough for faith that the whole creation groans in mortal frailty, strives with unconquerable constancy. Surely not all in vain.'"

Nell asked him to repeat the quotation but instead of doing so he wrote it down for her on the back of an envelope. She thought about it very seriously as she went home—through the wicket-gate and up the hill. There was something brave and comforting in the words.

## CHAPTER ELEVEN

THE WAR was several weeks old when a letter was received from Roger to say that he had got a few days' leave and was coming home. He would arrive on Sunday evening after dinner.

They were having coffee in the drawing-room when the door opened and he walked in. He was in uniform of course and looked fit and well, and he had an air of confidence about him which was good to see. Nell thought he was like a fresh breeze blowing into the room, which to her seemed stuffy with unexpressed feelings.

" Roger! " exclaimed his father in surprise. " We didn't expect you so soon. Have you had dinner? "

" I stopped for it on the way," replied Roger smiling. ' The little old bus was going like a bird." He kissed Mrs. Ayrton and Nell and shook hands with his father.

" How did you get away? " asked Mrs. Ayrton who obviously thought the war could not proceed without her stepson.

" Embarkation leave," replied Roger, sitting down and accepting a cup of coffee. " Everybody gets it—if possible—before they go abroad. We're off to France one of these days."

" Perhaps you'd like some shooting while you're here," suggested Mr. Ayrton.

Roger hesitated. " Well, I don't know," he said. " I haven't got very long and I want to have a look round Amberwell . . . and I shan't be sorry to have a rest; the last fortnight has been pretty hectic. How are Connie and Anne? "

" Connie is very well," replied Mrs. Ayrton. " She didn't like Glasgow at first but now that they have moved into their new house she is settling down and feeling much happier. They have got to know some very nice people and they seem to go out a lot."

" But hasn't Gerald been called up? " asked Roger.

" Called up! " exclaimed Mr. Ayrton. " Certainly not. Gerald is much too valuable. You seem to forget he's in a shipbuilding firm."

" Isn't it lucky? " said Mrs. Ayrton. " I mean if he were in any other sort of business he would have to go and I don't know what Connie would do—they're so devoted to each other. As it is the war won't affect them at all, except that they'll have to build more ships, and that means more money of course."

" How nice for them," said Roger with a little twist of his lips.

" Yes, it *is* nice," agreed Mrs. Ayrton. " There's no need to worry about Connie, her marriage is a great success in every way . . ." and she went on talking about Connie and Gerald and the new house.

When Roger could get a word in he asked again about Anne but Mr. Ayrton merely said that as far as he knew she was well and turned the conversation to other matters.

" I don't know how we are going to keep up the gardens," declared Mr. Ayrton. " The two under-gardeners are leaving to join the Army and it seems impossible to replace them. Gray still has a boy, but——"

" There's a war on," said Roger.

" We know that, dear," said Mrs. Ayrton. " We know it only too well; it isn't only the gardens. The head-housemaid is leaving next week. She's going into the Wrens. It seems quite ridiculous. Janet is a good house-maid but what use will she be in the Wrens?"

"She will learn to Serve her Country in its Hour of Need," said Roger with a mirthless laugh.

Nell glanced at him and saw that his face had gone white and his jaw hardened. She said timidly, "We want to hear about Roger's plans, don't we?"

"Of course," agreed Mr. Ayrton. "But I expect Roger's plans will be arranged for him; he won't have much say in the matter. I wanted to ask your advice," he continued turning to Roger. "I have been trying to find out how I could get the garden-boy exempted. If he has to go I don't know what we shall do."

"Get a woman," said Roger shortly.

"Good heavens, Gray wouldn't like that! Fergus is a very good lad and he understands vegetables. I thought you might be able to tell me——"

"No, I can't," replied Roger. He added in a low voice, "and I wouldn't if I could."

"I don't understand your attitude," declared Mr. Ayrton in annoyance. "One would think you would take some interest in the gardens. The place will belong to you some day."

"We've got to win the war."

"But we shall need food," Mr. Ayrton pointed out. "To my mind it's very short-sighted policy to call up all the able-bodied men."

"We shall need every able-bodied man to beat the Germans," said Roger. "When we've won the war we can tidy up the gardens—if there are any gardens left."

"The war will be over before the men are trained," declared Mr. Ayrton. "It's a waste of time calling up

E

thousands of men from all over the country—and a waste of money as well."

" People said that in the last war, didn't they? "

The argument continued, it went round and round and got nowhere. Nell became more miserable every minute. It seemed so dreadful. Roger had come home to say good-bye before going to France—they might never see him again—and they were wasting the precious hours arguing about gardeners and housemaids. Nell did not know what they should be talking about—but surely something important, something worthwhile. At last she could bear it no longer so she rose and said she was going to bed.

" Going to bed already! " exclaimed Mrs. Ayrton in surprise.

" I've got a headache," said Nell.

2

Nell's quiet room welcomed her and soothed her as it always did. Anne's bed stood beside her own and (although there was no Anne to lie beside her and talk to her) she found its presence comforting. Nannie had suggested moving it to give her more room, but she would not have it moved. Anne had been banished from Amberwell but her bed would remain in Nell's room.

When Nell had undressed and put out the light she opened the window wide and lay looking out at the stars . . . and presently the moon rose from behind the hill like a great golden ball. Nell's head ached and her heart ached too. She was too unhappy to sleep.

Presently there was a tap on the door and it opened softly.

" Nell, can I come in? " asked Roger.

All at once Nell was reminded of the night when Tom had turned on the fountain; there was the same feeling of secrecy about this clandestine visit, and the same shaft of moonlight was streaming into the room.

" I've got to speak to you," said Roger, closing the door softly and coming to sit down upon her bed. " I've got to speak to somebody. They don't understand at all. They're absolutely mad. The whole world is falling to pieces and they go on discussing weeds in the rose-beds."

" I know," said Nell. She could see his face in the moonlight. It was white and strained.

" You said nothing," continued Roger. " I could see you felt wretched."

" We should have been talking to you about—about things that matter."

" It made me angry," Roger admitted. " When they said Gerald was too valuable—silly to be angry of course—and the garden-boy is valuable too! But never mind that. The thing that really upset me was that it's all such a waste of time. I came home hoping that Father would talk to me sensibly about plans—about business affairs. Other fellows know all about their parents' affairs but I know nothing. Sometimes Father behaves as if he had lashings of money and sometimes he talks as if he could hardly make ends meet, so I don't know where I am. Other fellows get a definite allowance, or else not, so they know whether they ought to save or whether they can afford to splash it about; they know what's behind them. Father doesn't seem to want to do that. He gives me a present of money now and then—sometimes quite a lot—and of course I'm grateful, but I'd rather know exactly how I stood—if you see what I mean."

Nell saw.  As a matter of fact she was treated in the same way.  She had no definite allowance but just an occasional present.  She never knew where she was.  It was inconvenient for her but it was far worse for Roger.

She said in a low voice, " I've got a little in the Savings Bank.  Perhaps you'll—need it—in France."

" Dear lamb, I shan't need it in France!  There'll be nothing to spend it on.  But it's very sweet of you all the same."

" Oh, Roger, I wish you weren't going."

" That's all right," he said quickly.  " I've been trained for this and in some ways I'm glad it's come.  We've all been expecting it for ages.  The only thing is I'd like to have—to have something to hold on to—at home.  Other fellows have families that are part of them.  It's difficult to explain what I mean."

" They *do* love you," whispered Nell.

" Not really," said Roger thoughtfully.  " Father is proud of me because I've done quite well and got my captaincy, but he doesn't love me."

" I think——"

" No, honestly.  He doesn't love me because he doesn't know me.  You can't love somebody you don't know.  They've never bothered to get to know any of us.  They've never made the slightest attempt to understand."

This was so true that Nell could find no comforting reply.

" Funnily enough," continued Roger thoughtfully.  " Funnily enough I never realised this before.  It was only when I heard other fellows talking about their parents and saw them getting long letters from home . . ."

Nell could imagine it: Roger's friends opening their bulky letters and reading them with avidity while Roger sat apart, looking at the papers.  She could see it happening as if it were happening before her eyes. "Oh Roger!" she said in a trembling voice.

"It can't be helped," said Roger. "Don't let's worry about that. Tell me about Anne."

"About—Anne?"

"What's happened, Nell? Where is the poor little creature? All I know is that she's married some fellow that they don't approve of—Father wrote and told me—but of course I want to know the whole story."

"I don't know anything," said Nell in a shaky voice. "I don't know where she is or—or anything."

"You don't know? D'you mean she hasn't written to you?"

Nell's tears were beginning to flow. She could feel them running down her cheeks and taste the salt of them on her lips.

"Don't cry," said Roger uncomfortably. He took her hand and held it firmly. His hand was hard and strong—a man's hand.

"I can't—help crying," whispered Nell. "I've been —bearing it all alone—for so long. If only we could—find her. If we could—just find her and see—see if she's happy —and—and has enough money——"

"I asked them," said Roger. "I asked them about her after you'd gone up to bed, but they wouldn't draw."

"Oh, Roger, please find her," sobbed Nell.

"But how can I? There's no time to make inquiries —even if I knew how to begin—I've got to report for duty on Wednesday and then it's France. You had better tell me what you *do* know about her. You must know something."

Nell pulled herself together and told him. There was very little to tell.

"I can't understand it," declared Roger in amazement.

" The whole things seems crazy: it seems so unlike Anne
... and she *must* have written to you. Goodness me, you
were like Siamese twins! Nobody ever saw one of you
without the other. Of course she must have written. The
letter must have got lost or something. Perhaps they've
told her not to write to you."

It was somehow comforting to Nell to have her own secret
idea confirmed. " Yes, it might be that," she agreed.

" What about Aunt Beatrice? She must know Anne's
address."

" I wrote and asked her but she didn't reply."

There was a little silence.

" It seems rather hopeless," said Roger at last. " I don't
see what we can do except wait. Perhaps she will write to
me or—or to somebody else."

" She's been cut off. I expect she thinks we're all against
her—all furious with her. You know how you would feel
yourself. If only we could find her and tell her that we
still love her——"

" But I haven't time to do anything; that's the trouble."

" Perhaps Tom could do something."

" Tom won't have much time either. He's sent in his
name to the Admiralty. It's a secret, Nell, but you won't
say anything will you? "

" To the Admiralty! " Nell exclaimed.

" They'll take him as a doctor—a surgeon lieutenant
commander or something—they want hundreds of young
doctors in the Navy. Tom always wanted to go into the
Navy, you know. He'll tell Father when it's all fixed up;
that's Tom's idea. There would have been a fuss if he had
told Father before."

" There will be a fuss! "

" But by that time it will be too late." Roger paused
and looked at her curiously and then he added, " Amberwell

is so quiet—it's a sort of backwater—you didn't realise there was a war on, did you?"

It was true. She had not realised that the world was turning upside down.

"Poor little kid," said Roger, pressing her hand gently. "You've been having a frightful time—and you're in for a whole lot more trouble. This war isn't going to be a picnic. Before we're through there won't be any gardeners or house-maids at all. It will be your job to look after Amberwell and keep the wheels turning."

Nell gazed at him in astonishment, for she had never been encouraged to take the slightest interest in the house; she was not even allowed to arrange the flowers. "My job!" she exclaimed. "But Roger——"

"I don't see who else there is. There's Connie of course. I thought old Gerald would be sure to join up and Connie could have come home and helped . . . but apparently Gerald is too valuable to fight, so that's no use."

"They wouldn't let me help," declared Nell.

"My dear lamb!" exclaimed Roger and for the first time there was a real smile in his eyes. "My dear lamb you *still* don't understand. They'll be mighty glad of your help. I can see you cooking the dinner and sweeping the floors—perhaps even weeding the rose-beds."

"But I don't know how to do anything!"

"You'll learn," said Roger. It sounded like a prophecy —or perhaps a threat. He rose as he spoke and stood looking down at her, a giant in the moonlight. His face was in shadow now.

"Roger," said Nell a little breathlessly. "I'm beginning to understand. I'll try to keep Amberwell in good order— for you."

"And I'll try to keep myself in good order for Amberwell,"

returned Roger. He said the words lightly—almost jokingly—but Nell did not feel inclined to smile.

"I'll write to you," Nell said.

"Yes, do. Tell me everything that happens—all the silly
things."

Nell nodded.

"And I'll write to you. The letters will be for you only.
They won't be the sort of letters to be handed round at
breakfast. You understand, don't you?"

She understood. "Yes, but it won't be easy. Mother
always reads my letters. She always has."

"I'll address them to the Post Office and you can fetch
them yourself. That's the best way." He sighed and added,
"I'm frightfully tired."

"You must go to bed," Nell told him. "You'll have all
to-morrow. You want to go round Amberwell and see
everything, don't you. Do you want to go alone?"

"No, with you," said Roger quickly. "We'll escape
directly after breakfast before they can fix anything else.
You'll come, won't you?"

"Yes, of course," said Nell.

When he had gone Nell lay awake for a long time trying
to tidy up the chaos in her mind. It was not easy. She
had always thought of herself as a complete nonentity,
unimportant and ineffectual; but now, all of a sudden, she
had had heavy responsibilities placed upon her shoulders,
and placed there quite confidently. Roger obviously had
no doubt at all of her ability to cope. The first responsibility was Roger. He needed her as a confidante, as somebody to whom he could open his mind. That alone gave
her a feeling of importance. Then there were her letters
to Roger which would tell him all that went on at Amberwell
and give him "something to hold on to" when he was far
away. She would write regularly. Never again would

Roger have to watch other fellows opening their letters and receive none himself.

The other responsibilities prophesied by Roger would be more arduous but they would come gradually and she would have time to prepare for them. Nell reviewed the household staff: Mrs. Duff would probably remain at Amberwell (she was too old to join any of the services) and the same went for Nannie, but all the others were comparatively young and sooner or later they would all go. The prospect of running Amberwell House with two elderly women—neither of whom had done any real work for years—would have daunted the stoutest heart and Nell was no heroine. Goodness! thought Nell. What on earth shall I do? Well, it's no use worrying. I must wait and see.

One thing she could do—and must do immediately—she must prepare herself for the battle by taking cooking lessons from Mrs. Duff. If she could cook a reasonably good meal for herself and her parents she would not feel so helpless.

Nell's last thought as she drifted off to sleep was of her expedition with Roger to-morrow morning (but it was really to-day) " Oh God, please let it be fine and sunny—for Roger," she murmured.


3


" I didn't know you loved Amberwell like that," said Nell.

She and Roger were sitting on the big mossy stone at the edge of the woods and looking down upon the house and gardens. Nell's prayer had been answered, it was a perfect day, the whole place seemed to bask in the mellow Autumn sunshine. The house of Amberwell was deep-seated in its bowl of flowers and trees; the leaves were turning scarlet and gold, the flower gardens were glowing with chrysanthemums and dahlias. Just below them lay the bowling-green surrounded by its dark green hedge. A boy was mowing the grass with a petrol-driven mower; he was walking quickly up and down leaving behind him broad bands of differently-coloured grass, so that the lawn looked for all the world like a striped green ribbon. It was a peaceful scene; so peaceful that it was difficult to believe the greatest war in all history had begun.

" How do you mean you didn't know I loved Amberwell *like that*? " asked Roger after a little pause.

" It was the way you put your hand on the rock," explained Nell. " As if it were alive—as if it could feel you doing it."

" Yes," said Roger smiling at her rather shyly. " As a matter of fact I've always loved Amberwell like that—as if it were alive—but I used to think it was a bit soppy. Somehow it doesn't seem to matter now—being soppy, I mean."

Nell looked at his neat fair head with the sun shining on it. She knew what he was thinking: perhaps this was his good-bye to Amberwell.

" It doesn't matter at all," she said, and then she added, " Anne used to feel like that."

" Anne! " exclaimed Roger in surprise. " But Anne left Amberwell and went away! "

" I think that was why," said Nell slowly. " It was something she said."

" What did she say? "

Nell hesitated, trying to remember. " We were looking at the old chestnut tree in the wood; it was Spring and there were fat sticky buds on the branches. Anne said it was a part of Amberwell, its roots were in Amberwell ground and its leaves breathed Amberwell air. 'It's like us,' I said. Anne didn't say anything for a few moments and then she said, 'Yes, but it will die here. People won't pull it up by its roots and move it somewhere else.' "

" What on earth did she mean? "

" I didn't understand at the time, but I do now. She knew she would have to leave Amberwell some day. That's what she meant."

" But why? " asked Roger in bewilderment. " She needn't have gone away. Amberwell was her home, just as it's your home—and mine."

" It's your home," said Nell, smiling a little.

Roger was silent for a minute. " You're thinking I shall marry and turn you out! That's absolutely ridiculous. Amberwell will always be home for all of us if I have any say in the matter."

" Your wife might have something to say."

" I shan't marry," said Roger soberly. " I know it sounds silly. Fellows who say they're never going to get married usually meet some fascinating girl and get married within a year, but—well—it's different in my case. I mean I've met the girl I want to marry—and it's no good. She isn't for me."

" Isn't for you? "

He shook his head. " She's so wonderful," he said with a little sigh. Then he smiled and added, " Don't worry, I'm not going to drivel about her, but you take it from me she really *is* wonderful. Now that I've seen her I shall never want to marry anybody else."

" But Roger, perhaps——"

" No, it's hopeless. She's engaged to another fellow. As a matter of fact he's one of my best friends—a frightfully good chap—in the regiment—so you see——"

Nell saw. She did not know what to say.

" Well, come on! " exclaimed Roger leaping to his feet.
" We haven't been to the rocks yet; I must see the Smug-
gler's Cave. And we haven't been to Ponticum. Come on,
Nell! Let's go to Ponticum first."

It was difficult for Roger to squeeze in between the
gnarled branch of rhododendron and the wall, for he was
large and solid, but he managed it somehow and sat down
upon a stool.

" Gosh, how small it is! " he exclaimed. " I thought it
was much bigger. I haven't been here for years. What
fun we had! "

Nell nodded. There had been five of them, having
fun: now there were only two, and the world seemed joy-
less.

Roger was looking round and remembering. He said,
" I wonder what became of that funny little lead soldier
that you found."

" It's here," she replied, opening the treasure-box and
taking it out. " We always kept it here——"

" Well I never! " exclaimed Roger. " It's the uniform
our chaps wore at the Battle of Waterloo. Yes, honestly,
Nell. This little man is one of Wellington's soldiers."

" More than a hundred years old! "

" Much more, my girl. The Battle of Waterloo was
fought in 1815."

They tried to count backwards and to decide which of
their ancestors could have possessed the lead soldier (and
lost him amongst the accumulated leaves of Ponticum) and
finally decided that it must have been Stephen. Their
father could have told them of course. As a matter of fact
Mr. Ayrton would have been interested in the little lead
soldier (he would have looked up dates in the Family Bible
and enjoyed himself immensely) but never for one moment

did it occur to Roger and Nell to show their father the treasure.

4

Roger was a good deal more worried about Anne than appeared on the surface. He decided that the only thing to do was to ring up Aunt Beatrice and see if he could get any satisfaction out of her. So after tea, without saying anything to Nell, he walked down to the Post Office and put a call through to her flat. It was better to do this from the Post Office where he could speak to her in private and undisturbed. Fortunately Beatrice Ayrton answered the phone herself and Roger was able to surprise her with his question.

"Oh—Roger!" she exclaimed. "But I can't give you Anne's address because . . ." She hesitated and then added, "Besides your father said I wasn't to tell you anything about her."

Roger realised that she was wavering and followed up his advantage. "I must know," he said firmly. "Please tell me all about Anne. I'm very worried—and so is Nell."

"I'm worried too. I mean of course she will be all right with Martin. He's such a delightful creature. But I can't understand why they haven't written to me."

"If you would give me their address——"

"But they've moved," Aunt Beatrice explained. "I wrote twice to Martin's flat in London. They never answered the first letter and the second letter was returned by the Post Office marked GONE AWAY. ADDRESS NOT KNOWN."

"But we can't leave it like that!" cried Roger in dismay.

" I didn't leave it like that," retorted Aunt Beatrice crossly. " I did all I could. I went to London myself and called at the flat. It was empty and none of the neighbours knew anything about them. So then I went to the school where Martin taught and saw the headmaster. He said Martin had left to join the Army—and that was all he knew."

" Good heavens! But what's become of Anne! "

" I told you I don't know," declared Aunt Beatrice, beginning to lose her temper, which was never very firmly under control. " As a matter of fact I think it's very unkind of Anne not to write and tell me where they've gone. She promised she would write and I've never heard a word. I did all I could to help her—I arranged everything—and that's all the thanks I get! I've been very badly treated by the whole family—your father wrote me a dreadful letter. I shall never forgive him for the things he said . . ."

Now that she had started she could not stop; she was becoming more and more furious every moment. Roger could do nothing but hang on to the end of the line and listen.

" Look here, Aunt Beatrice! " he cried at last. " Why did you let her do it? Why didn't you make her wait and get Father's consent? "

" Would he have given his consent? Of course he wouldn't! He's utterly selfish and unreasonable—you know that as well as I do! "

Roger was taken aback and was still searching for a reply when he heard the sound of the receiver being replaced violently. The conversation was at an end and he could see no point in trying to reopen it. As he walked back to Amberwell he tried to make up his mind whether or not he should tell Nell what he had done and what he had learned about Anne's affairs. He had learned very little

. . . and that little was bad. Nell would be more distressed than ever to hear that Martin Selby had left his post at the school and joined the Army—and Nell had as much as she could bear already—it seemed useless to tell her. Roger decided to keep secret his conversation with Aunt Beatrice. He felt certain that sooner or later (and probably sooner) Anne would write to Nell and tell her everything.

## CHAPTER TWELVE

NELL DROVE Roger to the station and saw him off. She managed to see him off cheerfully. She managed to wave her handkerchief and to call out " Haste ye back! " in the good old Scottish tradition. But somehow the words (which had often been said in fun when Roger and Tom went off to school after the Summer Holidays) were now so full of hidden meaning and emotion that she was suddenly swamped with tears.

Fortunately by this time the train was steaming off and there was nobody on the platform but the station-master —who appeared not to notice. She groped her way to the car and climbed in and sat there in the station-yard until she had recovered sufficiently to be able to see where she was going.

On the way home Nell decided that the car was another responsibility which would shortly be placed upon her shoulders. She knew how to drive it, of course, but its inward parts were a complete mystery to her. Cameron would have to teach her before he left how to look after the car and keep it in order.

Lessons from Cameron and from Mrs. Duff began forthwith and these, in addition to Roger's letters, kept Nell busy. She wrote long letters to Roger, as she had promised, and called at the Post Office in Westkirk for Roger's replies. Sometimes his letters were very short—a few words scrawled in pencil—and sometimes they were very long indeed. Nell reported faithfully all that happened; it was small beer of course, but small beer was what Roger wanted.

" Your last letter arrived when I was feeling blue," wrote Roger. " You can't think how comforting it was to read about the snowdrops coming out in Stark Woods —and about your visit to Mrs. Gray. It was frightfully decent of her to make tablet for me—I always loved Mrs. Gray's tablet. I hope it will arrive safely and nobody will pinch it on the way. The socks are A.1. Did you really make them yourself? I didn't know you could knit socks—but there's quite a lot I didn't know about you. Sorry to hear there was such an awful blizzard about Tom, but they'll get over it all right— you'll see. Tom is off to the Mediterranean so he'll see all the places he's always wanted to see. He's as happy as a sand-boy. It seems funny that it should take a beastly, bloody war to give Tom his heart's desire. Good thing somebody is happy anyway. I suppose Connie is happy too. She wanted a son, didn't she? Connie always does the right thing. Your story about Mr. Gray and the Land Girl was awfully amusing, I laughed and laughed. Write lots more, won't you? There's no need to worry about me; this war isn't dangerous, in fact it's frightfully boring. If you could lay your hands on a French Grammar it would be useful. I find I've forgotten most of the French I learnt at school . . ."

Nell took Roger's letters to Ponticum and read them there, sitting on the treasure-box in the damp green gloom. It was a good place to read them not only because she was safe from interruption but also because she could almost imagine Roger was there. Sometimes she took out the small figure of Wellington's soldier and held it in her hand while she read and re-read Roger's letters. It was frightfully silly of course—Nell knew that—but nobody could see her so it did not matter.

2

As the weeks went by it became increasingly important for Nell to have some place where she was safe from interruption, for as Roger had prophesied the staff of Amberwell melted away and Mrs. Ayrton (who had run the house perfectly for twenty-five years with eight well-trained servants) was quite unable to cope with the new conditions. Gradually Nell took over everything; she battled with rationing and food cards, she made the beds, prepared all the vegetables and helped Mrs. Duff with the cooking. As a matter of fact Nell liked it; she enjoyed working in the big square kitchen with its tiled floor and wide windows, and she enjoyed Mrs. Duff. Nell had scarcely ever been in the kitchen before and Mrs. Duff had been a shadowy sort of figure—not really human. But now Nell got to know the kitchen well, and discovered that Mrs. Duff was very human indeed. Mrs. Duff and her sayings provided good material for Nell's letters to Roger.

Nannie worked about the house (clad in a flowered overall, instead of her large, starched apron) and Nell was fortunate enough to find a girl in Westkirk who was willing to come daily. The girl was lame and therefore unfit for the services but she was a good worker.

With this little band Nell coped as best she could with all the hundred and one tasks of the household; she was so busy that there was not much time to think about Anne, there was no time at all to brood upon her troubles . . . and the disquieting idea that she was " not quite right in the head " vanished completely.

In March Roger wrote that he was getting ten days' leave but was not coming straight to Amberwell:

You remember I told you about Clare? Well, I made an idiotic mistake, she isn't engaged to John McDermott after all. He's engaged to a friend of Clare's and they are going to be married soon—so there may be a chance for me. Clare is nursing in a hospital in London so I'm going to see her and try my luck. I don't know whether there is any chance but it's worth trying. If it's quite hopeless I'll come on to Amberwell. I'll let you know what happens.

Nell said nothing to her parents for it was all so vague and if Roger wanted them to know he would tell them . . . but of course she thought about it constantly and wished she knew more about it. She wondered who Clare was. Roger had said she was " wonderful " but that was all. It did not tell you very much, thought Nell, who would have liked to know whether she was tall like a goddess, or small like a fairy; whether she had fair hair or dark; blue eyes or brown . . . and most important of all whether she had a friendly nature. Probably Roger was under the impression that he had told Nell more about Clare—he could scarcely have told her less. Would there be " any chance " for Roger? Nell could not believe that any girl in her sane senses would refuse to marry Roger—but you never knew.

For nearly a week there were no letters and then one morning when Nell came down to breakfast there were three letters lying on the table, one for each of the family.

" Three letters from Roger! " exclaimed Mrs. Ayrton in surprise.

" It's about time we heard from him," commented his father. " Roger never writes . . . and Thomas is almost as bad. When I was young I used to write home regularly once a week."

Nell seized her letter and tore it open. The letter was long and incoherent; Roger had let himself go.

It's all right—she's going to marry me—it's too marvellous for words. She loved me all the time—wasn't I a fool? I told you she was wonderful. Oh Nell, you'll love her, I know you will! I've told her all about you—and all about Amberwell. She's the sort of person you can tell things to. She understands. This letter is crazy of course, but I've written to the parents quite sensibly and I think it's pretty sure to be all right. Clare's grandfather is Lord Richmore so that should please them, shouldn't it? It will be better for Clare's sake if they're pleased. Personally I don't care a damn. I would marry Clare if her grandfather was a gaol-bird, but if it's going to make things easier rub in Lord Richmore for all you're worth . . .

Nell glanced at her father, but she saw there was no need to rub in Lord Richmore. Mr. Ayrton was reading his letter with a complacent smile.

" Clare's parents are dead," continued Roger. " She has nobody belonging to her except her grandfather. He's a queer old boy but fortunately he seems to like me and he's told us to go ahead. Clare wants to be married at once. She says she wants me to belong to her before I go back to France, so we're getting a Special Licence. I don't know if you could manage to come to London for the wedding—it would be great if you could —but it's all a bit of a muddle and I can't tell you what day it will be—perhaps Thursday. It's too marvellous to be true. I can't believe it. Something will happen to prevent it . . ."

Mrs. Ayrton was reading her letter too. "Goodness, Roger says he's going to be married!" she exclaimed.

Mr. Ayrton chuckled. "The young rascal! He seems to have done pretty well for himself as far as I can see. Old Lord Richmore's granddaughter! He's going to be married at once."

"But he can't—all in a hurry," objected Mrs. Ayrton. "I mean we must go to London or else they must come here. It would be nice to have Roger's wedding at St. Stephens."

"There's no time," said Mr. Ayrton. "He's only got ten days' leave and he says they intend to be married on Thursday by Special Licence. Lord Richmore is making all the arrangements so we had better not interfere. As for going to London it's quite out of the question for me—at the moment—and if you take my advice you will remain safely at home."

"You mean because of the air-raids?" asked Mrs. Ayrton nervously. "Well, perhaps it would be rather silly to go——"

"May I go?" asked Nell eagerly.

"No dear," replied Mrs. Ayrton. "You couldn't possibly go alone."

"But I'd like to," declared Nell. "I want to meet Clare—and it seems—it seems dreadful for Roger to be married with none of us there. I could easily——"

"No, dear," said Mrs. Ayrton.

"But Mother——" began Nell, and then she stopped for Mrs. Ayrton was not listening. It was Mrs. Ayrton's usual technique and (as Nell had found before) it was impossible to argue with somebody who did not listen—or at any rate pretended not to hear what one was saying.

"I shall wire him a hundred pounds," declared Mr. Ayrton, rising. "That ought to see him through . . . and I must write to Dalgleish and arrange about settlements. Heaven knows what Dalgleish will say. He took three months to draw up Connie's marriage contract and complained that I was hurrying him. I had better write to Lord Richmore too. Are you going to write, Marion? There's no time to be lost if the letters are to catch the post."

"I wonder what she's like," said Mrs. Ayrton anxiously. "What does your letter say, Nell?"

"The same as yours, I expect."

"Let me read it, dear."

Nell took no notice of the outstretched hand; she pretended not to see nor hear. It had suddenly occurred to her that there was a good deal to be learnt from her parents. She rose and slipping the letter into the pocket of her cardigan followed her father out of the room.

It was a victory—a very small victory of course, but at least it was a beginning—and Nell was absurdly elated by her own courage. After this she would keep her correspondence to herself. She would tell Roger that he could write to her direct instead of addressing his letters to the Post Office . . . but perhaps Roger's letters would not be so frequent now, nor so private.

Nell had enjoyed her position as Roger's confidante but she was not jealous of Clare—not the tiniest bit—she was sincerely glad that Roger had got what he wanted, and because she knew Roger so well she was sure he had chosen the right girl and that they would be happy. It was a pity she could not go to the wedding, thought Nell with a little sigh, but it would have been difficult to get away (so much depended upon her) and later on Roger would bring Clare to Amberwell. That would be something lovely to look forward to.

Nell wrote a long letter to Roger and one to Clare as well and they both replied by return of post. Clare's letter was charming, it was friendly and understanding; she enclosed a little snapshot of herself (which Roger had taken) and asked for a photograph of Nell. It was obvious from her letter that she adored Roger and thought the world of him—which was as it should be, of course. Clare said that when Roger returned to France she was going back to the hospital; she thought it would be easier to bear the separation if she had plenty to do. She asked Nell to write to her as often as possible and to tell her about Roger when he was a boy—what he had done and said.

" Roger has talked such a lot about Amberwell," wrote Clare. " Sometimes I almost feel as if I had been there. It will be wonderful to see it—the beautiful gardens and the woods where you used to play Indians, and of course the mermaid fountain. Roger told me about the night when he and Tom got you and Anne out of bed and turned it on for you to see. It must have been thrilling. I have no brothers or sisters so I have missed all that sort of fun. I am awfully sorry you can't come to the wedding, but I quite understand how difficult it would be for you to get away. We shall have three days together before Roger goes back to France and I have made up my mind that those three days are going to be blissfully happy—I am going to enjoy every hour and not think about what will happen when they are over. I think one can do that, don't you? I mean, live completely in the present. Roger is going to try and do the same. I hope you don't think it is horrid of us not to come to Amberwell—I am afraid it is rather selfish—but I want Roger all to myself for the three days and he says he feels the same about me . . ."

Nell liked Clare's letter—it was exactly right, she thought —and the little photograph was enchanting. Clare had a small eager face and her eyes sparkled with humour. Unfortunately Nell had no photograph of herself to send in return.

3

Roger and Clare had their three days' honeymoon and then Roger went back to France; but he had not been in France more than a fortnight when he was badly wounded in the leg and was sent home to a hospital near Coventry. Although this seemed a major catastrophe to Roger's relations it was really very fortunate, for he was in hospital when the Retreat to Dunkirk took place and he escaped all the horrors suffered by his regiment. He was in hospital for weeks and then went to Salisbury Plain where Regular Officers were needed for training.

Clare went with him to Salisbury; they found a little house and settled down together. A baby was expected at Christmas time, and Clare (who had worn herself out nursing at the hospital) was not very well so the visit to Amberwell had to be put off until she was better. They were both very anxious for Nell to go and stay with them but by this time it was impossible for her to leave home even for a few days because her father was unwell.

Mr. Ayrton had been ailing for some time, he was troubled by attacks of dizziness and a pain in his chest; at first he refused to see Dr. Maddon (saying that he had never been ill in his life and he was not ill now, and he was sure he would be all right to-morrow) but instead of getting better he got worse. The doctor was consulted and diagnosed the complaint as high blood-pressure.

" What does that mean? " asked Mr. Ayrton crossly.

" It means that you must take care of yourself," replied Dr. Maddon. " We shall have to put you on a strict diet, I'm afraid, and you mustn't get overtired or over-excited."

Dr. Maddon repeated his instructions to Nell and to Mrs. Ayrton, warning them that Mr. Ayrton's condition was serious and that he really must take care.

Unfortunately the doctor's instructions were not very easy to observe in the summer of 1940, and Mr. Ayrton's temperament did not help matters. Sometimes he became frightened and carried out his régime to the letter and at other times he rebelled against his uninteresting food.

Then there was his port: Mr. Ayrton had always enjoyed a couple of glasses of port after dinner and now this pleasure was denied him. Every evening the same conflict took place.

" That doctor is a perfect fool," Mr. Ayrton would declare as he sipped a glass of orange juice and screwed up his mouth in distaste. " As if a glass of port could do a man any harm! I've a good mind to open a bottle."

" Oh William! " Mrs. Ayrton would exclaim. " Orange juice is so much better for you and it's really very nice."

" It is not nice. It is absolutely disgusting—and you needn't offer me lemon juice, that's worse."

" Don't get excited, William. It's so bad for you to get excited."

" Excited! " he would cry, seizing a couple of walnuts and cracking them viciously. " Why should I get excited? There's nothing to get excited about."

Sometimes Mrs. Ayrton would give in and say weakly, " Well, perhaps one glass of port——" but this was not right either.

Mr. Ayrton would glare at her across the table and reply, " I suppose you've forgotten that the doctor said I wasn't to touch port! "

He certainly was a very difficult patient. Nell thought it would have been better if Dr. Maddon had allowed him to eat and drink what he pleased—better not only for his family but also for himself.

The summer slipped away; it was a stormy summer in the outside world but Amberwell had settled down into its war-time routine and the household was peaceful. Nell, working early and late, found time to pick fruit (in addition to her other activities) and she and Mrs. Duff bottled it and made jam. Everybody was co-operative and there was a pleasant friendly spirit in the house—a very much more friendly spirit than had prevailed when Amberwell was staffed with its proper complement of servants. Nell could not help smiling when she went into the kitchen and found Nannie sitting at the table cutting up vegetables while Mrs. Duff stirred the jam.

" I thought I'd give Kate a hand," said Nannie apologetically. " I just gave the house a lick and a promise this morning."

Nell saw they were perfectly happy. She wondered what Nannie would have said a year ago if anybody had dared to suggest she should soil her hands by cutting up vegetables.

Mr. Ayrton was not able to go about much during the summer (he spent most of his time in the library, or sitting on the terrace in a shady corner) but he seemed better in the Autumn for the cooler weather agreed with him. One afternoon when Mrs. Ayrton was resting and Nell was busy in the kitchen he suddenly decided to take a walk round the gardens. He knew perfectly well that the place was not being properly cared for, of course (he knew the men had gone and that Mr. Gray was struggling along with nobody to help him except a Land Girl) but Mr. Ayrton was lacking in imagination and it was not until he saw the gardens with his own eyes that he realised their condition.

He returned home tired out and very angry indeed: everything was going to pieces; the weeds were rampant; the bowling-green had not been cut for weeks; the lily-pool was covered with green slime!

Nell was alarmed at his appearance and did her best to calm him, but nothing she could say had any effect. He went into his library and shut the door. For a few minutes she waited outside and heard him pacing up and down the room . . . and then his chair creaked as he settled into it.

Better to leave him, thought Nell. It would only annoy him if she went in and fussed. Perhaps the best thing to do would be to get Nannie to make him some tea and take it to him, for as a matter of fact Nannie was the only person who could manage him. Nannie treated Mr. Ayrton with cheerful kindness, in much the same manner as she would have treated a rather troublesome small boy recovering from a severe attack of measles.

" Yes, very well," agreed Nannie. " Don't you worry about him, Nell. I'll make him a nice pot of tea. It was naughty of him to go out like that without a word to anybody —and of course the place is in a bit of a mess."

" Do you think we should ring up Dr. Maddon? "

" Well, we'll see," said Nannie. " Maybe it would just upset him. I'll see what like he is when I go in with his tea."

But when Nannie went in with Mr. Ayrton's tea she found that he had died. He was sitting in his chair by the fire as if he were asleep and looked strangely peaceful.

The doctor had warned them that this might happen, and in a way they had been prepared for it, but death is always a shock to those who are left behind. Mrs. Ayrton was prostrated, she could do nothing, and all the arrangements devolved upon Nell.

As she went about her tasks—writing letters, answering

telephone calls and putting the house in order—Nell reflected that the war had killed her father just as surely as if he had been shot through the heart by a German bullet. It seemed odd that he, who had stayed at home in peaceful Amberwell, should be the first casualty in the Ayrton family.

## CHAPTER THIRTEEN

THERE WERE so many preparations to be made for Mr. Ayrton's funeral that Nell had no time to grieve. Many of the rooms had been shut up, to make less work, and now they had to be opened. Roger came from Salisbury, but without Clare (for Clare's baby was expected in December and the long journey, with all the discomforts of war-time travelling, would have been too tiring for her) ; Connie and Gerald arrived from Glasgow in their fine new car: Tom, whose ship happened to be lying at Rosyth, managed to get a few days' leave and turned up unexpectedly.

Nell was delighted to have them all, it helped a lot, but the sudden influx made housekeeping very difficult. Food was the problem; Nell thought about food most of the time; she even dreamt about food.

The young people were sorry and somewhat awed by their father's death but it was impossible for them to feel very distressed (as Roger had said, he had never taken the trouble to know his children, he had never been a real friend to them): so it was natural that after the funeral, when Mrs. Ayrton had retired to bed, the conversation should become reasonably cheerful. They had not seen each other for so long and they wanted to know all about each other's doings. They settled themselves comfortably round the fire and chatted amicably. Nell was the silent one. We're all here except Anne, she thought. If only Anne were here! She wondered if any of the others were thinking about the missing member of the family.

It was Roger's prerogative to take the lead and after a bit he did so, a trifle apologetically. "Look here, all of you," he said, breaking into Connie's story about the cleverness of young Gerry. "Look here, I want to talk to you all about something important."

"Go ahead!" said Tom cheekily. "You're the skipper."

"I know," agreed Roger. "That's what I want to talk about. You see Amberwell is supposed to belong to me now. I can't really believe it—but Mr. Dalgleish says it does. Of course I'm not going to turn Mother out into the street or anything. I'm not going to turn out anybody. We've all grown up at Amberwell and as long as I'm alive Amberwell will continue to be 'home' for all of us. Clare agrees, of course. What I mean is Tom can come here any time he likes—and if he marries, his wife will be welcome. Connie can come whenever she likes and bring her family. Nell will go on being the boss; she's doing a splendid job, you'll all agree. Goodness knows what would have happened to Amberwell without Nell." He paused and looked round. "Then there's Anne," he said. "I intend to find Anne if I possibly can."

"Anne!" exclaimed Connie. "Father said we weren't to have anything more to do with her. She's chosen her own way. She's cut herself off from everybody."

"She's been cut off," said Nell in a low voice.

"Anne is one of the family," said Roger firmly.

"But Roger——" began Connie.

"There are no 'buts,'" said Roger smiling at her. "If Anne can be found she will be welcome at Amberwell. I want you all to understand that."

"But you'll have to ask Mother," objected Connie. "And I know what she'll say."

Gerald leaned forward and put his hand on her knee.

"You don't understand," he said. "Amberwell doesn't belong to your mother."

"Oh, but surely——"

"It belongs to Roger. He's just told you so."

Connie looked bewildered, and somewhat annoyed. She said, "Well, I think it's rather—rather horrid to talk like this when Father has just died."

"I don't," declared Tom. "Roger is right to talk straight out and say what he means. Then we know where we are. This family would have been a lot better if there had been more straight talk."

"Oh yes!" exclaimed Nell with feeling.

"That's what I think too," Roger declared. "Let's have everything straight and above board. That's why I'm talking like this to-night. We're all here together and it may be years before we all meet again."

"Carried unanimously," said Tom. "For my part I'd like to add that I think it's most awfully decent of Roger to say we're to come to Amberwell whenever we like and to consider it our home. I'm jolly grateful and I intend to take him at his word. It's a good thing to know you've got a home to come to; especially in war-time."

"Oh yes," agreed Connie. "I only mean—I mean Father has just died."

"Well, of course we're all sorry," said Tom. "But people are dying every day and Father had a jolly good innings. That's how I look at it."

"You're absolutely heartless!" cried Connie in shocked tones.

"People are dying every day," repeated Tom. "Young people who haven't had a life at all. Nowadays you've got to be 'heartless,' as you call it, or you just couldn't go on."

"You shouldn't be heartless, Tom," said Connie reprovingly.

Suddenly his eyes blazed. "You don't know what you're talking about!" he cried. "Perhaps if you'd seen one of your best friends brought into the sick-bay on a stretcher and watched him die before your eyes you'd begin to understand."

There was a horrified silence.

"Go it easy, Tom," murmured Roger, picking up a log and throwing it on to the fire.

"Sorry!" said Tom quickly. "I didn't mean to bleat. Let's talk about Anne. As a matter of fact I've thought about Anne a lot and I agree with Roger that she ought to be found, but I don't know how we're going to do it."

"I thought perhaps Aunt Beatrice——" began Nell.

"No good," said Tom, interrupting her. "Aunt Beatrice doesn't know. As a matter of fact I went to lunch with her the other day. She heard my ship was at Rosyth and wrote and asked me. Aunt Beatrice has got a lot older. I couldn't help feeling sorry for her."

"You shouldn't have gone to see her," Connie declared. "Father and Mother were frightfully angry with her, and no wonder! You're making such a fuss about Anne—well, it was all Aunt Beatrice's fault. You can't deny that."

Nobody could deny it.

"Oh well," said Tom uncomfortably, "it's silly to keep up feuds for ever. As a matter of fact she's rather a nice old trout. D'you remember that Christmas Party when I kissed her under the mistletoe? Anyway she was delighted to see me—it was quite pathetic really—and she gave me a rattling good lunch."

"What did she say about Anne?" asked Nell, who was more interested in Anne than in Tom's reminiscences.

Roger said nothing. He was aware that Aunt Beatrice knew very little about Anne.

"Aunt Beatrice was no good at all," declared Tom.

" Her letters to Anne were returned through the Post Office and when she went to London to find out what had happened she came up against a blank wall. They had moved from the flat where they were staying and had left no address. She asked at the school where Selby had been teaching and was told he had resigned his post and enlisted. As a matter of fact the headmaster was rather fed up about it and wasn't inclined to be helpful."

" But that's awful! " cried Nell in horrified tones. "It means Anne is alone—in London! "

" Not necessarily," said Roger. " If he's been sent to a Training Camp she may have been able to get lodgings near-by——"

" Or she may have joined the Wrens," suggested Connie. " Lots of girls have joined the Services; they have a very good time. If I wasn't married that's what I'd do."

" If only we knew! " exclaimed Nell. " If only we could find her! "

" I'm sure she'll write to one of us soon," Roger declared.

" Well, we can't do anything more," said Gerald. There was a suggestion of relief in his voice for he agreed with his wife upon the subject. He had liked Anne, but she had behaved very badly. Gerald felt that when people insisted upon making their own beds they should be left to lie upon them, even if the beds were slightly uncomfortable.

" Did Aunt Beatrice say——" began Nell and then she found that her voice had failed her and she could not go on.

" Yes, she told me a lot," said Tom. " She said he was a very good fellow and devoted to Anne and she was sure they would be happy."

" Well, why worry any more? " asked Connie.

Tom hesitated. " I don't know, really. I don't think you can go by what she says—not entirely."

F

"Yes, Aunt Beatrice is a bit queer," added Roger thoughtfully.

2

Nell had no opportunity to talk to Roger privately and there were several matters upon which she wanted his advice. She wondered, as she went to bed, whether Roger would come to her room as he had done before. There was no real reason why he should, but she had a feeling that he might . . . and sure enough she had not been in bed for more than a few minutes when there was a tap on the door and there he was. Nell was reading, so the curtains were drawn across the window and the bedside lamp was lighted. The room looked quite different from the last time Roger had visited it—cosier and more intimate.

"May I come in?" asked Roger.

She nodded, but put her finger to her lips, and he came in quietly and shut the door behind him.

"Connie and Gerald are next door," whispered Nell.

"Would they be shocked?" asked Roger, sitting down upon the end of her bed and smiling at her.

Nell was not sure whether they would be or not.

"Connie is very proper isn't she?" continued Roger. "She's one of the lucky people who don't know there's a war on. As a matter of fact she gets my goat; I was quite glad when Tom rounded on her."

"Poor Tom," said Nell with a sigh.

"Yes, he's a bit nervy," agreed Roger. "He's not heartless enough—for a war. Old Tom has always been frightfully sensitive; you wouldn't think so unless you knew him well." He looked round the room and added, "What a lot has happened since the last time I was here! It's only a little more than a year but it seems like a lifetime."

" We were both very young."

" And very unimportant."

" And now you're the head of the family."

Roger nodded. " Did you think I was—all right? " he asked boyishly.

Nell could reply to that very easily; she had thought him splendid. He had taken his place with just the right mixture of dignity and diffidence.

" I'm glad you approved," he said. " Somebody has got to take the lead and I wanted to make it clear that I shall back you up for all I'm worth. I had a talk with Mr. Dalgleish and you're to have Power of Attorney ... Don't worry, it only means you can sign cheques to pay for repairs and the wages and all that sort of thing. I'll explain about it to-morrow. I didn't come to talk to you about business matters. I came to tell you about our plans."

" Are you leaving Salisbury? " Nell asked in surprise.

" Yes, I've got a job at the War House. It's promotion of course but we're both sorry to leave our nice little home. We're going to live with Lord Richmore. It's decent of the old chap to have us but it won't be quite the same."

" But Roger, couldn't you find a place of your own? "

" It wouldn't be worth while. The job is only temporary."

" You're not—going abroad again? " asked Nell with a sinking heart.

He nodded. " Probably some time early next year. I ought not to tell you really, so don't breathe a word. It will be Egypt I expect."

There was a little silence and then Nell said, " Roger, I don't want to interfere, but wouldn't it be a good plan for Clare to come to Amberwell to have her baby? "

"It would be an excellent plan—but she won't." He smiled ruefully and added, "I should like our child to be born and brought up at Amberwell—to have roots in Amberwell ground and breathe Amberwell air—but Clare is determined to come to London with me. She says she wants to be with me as long as she possibly can. So there you are—Stephen is to be born in London."

"Stephen?" asked Nell.

"That's the idea—after his great, great, great grand-father—or, if it's a girl, she's to be Elinor—after her aunt."

"Oh Roger!" exclaimed Nell, blushing with pleasure.

"But I expect it will be Stephen," said Roger smiling. "Clare says she's sure it's Stephen. Perhaps Elinor will follow in due course."

# PART THREE

As long as skies are blue and fields are green
Evening must usher night, night urge the morrow,
Month follow month with woe, and year wake year
                                    to sorrow

PERCY BYSSHE SHELLEY

## CHAPTER FOURTEEN

SOMETIMES COMING events cast their shadows before, but more often a thunderbolt strikes suddenly, falling from a calm blue sky. Certainly Nell had no premonition of disaster when she rose from her bed one morning in February and hastily dressed. She hummed cheerfully as she ran downstairs to help Mrs. Duff with the breakfast . . . and Mrs. Duff was cheerful too.

" The mornings are a wee bit lighter," declared Mrs. Duff. " It makes a change. Will I take up the mistress's breakfast-tray or will you? "

Mrs. Duff's question was merely rhetorical for Nell took it up every morning of her life. Mrs. Duff would have been considerably astonished if Nell had replied, " You take it."

But of course Nell said nothing of the sort; she carried the tray upstairs, drew back the curtains and settled her mother's pillows in a comfortable heap . . . and then she asked (as she asked every morning) what sort of night her mother had had.

" Not too bad, dear," Mrs. Ayrton replied. " Those new tablets are helping me a lot. Oh, here's a letter from Connie —how delightful! "

Mrs. Ayrton had been breakfasting in bed ever since her husband's death, but she was now gradually recovering her energy and threatening to get up for breakfast. " Threatening " was Nell's word for her mother's avowed intention; it was so very much easier to carry up her mother's tray than to have her mother coming down expecting to find breakfast set out upon the table and everything in order.

The morning continued to be quite a usual sort of morning; if anything rather better than usual. Nell helped to wash the dishes and to make the beds and then she seized a moment for a very special job to which she had been looking forward. Yesterday she had been to the woods and gathered a basketful of snowdrops—Amberwell snowdrops for Clare and little Stephen—and to-day she was going to pack them in damp moss and send them off to London.

Clare and her baby had left the hospital and were staying with Lord Richmore; Roger was there too. Roger had got his orders and was going to Egypt, but of course Nell did not know the actual date of his departure. The sailing orders of ships were very secret matters in the spring of 1941. It was horrible to think of Roger going abroad, but it was no use thinking about it; Nell was thinking about another plan. She hoped that when Roger had gone she might be able to entice Clare to Amberwell. As a matter of fact she had picked the snowdrops with this end in view; perhaps when Clare saw them and smelt their woody freshness she would want to come and bring little Stephen to his home.

Nell found an old shoe-box and began to pack the snowdrops in their bed of moss. She was still busy with her pleasant task when the telephone-bell rang; her mind was full of Clare when she picked up the receiver.

It was a trunk call and there seemed to be trouble on the line; she stood there for some moments waiting for the call to come through and looking at the sunshine streaming in at the window on to the faded carpet. It's spring— almost—she thought. Winter is nearly over. The days are getting longer——

"Hallo, is that Nell?" said a voice. "This is Roger."

"Hallo—yes, it's Nell!" exclaimed Nell in surprise.

"Thank goodness I've got you! I've had an awful job

getting through. There's been a bad raid. Everything is upside down. Can you hear me?"

"Yes—but not very well," replied Nell. The line seemed dreadfully bad, there were queer cracklings, and Roger's voice sounded a long way off. Somehow it did not sound like Roger's voice at all, there was a sort of flatness about it.

"Are you all right?" asked Nell anxiously.

"Nell, I don't know how to tell you, but there's no time to waste. They'll cut me off in a minute. Nell—Clare has been killed."

"Roger!"

"I know," said the flat expressionless voice. "It's frightful. They were having supper together—Clare and her grandfather—and the bomb fell in the street outside. I was delayed. I was late getting back from the War Office. When I got there the whole place was in ruins, smashed to bits. The baby was sleeping in the back room and we managed to get him out. Are you there, Nell?"

"Yes, I'm here, Roger. Shall I come?"

"What did you say? I can't hear."

"Shall I come?"

"Come?" asked Roger's voice in a bewildered tone.

"I'll come now—at once," Nell told him. "I can get a train——"

"No, I don't want you to come. It would be no use. I'm leaving to-night."

"But Roger——"

"Listen Nell, there's no time. We'll be cut off any minute. Can you have the baby at Amberwell? I mean I don't know what to do with him. He's here at the hotel. The chambermaid is looking after him. Could you possibly——"

"Yes, of course!"

"The chambermaid says she'll take him as far as Carlisle, so if you could meet her——"

" Yes, I'll meet her.  I'll do anything you want."

" What did you say? "

" I said yes! " cried Nell.  " I'll meet her at Carlisle."

" There's a train from Euston about one o'clock.  I'll put them into it," said the weary voice.

" Do you mean to-day? "

" Yes, to-day.  Nell, I'm terribly sorry to—to foist him on to you like this, but I don't know what else to do."

" I want him! " cried Nell.  " I want him! "

" He's ill, I'm afraid.  I don't know much about babies, but he seems very ill.  Perhaps he'll die.  I hope not, because he's all that's left—but you mustn't worry too much."

" Nannie will look after him."

" Yes, that's what I thought.  Nannie and you.  Listen Nell, this is important," said Roger and for the first time there was an echo of the old Roger in his voice.  " Listen, Nell, he's yours.  Stephen is yours.  Do you understand? He's not to be messed about by other people; I'm leaving him with you."

A voice broke in saying, " Your time's up."

" Roger! " cried Nell.  " Roger, take care of yourself! "

" All right, I won't try to get killed—if that's what you mean."

It was what she had meant, and she was thankful for the assurance; there was not much else to be thankful for.

The line had gone dead, they were cut off, and there were a dozen questions she should have asked.  She should have asked what the woman was like—the woman she was to meet at Carlisle—she should have asked the woman's name; she should have arranged some sign by which to recognise her.  All she knew was that she was to meet a woman with a baby sometime to-night at Carlisle station.

Nell put down the receiver and stood there for a few

moments with her hands pressed against her heart. The sunshine was still streaming in at the window on to the shabby carpet; the shoe-box was standing on the table half packed.

"Clare!" whispered Nell. "Oh Clare! Oh poor Roger! But I mustn't think. There's no time. Oh God, please help me."

2

It was dark when Nell got to Carlisle; the station was filled with dim blue light, a weird sort of light which scarcely relieved the darkness. There had been another raid to-night, somewhere in the Midlands, and traffic from the south was completely disorganised. Trains were arriving hours late, crammed with people, and it was impossible to find out what time the midday train from Euston would arrive, or at which platform. She asked every official she could find and they all told her something different: the train had been held up at Crewe; the train had been diverted; the train would not arrive for at least two hours; the train was arriving now, at a platform on the other side of the station.

Nell ran wildly from one side of the station to the other, she climbed backwards and forwards over the bridge. She was jostled by crowds of people who were doing the same thing, trying to locate a train or to find a lost friend. There were hundreds of soldiers with packs on their backs —some with white-faced girls clinging to their arms. There were women in uniform, neat and tidy, and women not in uniform with made-up faces and incongruously perky hats; there were little children, tired and dirty and whimpering, being pulled along by one arm. There were women with babies—dozens of them. Nell accosted several and asked if this were Captain Ayrton's baby. Some of the women were annoyed at the impertinent question, others merely answered wearily that it was not.

The scene was macabre. It was like hell—surely hell could not be worse! All these people, with their strained anxious faces, hurrying hither and thither in confusion in the dim blue light! Even the young ruddy faces of the soldiers looked ghastly.

Trains came in constantly to different platforms and people poured out of them and streamed away. Nell ran from one platform to another, becoming more desperate every moment. This is frightful, she thought as she pushed her way through the crowds. If I'm not there when the train arrives I shall never find her at all—it's crazy—I don't even know her name. What will happen if I can't find her?

At last she saw a young Air Force officer who was looking round vaguely and she went up and spoke to him (afterwards when Nell thought of it she could not understand why she had done it; why had she selected this man out of the throng? And she could not understand how she had done it either; for she was one of the shyest people on earth).

" The London train? " said the boy. " It came in half an hour ago at this very platform. As a matter of fact I can tell you that quite definitely because I was in it."

" Oh Goodness! " Nell exclaimed. " I'm meeting a woman with a baby. Where can she have gone! "

" If she's got any sense she will have waited here," said the boy. He looked round and added, " *There's* a woman with a baby! I suppose she wouldn't be the one you're looking for? "

The woman was sitting on a pile of luggage with a little basket beside her, and on her knee was a baby wrapped in a dirty shawl. The woman was dressed in a green coat;

her face was very much made-up but in spite of the paint
and powder she looked dead-tired and half asleep.

"No, it wouldn't be her, of course," said the young Air
Force officer after another glance at Nell.

"It might be," said Nell. "Thank you very much
anyhow."

Nell had spoken to so many women with babies that she
had become hardened. She went up to the woman and
said: "Excuse me, but is this by any chance Captain
Ayrton's baby?"

"Crumbs!" exclaimed the woman. "Are you Miss
Ayrton? I was beginning to think you wasn't coming.
I've been in a good many jams but this seemed about the
worst. I was wondering what on earth to do?" She rose
as she spoke and handed the baby to Nell.

Nell took him in her arms. He was so small and so unexpectedly light that she nearly dropped him.

"He's a bit dirty," said the woman apologetically. "I'd
have washed his shawl but there wasn't time to get it dried
and I hadn't got anything else to put on him."

"It doesn't matter," said Nell. She held him close and
her heart seemed to swell. Roger's little son!

"I've had an awful time with him," declared the woman.
"He's been crying on and off all day. I tried to give him
a bottle but he wouldn't have nothing to do with it. He
hasn't had a drop past his lips. His mother was feeding
him—that's why."

"He's very quiet now."

"Pore little soul, he's tired himself out crying!"

The small puckered face was greyish-blue in the grim
light. The tiny hands were limp and cold.

"He's very—pale!" exclaimed Nell in alarm. "Do
you think——"

Their eyes met.

"Babies are queer," said the woman. "I've had a good deal to do with babies—one way and another. Some babies want to live and 'll come through a lot and others don't seem to think it's worth the bother."

The woman meant to be kind—it was a warning—and looking at the tiny wan face of her nephew Nell realised that the warning was justified. It certainly did not seem as if this pathetic little creature had the will to live—and if he thought life wasn't worth the bother you could hardly blame him. Nell's arms tightened round him . . . but he shan't die, she thought. If I can only get him to Nannie! I must get him to Nannie as quickly as I can.

"Well, cheeri-ho!" said the woman. "I done what I said and I don't regret it—not now. I don't mind telling you I *was* regretting it when there was nobody here to meet me—calling myself all sorts of a fool for being such a softy."

"It was good of you to come," Nell told her.

"Well, I was sorry for Captain Ayrton. I was so sorry for the poor young fellow I'd have done almost anything . . . No, thank you, miss. Captain Ayrton paid me; he paid me handsome, I *will* say that."

"Is this the luggage?" asked Nell, pointing to the suit-cases upon which the woman had been sitting.

The woman laughed. "Luggage!" she exclaimed. "There isn't a thing belonging to the baby but what he's got on. There isn't even a nappie; I had to tear up some towels. The house was all smashed to bits and they got him out of the ruins. His Daddy crept in under a heap of rubble and got him out—that's what the policeman said. Well anyhow there he is, pore little soul. You'll do your best for him, I can see that." She took one of the tiny hands and kissed it and turned away. "Cheeri-ho!" she said again.

"Where are you going? Can't I help you?" cried Nell.

The woman waved and hurried off.

## 3

The journey back to Westkirk was a nightmare to Nell. She was so tired that everything seemed vague and shadowy. She managed to find a north-bound train and getting out at Lockerbie she took a taxi to Dumfries; after hanging about in Dumfries station for more than an hour she got a train to Westkirk. All the trains were packed—especially the train from Carlisle to Lockerbie—but Nell was thankful to get in. She stood in the corridor with the baby in her arms until a sailor seeing her plight rose and gave her his seat.

For most of the journey the baby seemed to be asleep, or in a sort of coma (Nell knew so little about babies that she did not know which) but once or twice he woke up a little and whimpered miserably. At Dumfries she got some milk and hot water and tried to feed him with a spoon, but it was useless. Then she tried dipping her finger in the milk and moistening his lips. Nannie would have been horrified, she knew, but she was so desperate by this time that she would have tried anything . . . and the plan worked. She actually managed to get a few drops of milk between his lips. After that he slept again—and slept so quietly it seemed to Nell that he had stopped breathing. She put her cheek against his face and it was as cold as death. She was so terrified that she took out her powder compact and held the mirror to his mouth. The glass misted . . . which meant he was still alive.

Nell arrived at Westkirk at last. It was half-past five in the morning and pitch dark but fortunately not raining. At that hour Westkirk station was deserted; there was no taxi, nor any sort of conveyance, so she was obliged to walk.

The baby had seemed light when she took him in her arms but now she had had him in her arms for hours and he seemed to get heavier at every step. She turned in at Amberwell gates and walked up the avenue . . . and now she began to wonder how she was going to get into the house for the house would be shut up at this hour and everybody asleep. She would have to ring and knock until somebody came; perhaps Mrs. Duff would hear.

Then, as she turned the corner of the drive, she saw that the front door stood wide open and there was a light in the hall.

Nell dragged herself wearily up the steps and as she did so Nannie came out of the baize door which led to the kitchen premises—Nannie looking brisk and cheerful, dressed in the large white apron which was her badge of office.

"Nannie!" cried Nell with a sob. "Oh Nannie—I think he's dying!"

"Oh, the puir wee lamb!" exclaimed Nannie. She took the dirty little bundle from Nell's arms and held it against her heart.

"He's—dying," repeated Nell. "I've tried—to feed him——"

"Oh, the wee doo!" crooned Nannie. "We'll get some food into him somehow. We'll not let him die. Away off to bed with you, Nell. You've done your bit." She turned as she spoke and hurried up the stairs with the precious bundle.

Nell was too tired to go to bed. She sat down on the chest in the hall and began to cry weakly.

Nannie paused on the stairs and looked back. "Nell," she said crossly. "There's no sense in sitting there crying. Away to bed—I've put in a hot bottle for you—you can cry much more comfortably in your bed."

## CHAPTER FIFTEEN

It was dark when Nell woke. She looked at the clock and saw to her amazement that it was half-past ten—so she must have slept for fourteen hours! She put on her dressing-gown and came out on to the landing—and listened. There was no sound, the house was perfectly still, but she saw a light under the door of the nursery.

For a few moments Nell hesitated, afraid to go in, and then she turned the handle quietly. Nannie was sitting by the fire darning some stockings; she looked up and put her finger to her lips . . . so he was still alive!

A bassinet stood beside Nannie's chair; Nannie pointed to it and whispered softly, " He's asleep."

" Is he . . ."

" A wee bit better," said Nannie nodding. " I've been feeding him every two hours all day—with a medicine dropper. It takes a long time but I had to get food into him somehow. It's been a battle between him and me. I had a sort of feeling he wanted to go after his mother. Maybe it was silly, but that's what I felt. Once or twice I thought he was going, but I just hung on. I gave him a few drops of brandy."

Nell bent over the little bed and looked at the baby and was astonished at the change; the wee face had smoothed out—it was no longer wrinkled like the face of an old man—and it had lost the grey tinge which had alarmed her so much.

" You see a difference? " asked Nannie anxiously.

Nell nodded. She put one of her fingers into the tiny hand and the hand closed over it tightly. She was so pleased that her eyes filled with tears.

" He's grimed with dirt," said Nannie with a sigh. " I've not dared to wash him. I've just fed him and kept him warm with hot-water bottles all round him." She got up and added, " It's time for another feed."

" What about the doctor? " asked Nell.

" We got him to come this morning. It was that young Doctor Brown. He just looked at the wee lamb and said to keep him warm. I knew that already—and I knew what he was thinking too."

" You mean he thought——"

" He thought it wasn't much use bothering," said Nannie grimly. " That's what he thought. Mind you I'm not blaming the man. If it hadn't been Roger's wee son I'd have given up hope myself—and that's the truth."

By this time Nannie had measured out the milk and was heating it in a small saucepan. She went on talking. " Listen Nell, you'll need to sit up with him to-night and let me get a sleep; I'm not as young as I was and it's been an awful day—it's been about the worst day I can remember. If you come here a minute I'll show you what you're to do; it'll not be difficult because I'll leave everything ready. I'm giving him milk and water and sugar of milk every two hours—and you'll need to keep on filling the hot-water bottles. Not too hot, mind; just nice and warm."

When the feed was prepared Nannie arranged all the paraphernalia on the table beside the fire and lifted the baby. He began to cry. It was not a loud cry but it was a very different sound from the pathetic whimper which Nell remembered, and which she did not think she would ever forget.

" There now," said Nannie cheerfully. " That's more

like the thing. Let's see if you'll take it out of a bottle like a proper man." She cuddled him tightly against her and moistening the teat with milk put it to his lips. At first he would have nothing to do with it, he turned his head and shut his lips firmly.

"Come away now, Stephen," Nannie adjured him in wheedling tones. "Come away, there's my wee doo . . ."

Nell watched breathlessly while Nannie coaxed him and after a few moments the teat slipped into the tiny mouth and the baby began to suck feebly. "He's taking it!" she axclaimed.

Nannie was smiling. "We're over the worst," she said. "You'll not have much trouble with him now he's started."

"Do you really think I could manage?" asked Nell doubtfully.

"You'll manage all right," declared Nannie. "See, he's enjoying it now! If you're worried you can come and wake me."

2

Babies are queer, as the woman had said (the woman whose name Nell did not know but whose face remained quite clearly in her memory). Little Stephen, having been persuaded to live, recovered from his terrible experiences with remarkable rapidity. In a few days he was taking an interest in life and yelling for his bottle at the pitch of his voice if it did not appear at exactly the right moment. His face would pucker and become crimson with rage; he would beat the air with his doubled fists and go on yelling until he was gagged by the teat being thrust into his open mouth. Then and not till then there would be silence. Nell could not help laughing every time she witnessed this performance—but her laughter was not very far from tears.

Mrs. Ayrton took little interest in the baby. She was glad he was better of course but his presence at Amberwell disorganised the household. Nannie was too busy to look after the house and Nell was so besotted with little Stephen that she could think of nothing else. When Mrs. Ayrton's own children were small they had been kept in the background—properly cared for of course but not allowed to be a nuisance to their adult relations. Stephen definitely was a nuisance; his pram stood upon the terrace outside the morning-room window, because that was the most sheltered place and Nell could hear him if he cried . . . and if he cried Nell or Nannie—or sometimes both of them—would leave whatever they happened to be doing and rush to his assistance. Lunch was always late because Nell was upstairs in the nursery with Stephen and could not tear herself away from his charms at the proper hour. Tea-time was worse because Nannie had tea with Mrs. Duff (under the new régime) and Stephen was brought into the morning-room and laid upon the sofa where he kicked and gurgled and usurped all his aunt's attention so that she was quite unfit for any sort of reasonable conversation.

Mrs. Ayrton bore it as long as she could and then she rebelled.

" Nell," said Mrs. Ayrton at dinner one evening (it was the only peaceful meal). " Nell, don't you think it would be a good plan if Connie had the baby? "

" What! " exclaimed Nell.

" Connie is quite willing to have him and bring him up with Gerry. She has a very good nurse, you know. Roger can pay her a little for having him. It seems an excellent plan."

Nell was so dismayed that she was speechless.

" It will be better for little Stephen too," continued

Mrs. Ayrton complacently. " Gerry will be company for him. It isn't good for children to be brought up alone. I'll write to Connie to-night and——"

" No! " cried Nell.

" Oh my dear, do be sensible! We can't keep him here."

" Why not? "

" There's nobody to look after him. Nannie is getting too old."

" Not if I help her. Nannie and I are perfectly capable of looking after him between us."

" But Nell——"

" This is Stephen's home," said Nell firmly.

Mrs. Ayrton looked at her meek daughter in amazement. As a matter of fact Nell was surprised at herself; she had not known before that there was a tigress inside her.

" Really, Nell," said Mrs. Ayrton crossly. " You're behaving very strangely. If I choose to make an arrangement with Connie——"

Nell's fury rose like a flood. " You don't seem to understand," she exclaimed, trying without much success to control her voice. " You seem to forget Amberwell belongs to Roger. Stephen has far more right to live here than either you or I."

There was a moment's horrified silence. Mrs. Ayrton's face went as white as a sheet—and at the sight of her mother's face Nell's anger evaporated.

" I'm sorry," she murmured. " I'm terribly sorry, Mother. I didn't mean to say that."

Mrs. Ayrton did not speak and the subject was closed —nor was it ever reopened—but Mrs. Ayrton did not forget what Nell had said and the relations between mother and daughter which had never been cordial were considerably worsened. Perhaps Mrs. Ayrton did not realise this clearly herself, but the fact remains that after that unfortunate

conversation her heart was closed to Nell. There was no
outward breach, they spoke to each other as usual about
everyday matters, but there was no real communication
between them. This withdrawal affected Mrs. Ayrton far
more seriously than Nell, for Nell had Stephen to love and
care for, and Nell had staunch friends in Nannie and Mrs.
Duff and Mr. Gray. Mrs. Ayrton had nobody. Her friends
in the district were far too busy to come and see her, and
they had no petrol to spare for social occasions. The
Lamberts might have looked in occasionally of course, for
they were within easy walking distance, but Poppet was
not particularly fond of Marion—it was Will she liked—
so it never occurred to her to visit Amberwell. Mrs.
Ayrton was completely isolated; she had nothing to do,
she never helped in the house, and she did not care for
reading. It was no wonder that she brooded upon her
troubles and became self-centred.

3

Roger had wanted his son to grow up at Amberwell; he
had wanted Stephen to have his roots in Amberwell ground
and to breathe Amberwell air and his wish was fulfilled.
Little Stephen was out in his pram most of the day and his
first conscious memory was of green leaves swaying gently
above his head. Faces became important: the wrinkled
face of Nannie, the smiling face of Aunt Nell. Incredibly
soon Stephen could sit upon a rug on the nursery floor
surrounded by a motley collection of rattles and woolly
balls and teddy-bears, and after that it seemed no time at
all until Stephen was staggering across the lawn. He was
the most wonderful child in the world—according to his
aunt.

Roger was first in Egypt and then in the desert; he won the M.C. for Gallantry in Action at the Battle of El Alamein in October 1942. Nell was proud of Roger, but she was also very anxious and when she wrote to him to congratulate him upon his prowess she reminded him of his promise that he " would not try to get himself killed."

Roger wrote fairly regularly—all through the Desert Campaign—but his letters were not spontaneous as they had been before; they might have been written by anybody, there was nothing of the real Roger in them. All that he had suffered was shut up inside him and the box was firmly locked. Nell wrote to Roger of course, but she was wise enough not to tell him too much about Stephen (it would have been easy to fill all her letters with Stephen's doings but she resisted the temptation), instead she told Roger about Mrs. Duff's latest saying, about the comic things that had happened at the Red Cross Fête and other local affairs. Unfortunately there were sad tidings as well, which had to be reported to Roger. Ian Findlater was killed (he was the elder of the two Findlater boys who used to play with Roger and Tom in the Amberwell gardens), Arnold Maddon, the doctor's son, was badly wounded, and the garden-boy, whom Mr. Ayrton had tried so hard to keep, was taken prisoner by the Japanese.

Tom wrote occasionally, but Tom's letters had never been very informative. He could not tell her where he was, of course, for censorship was strict, but Nell wished he would tell her something about himself and how he was getting on, and after some weeks of complete silence she wrote and told him so. He replied quite soon saying he was all right and she was not to worry and added that a poisonous snake had bitten Paul's hand but it had done him no harm—much to everyone's surprise. This stray piece of information puzzled Nell (she knew nobody called

Paul and it was unlike Tom to hand out news about his friends) and then suddenly she remembered St. Paul's adventure at Melita and came to the conclusion that Tom was informing her that his ship had called at Malta. The postscript clinched the matter:

P.S. *Don't let on about Paul. He doesn't want his people to know.*

Nell smiled as she folded up the letter and put it away.

## CHAPTER SIXTEEN

ONE MORNING when Nell went down to help Mrs. Duff with the breakfast she was surprised to hear a man's voice coming from the kitchen. In fact she was more than surprised, and stood for a moment with her hand upon the knob of the kitchen door, rooted to the ground with astonishment. Mr. Gray was the only man left at Amberwell —and those were certainly not the well-known rumbling tones of Mr. Gray.

After a few moments she pulled herself together and opened the door—and there was Tom! Tom whom she had last heard of in Malta! He was sitting at the kitchen table eating bacon and eggs and talking with his mouth full (which difficult feat was one of Tom's many accomplishments). In front of him stood Mrs. Duff watching with fond indulgence while the whole week's ration of the household rapidly disappeared before her eyes.

" Oh my! " Mrs. Duff was saying. " Oh maircy! Oh, Mr. Tom, it's like a story-book."

" Tom! " cried Nell. " Oh Tom, how lovely? Where have you dropped from? "

" Hallo, Nellie! " exclaimed Tom, rising and wiping his mouth and kissing her with brotherly affection. Nobody but Tom ever called her Nellie. " Hallo, Nellie! Let me look at you. Do you know that you're getting extraordinarily pretty? "

" Where have you come from? " asked Nell smiling. " I thought you were at Malta! "

" Ah, so you understood," said Tom. " I wondered if you would have sufficient intelligence. Yes, I was at Malta but now I'm here."

" Why didn't you let us know you were coming? "

" I didn't want Hitler to hear about it," replied Tom in hushed accents.

" He's awful," declared Mrs. Duff. " I was telling him he ought to be having his breakfast in the dining-room, but you know what he is, Miss Nell."

" It's much nicer here," said Tom. " I like my bacon straight out of the pan and I like Mrs. Duff to talk to while I'm eating."

" It's not the right thing, Mr. Tom. I told you——"

" You told me Nellie would be cross. Is she cross? Look at her! No."

" He slept in his bed with no sheets, Miss Nell."

" I did indeed," nodded Tom. " It was a frightful hardship. Fancy having to sleep in a bed with blankets and no sheets! And this house is terribly difficult to break into. It took me the best part of twenty minutes to force an entrance. Well, well, what a homecoming! "

" If you'd told us you were coming——" began Mrs. Duff.

" You should have known," declared Tom. " You should study telepathy and then you'd know the proper moment to hang out the flags and roll out the red carpet." He sat down and went on with his breakfast.

" You always was the worst! " exclaimed Mrs. Duff laughing.

Tom nodded. " I always was the worst and you always loved me best, didn't you, Duffy? "

" Yes," said Mrs. Duff blatantly.

" You broke into the house? " asked Nell, interrupting these fond exchanges. The news caused her anxiety.

Amberwell House was so big and rambling and she herself was the only able-bodied person in the place. She had spent quite a lot of time and thought—and money—in making Amberwell House burglar-proof, and here was evidence to show she had failed.

" It was difficult," replied Tom, taking a piece of bread and mopping up the remains of bacon-fat, in a manner which would have distressed Nannie considerably. " It was very difficult indeed. You've got new-fangled snibs on all the ground-floor windows; I couldn't open them with my knife."

" Good," said Nell smiling.

" Not good at all. I had to climb on to the scullery roof and crawl in through one of the bathroom windows."

" I'll put a snib on it," said Nell.

Tom had finished and cleaned his plate. " Look here, Duffy," he said. " If it wouldn't be a bother I'd like some more. Nobody cooks bacon like you."

" Oh, Mr. Tom, there's not a bit! " cried Mrs. Duff in dismay.

" No more bacon in the house? "

" There's a war on," Nell told him.

" You mean——"

" That was our week's ration, that was," said Nell and she began to laugh at Tom's horrified expression.

" Golly! " he exclaimed. " D'you mean to tell me I've eaten your whole week's ration? But that's awful! Duffy, why on earth did you let me? "

" Och, well, there's lots of eggs."

Tom pushed away his empty plate. " It's awful," he repeated. " Why didn't somebody tell me there was a war on? Fancy there being a war on and me not knowing a thing about it! All these months when I've been cruising about in a lovely ship, living on the fat of the land and basking in the warm sunshine, you've been enduring the rigours of war! I can hardly believe it."

He looked so earnest that Mrs. Duff was bewildered. " Oh, Mr. Tom, how you do run on! You knew it was war all the time. You've just been telling me about the enemy shooting at your ship and making a hole in it and the water pouring in."

" That was just my fun," explained Tom. Then, all at once, the gaiety and nonsense drained out of him and his face looked tired and old.

The change was alarming. Nell was quite horrified; she remembered Roger saying that old Tom was not heartless enough for a war. She did not know what to say, but she had to say something to break the unbearable silence that had fallen upon them so suddenly.

" Why don't you have a walk in the garden," suggested Nell. " We're going to have our breakfast now, but you don't want to sit and watch us eating. You'll find Mr. Gray somewhere about; he'll be awfully pleased to see you."

Tom rose without a word and went out.

" Oh, Miss Nell! " exclaimed Mrs. Duff. " Oh Goodness! I thought he was going to faint."

" I know," agreed Nell. " It was frightening. He's had a bad time. Perhaps he'll be better when he's had a few days leave."

" He's got a fortnight—that's what he said. I'll take a walk down to the lodge this afternoon and see if Mrs. Gray could lend me a wee bit of bacon for to-morrow morning," said Mrs. Duff.

2

Tom needed more than a few days to recover his equilibrium. He was terribly restless—sometimes unnaturally gay, sometimes silent and gloomy—Nell noticed that he could not bear to be in the room when her mother was there. Mrs. Ayrton's banal conversation irritated him and he had no patience with her when she got muddled and repeated herself. Tom did not say anything, he merely got up and went away.

Nell was so worried about Tom that she neglected some of her duties and went for long walks with him across the moors or along the shore, but she could not neglect all her duties and presently she discovered that, left to himself, Tom sought out the company of his nephew. Stephen was now two years old, walking sturdily and talking a great deal—though not very clearly. The two played together very happily, they sat upon a rug on the lawn and Tom built towers of small, gaily-coloured cardboard boxes for Stephen to knock over. It seemed a monotonous occupation but neither of them grew tired of it.

" You never saw Clare, did you? " said Tom one morning when Stephen had been dragged off by Nannie to have his rest.

" No," said Nell with a sigh.

" The kid's awfully like her, you know. I only saw Clare once—went and stayed with them in Salisbury for a week-end—they were terrifyingly happy."

" Terrifyingly? " asked Nell, sitting down beside him on the rug.

" Yes, it terrified me. I felt it couldn't last. Perfect things don't last."

" Imperfect things don't last either," said Nell thoughtfully. "I suppose even the war will be over some day. Tom, are you sorry you went into the Navy?"

"That's a funny thing to ask," said Tom. "I've been sorry lots of times and glad lots of times if you really want to know . . . sorry in the middle of a North Sea blizzard and glad when the sun shone and the sea was blue. You know, Nell, I wanted to go into the Navy when I was a kid and Father wouldn't let me. I was as sick as mud and I went about for years with a chip on my shoulder. It wasn't until Father was dead and I went to see the lawyer, Mr. Dalgleish, that I discovered why. I mean Father had quite good reasons; he had thought it all out and wanted to do the best for me. It wasn't just a whim. If only he had told me at the time it would have saved all the bitterness."

Tom was building another tower of boxes but there was nobody to knock them over. "I like kids," he said. "And Stephen is rather special. It's fun watching him. Sometimes he looks a bit like Roger—and he laughs like Anne—and then, at other times, he's all Clare. Odd, isn't it?"

"Yes," said Nell.

There was a little silence and then Tom looked up with his engaging grin which made him look so young—so like the Tom of long ago. "I'm better," he said. "I was pretty nearly round the bend. I expect you noticed. It's just as well I'm better because my leave is up. I'm off to-morrow at daybreak."

Nell knew this. She had been watching the days fly past.

"Amberwell has cured me," continued Tom in a reflective tone. "You and Stephen have helped a lot—but it was Amberwell, really. There was a fellow called Antæus that we learnt about at school. His mother was the earth. He fought terrific battles and every time his opponent got

him down and he fell on the ground his mother healed him
and he rose up stronger than before."

" So you're like Antæus? "

" Only in some ways. He was brave and I'm not."

" What nonsense, Tom! You were always the bravest.
It was always you who did the daring things."

" Daring things are easy—things that you do in the heat
of the moment. I mean I could lead a charge, waving my
flag and yelling like a savage; it's far more difficult to go
on and on bearing things day after day. That's what gets
me down. But don't worry about me," added Tom,
balancing the last and smallest box upon the top of the
tower with precision. " Just look at that! The old hand
is as steady as a rock."

" Good," said Nell, trying to smile.

" You are worrying," said Tom. " I wish you wouldn't.
No, that's not quite true. It's rather nice to know that
somebody is worrying a little, but don't worry too much."
He rose and added, " I promised Mr. Gray I'd do a bit of
digging."

Nell watched him as he strolled off; she would have
liked to bury Tom in a deep hole in the garden and keep
him there safely until this ghastly war was over.

It was a miserably wet morning for Tom's departure.
Nell got up very early to give him his breakfast but when
she went down to the kitchen Mrs. Duff was there already,
frying a large pan of bacon. Nell wondered where she had
managed to collect it, but forbore to inquire. As the
breakfast was under control she went out to get the car to
drive Tom to the station but here again she was forestalled.
Mr. Gray was in the garage; the car had been started and
was running smoothly.

At six o'clock it was still dark and raining heavily but in
spite of the weather conditions everybody in the place had

gathered round the door to see Tom depart (everybody except Mrs. Ayrton who was still in bed). The group consisted of Mr. and Mrs. Gray and the Land Girl, Mrs. Duff and Nannie and Stephen. Even Margaret, the daily help, who was not due to arrive at Amberwell until nine o'clock, had limped up from Westkirk through the rain to say good-bye.

Tom was in tearing spirits—or at least appeared to be— he kissed everybody with the single exception of Mr. Gray and leapt into the car beside Nell.

They shouted " Good-bye! " and waved.

" Haste ye back! " cried Mrs. Duff, bursting into tears.

## CHAPTER SEVENTEEN

ALL THIS time Mr. Gray had been doing his best with the gardens but except for the Land Girl he had nothing but casual labour to assist him and things were going from bad to worse. Nell would have helped if she had had time but her days were too full already. Amberwell was very quiet, there was no social life in the district because people could not use their cars to go about and visit their friends.

One streaming wet day in November Nell met Mary Findlater coming out of the butcher's. They were both thoroughly mackintoshed and hung about with baskets and bags.

" Nell! " exclaimed Mary. " Goodness, what years it is since I saw you! Have you got time for a cup of coffee? "

Nell decided to make time, for as Mary said it was years since they had met and Mary looked so tired and depressed that it would have been unkind to refuse her invitation.

They went into the little hotel together and sat down in the comfortable lounge before the fire.

" I'm just home for a fortnight's leave," said Mary. " I'm in the Wrens—but I expect you knew that."

" Do you like it? " asked Nell.

" Yes, it's fun," she replied. " The only trouble is I ought to be at home. I wish I were twins," she added with a sigh.

Nell understood this somewhat peculiar wish for she herself had often thought that there would be ample occupation for two Nells. She accepted a cup of coffee and sympathised.

" It's awful," said Mary. " It makes me miserable to come home and see the poor darlings looking so old and tired. When I saw Daddy washing up the dishes I almost cried—and Mummy beating up horrible potatoes in a little bowl! Oh dear!"

Nell tried to imagine Sir Andrew and Lady Findlater engaged in these unwonted pursuits but it was impossible. Her imagination boggled at the idea.

" I shouldn't have left them," continued Mary. " I wouldn't have if I'd known what was going to happen. I feel a perfect beast . . ."

She went on talking about it and Nell continued to listen and sympathise. They talked about other things too. They exchanged family news and reminisced about their childhood. They had never been great friends (Nell had never wanted any friend except Anne) but to-day it seemed different. She's nice, thought Nell, looking at the small piquant face, framed in curly brown hair. She really is a dear. I wonder why I didn't like her better.

Suddenly the clock struck twelve and Mary sprang to her feet.

" Goodness, it's twelve!" she cried. " I'm keeping them both in bed to-day so I must rush back and cook their lunch. It's been awfully good of you to listen to my moan. I feel a lot better—if that's any consolation. Remember me to Roger when you write—and Tom of course. You're lucky," she added as she put on her mackintosh hat.

Nell was aware that this was an oblique reference to Ian's death. " I know I'm lucky," she agreed. " We were terribly sorry. Where is Andy?"

" Quite safe at the moment, thank goodness," replied Mary with a sigh. " He's got a job as instructor—training

commandos—not far from Inverness. I'll tell him you asked
for him, shall I ? "

" Yes, do," said Nell.

" You've changed," declared Mary as they said good-bye.
" You used to be so—so shy—and—and——"

" Stupid," suggested Nell.

Mary laughed. " No, not stupid, but just—not very
interesting if you know what I mean."

The compliment pleased Nell and as she toiled home up
the hill with her heavy basket she thought about it seriously
and realised that what Mary had said was true. The hard
work and all the responsibilities and grinding anxieties had
changed her from a colourless nonentity into a useful sort
of human being who had a definite place in the world.
Perhaps Stephen had been the principal factor in the
metamorphosis of Nell; Stephen had become the most
important person in Nell's life. " Listen, Nell, he's yours,"
Roger had said. " He's not to be messed about by other
people." Nell could still hear the tone of Roger's voice as
it had sounded on the telephone—a desperately urgent
tone of voice, quite different from the flat weary voice in
which he had told her of the tragedy. At first it had been
quite easy, for all Stephen had needed was love and care,
but now that he was older—he was nearly four—there
were other things to be thought of. Nannie was inclined
to spoil him (which was odd, because she certainly had not
spoilt Connie and Nell and Anne) so it was left to Nell to
bring up Stephen in the way he should go, to teach him to
be considerate and kind . . . and above all to be obedient.
In one way the job was simple enough, for Stephen had a
delightfully happy nature, but in another way it was
difficult because Stephen's charm was hard to resist. Nell
would have liked to give him everything he wanted—and
more. It seemed odd to Nell that although she was strict

with Stephen he loved her better than Nannie, who was lenient.

All this time Roger had not been home to Amberwell. He had had leave on two occasions, but had gone to South Africa instead.

"Perhaps you think it queer," wrote Roger. "But I don't want to come home until we've finished the job."

Nell did think it "queer," and at first she was surprised and hurt, but after some thought she saw that Roger had a right to do as he pleased. Tom had come to Amberwell to steep himself in its atmosphere and be healed, but Roger wanted to "finish the job" before he returned. He loved Amberwell in a different sort of way.

2

Occasionally the peace of Amberwell was broken by a visit from Connie and her family but unfortunately these visits were not entirely enjoyable and became less welcome and more upsetting to the household as the family grew older; for Gerry and Joan were being brought up in the modern manner and were allowed at all times to "express their ego." This curious phrase, which Connie had culled from a book on child management, was always upon her lips and excused the most unsocial behaviour on the part of her offspring.

They came for a fortnight in the early spring of 1945 when Gerald was obliged to leave home on business.

Mrs. Ayrton had been looking forward to having Connie, and although she was not fond of children she was prepared to love Gerry and Joan for Connie's sake. She had become a great deal older in the last few years and she was lonely. She and Nell had never had anything in common but Connie was different.

Mrs. Ayrton had looked forward to long comfortable chats with Connie about matters which interested them both . . . but alas Connie was now " all mother " and was interested in nothing except her children. If they were present they claimed her full attention and if they were absent she talked about them all the time. Mrs. Ayrton did her best to make friends with Connie's children but they did not respond and they were so wild and rough that she was actually frightened of them. They ran about the house shouting and yelling; they climbed upon chairs and bounced up and down and then jumped off; they wandered round the room touching everything. Any ornament which attracted them was removed from the table upon which it happened to be standing and placed upon the floor. Usually they both wanted the same thing at the same time and quarrelled over it loudly and violently.

" It's mine, I saw it first! " Joan would cry.

" I want it! " Gerry would declare, trying to tear it out of her hands.

A struggle would ensue during which the bone of contention was sometimes broken.

Mrs. Ayrton had never been used to this sort of behaviour and she did not like it. " Connie dear, don't you think——" she would begin.

" No, Mother, we mustn't interfere," Connie would say earnestly. " It's so important for them to express their ego. Of course it's a pity the little shepherdess has lost her head but if I stick it on with glue it won't show at all. I often have to mend things at home and I know just how to do it."

Nell bore the " expressions of ego " as patiently as she

could, reminding herself from time to time that the days were passing and the visit would soon be over. She was obliged to remind Nannie too, for Nannie suffered severely —especially at meal-times.

" It's just awful," Nannie told her. " The nurse is quite a nice sort of woman but she's not allowed to check them. If she checks them they go straight off and tell their mother. You never saw anything like the way they behave; they don't like carrots so if there's carrots they throw their dinners on the floor—and they get down off their chairs and rampage round the room like savages."

" They're going away on Friday," said Nell comfortingly.

" Well, I hope I'll be able to last out," declared Nannie. " My hands itch to give them a good skelping."

There was one frightful day when Gerry and Joan excelled themselves in wickedness. They woke very early in the morning and demanded to be dressed. It was cold and rather misty but their nurse dared not thwart them so she dressed them and let them loose. As they clattered off down the stairs to the garden she wondered whether she ought to go after them and see what they were doing. But what was the use? thought the unhappy woman. She had no control over her charges so she might as well go back to bed.

Mr. Gray was taking a walk round the garden before starting his day's work and was alarmed to hear a series of loud crashes coming from the direction of the greenhouses; when he went to investigate he discovered Gerry and Joan throwing stones through the glass and screaming with delight.

" Stop that! " shouted Mr. Gray. " Stop it at once, you young devils! "

" We like doing it! " yelled Gerry, seizing another stone and sending it hurtling through the air.

" It's good for us! " shrieked Joan, following his example.

Roused beyond bearing Mr. Gray rushed upon them waving his stick, and chased them out of the garden, and the two children fleeing in fear and astonishment made straight for their mother's room.

" He was horrid to us! " wailed Joan. " He tried to hit us with his stick."

" He called us devils," added Gerry between his sobs.

Connie was very upset—but not because of the damage to the greenhouse—she explained to Nell that the glass could easily be replaced but the effect of Mr. Gray's behaviour might be irreparable. The book said fear and violence often produced complexes which could ruin a child for life. When Nell tried to comfort her by pointing out that Gerry and Joan seemed none the worse of their experience, but were chasing each other round the house and shouting lustily in their usual manner, Connie replied that the book said it would show later—perhaps not until they were grown-up.

Having failed to comfort Connie, Nell's next thought was to seek out Mr. Gray. She found him trying to stop up the holes in the greenhouse with pieces of cardboard.

" All my wee seedlings! " mourned Mr. Gray. " They were doing fine—and who knows but there might be frost to-night! "

Nell thought this unlikely and said so, but her assurance fell upon deaf ears.

" They're hooligans, that's what they are," declared Mr. Gray with unaccustomed frankness. " You say they don't know it's naughty—well, they ought to. Miss Connie —I mean Mrs. Lambert—ought to bring up her bairns to know right from wrong. None of you ever thought of spoiling things. All the years you ran about the gardens there was never a bit of damage done."

" They're going home on Friday," said Nell.

" The sooner the better," growled Mr. Gray.

The afternoon was fine and Connie proposed that she and Nell should take the children and have a picnic on the bowling-green. Nell suggested that they might go to the shore instead, but Connie would not hear of it.

" The bowling-green is more peaceful," said Connie. " I want them to have a very peaceful afternoon."

Peace was obtained by allowing the young Lamberts to do exactly as they wished; Gerry rode Stephen's tricycle round and round the lawn; Joan played with Stephen's wheel-barrow. Nell had brought a toy roller for Stephen to play with but after a few minutes Joan wanted that too, and Stephen surrendered it meekly. Stephen had learned that it was better for everybody if his cousins got what they wanted.

They had tea on the grass stage; it had been a favourite place for tea when Connie and Nell were children and it reminded them of byegone days. " Do you remember . . ." is a fascinating game to play, especially with a sister, and Connie became quite human. She was so interested in the conversation that she actually stopped worrying about her children.

" You're not talking to us, Mummy," complained Joan.

" Mummy is talking to Aunt Nell," said Connie. " Oh Nell, do you remember——"

But Nell was fated not to hear this memory for Joan took immediate action; she leant forward and emptied her mug of milk into her mother's lap.

For a moment Nell thought—and hoped—that Connie would lose her temper but Connie had trained herself too thoroughly to do anything so crude.

" Oh Joanie, you are a funny little girl," said Connie, taking out her handkerchief and trying to mop up the mess.

" You wanted Mummy to talk to you, didn't you? Naughty Mummy to talk to Aunt Nell! "

Joan was delighted of course for she had achieved her object but Gerry was not so pleased. Gerry was being neglected, nobody was taking any notice of him. Gerry's ego prompted him to seize a stick, which happened to be handy, and hit Stephen on the head.

The unexpected assault alarmed Stephen and he opened his mouth and howled.

" Don't do that, Gerry! " cried Nell.

" It was only in fun," declared Connie.

" It's fun! " said Gerry, laughing with glee and hitting his cousin again.

Nell leapt to her feet and snatched the stick from his grasp, and in a moment there was pandemonium. Gerry shrieked at the top of his voice, Stephen sobbed loudly and Connie added to the din by rounding upon Nell.

" It's horrid of you! " she raged. " You should never use violence to little children—it's a dreadful thing to do —you've upset poor little Gerry frightfully. He was just having fun with Stephen—that's all. Stephen shouldn't be such a baby. He's completely spoilt——"

All three children were now screaming so the remainder of Connie's diatribe was lost and Nell was so angry that she picked up Stephen and carried him into the house.

When Nell discovered that there were no wounds upon Stephen—not so much as a red mark—her rage died down and she was able to smile, but all the same a quite unmistakable chill developed in the relationship between herself and her elder sister and she was thankful when Friday came and the family packed up and went home—nor was Nell the only person who was thankful.

It isn't fair, thought Nell as she waved them away (but

without the usual valediction). It really isn't fair to *them* to allow them to make themselves so unpopular.

The visit had been an ordeal, and yet it was useful, for at least Nell had been given an object lesson on how not to bring up the young. Nannie had had an object lesson too, and was not quite so indulgent with Stephen as she had been before.

## CHAPTER EIGHTEEN

AMBERWELL WAS in Tom's thoughts as he stood on the bridge of the destroyer, *Starfish*, with Dennis Weatherby. He often talked to Dennis about Amberwell and Dennis listened and understood for he had a home in Yorkshire and loved it in much the same way. Dennis was some years older than Tom (he was a Lieutenant Commander and due for promotion) but in spite of the difference in age the two were firm friends.

The *Starfish* had had a pretty thin time all winter for she had been on convoy duty in the north but now she was making for Rosyth and her crew was looking forward to a well-earned spell of leave.

It was early April, but the night was warm—or at least it seemed warm to men who had braved the blizzards of a northern winter—there was no moon but the stars were so bright that it was not really dark. There were millions of stars to be seen and for a while the two young men looked at them in silence. Tom had always loved stars.

" I suppose you'll be going home," said Dennis at last.

" Yes, what about you? I mean would you like to come to Amberwell for a few days? It would be grand if you could."

" I'd love to, sometime. But they're expecting me at home, and—well, you know how it is. I mean one doesn't get home too often."

" Of course," agreed Tom quickly. " I just meant if you could manage to come——"

Silence fell. They understood one another and their

silences were companionable. What a splendid fellow Dennis is, thought Tom. You can depend upon him whatever happens . . . just as you can depend on Roger. The fact was Tom had always needed someone like that, someone solid and rock-like, to give him stability, to make him feel safe.

Tom leaned on the rail beside his friend and watched the stars dipping up and down to the gentle movement of the ship as she surged along through the dark water. Amberwell! thought Tom. Soon he would be there. Perhaps he should ring up from Edinburgh and say he was coming. Nellie would be pleased . . . and he would see Stephen . . . a nice kid, Stephen . . .

" Look, there's the Bell Rock! " said Dennis.

The rock was a thin dark streak on the starboard bow. It was so low in the water that one would not have noticed it but for the fringe of white lace where the sea broke upon the rocks. From the middle of the reef a finger stood pointing to the skies.

" You've seen it lighted of course," said Tom.

" Haven't you? " asked Dennis in surprise. " Oh no, of course not. I always forget you aren't a real sailor. It's wonderfully cheering to see the beams sweeping round the sky on a cold dark night—must have been a job building it, I must try to find out about it."

Tom knew quite a lot about the building of the Bell Rock Lighthouse for although he was not " a real sailor " he had always been interested in everything to do with the sea. " The reef is only uncovered at low water," said Tom. " They worked at it night and day whenever the tide went out. At night they used torches; there was no other form of lighting in the early years of the nineteenth century. The tower was designed by Robert Stevenson and he was on the spot himself to superintend the work."

" So it has stood there, battered by storms, for over a

hundred years," said Dennis thoughtfully. "You know, Tom, I'd like to do a job like that—a constructive job that would last after I was dead."

Tom was silent.

"It would be good to make something permanent," continued Dennis. "Something worth-while—so that in the year two thousand and forty-five two chaps would look at it and say, 'Dennis Weatherby built that.'"

"We can't all do that sort of job," said Tom. "We've helped to beat Hitler. That's something, isn't it?"

They were now approaching nearer the reef; soon they would be swinging westwards up the Firth of Forth. Dennis began to talk about the Firth in the days of peace, which seemed so long ago, when the lighthouses from the May and the Bass and Fidra flashed their welcoming beams, and the little towns on the shores of the wide estuary glittered like handfuls of jewels. To-night there was not a light to be seen; the land which they were approaching might have been an uninhabited desert.

"Soon we shall see the lights again," said Dennis cheerfully. "We're coming to the end of the tunnel. They can't hold out much longer. You know, Tom, I feel as if the war had been going on for about twenty years. It will be queer when it's over. Difficult to believe."

"Frightfully difficult," agreed Tom. "I've got a brother who has been all through the Desert and the Italian campaigns. He's all right so far—thank Heaven! Well, I think I'll turn in now."

"Wish I could," said Dennis enviously. "You wouldn't see me up here if I didn't have to be."

Tom paused at the top of the ladder and looked back. He said jokingly, "Keep a good look-out, won't you?"

"Don't worry," replied Dennis laughing. "You can go off to your nice comfy bed and dream of Amberwell."

Tom waved and turned away—and at that moment there was a terrific shattering crash. The ship seemed to leap into the air and a sheet of flame burst from beneath her bows. A burning blast of hurricane force swept Tom from the ladder as if he had been a withered leaf and hurled him into the water. He felt himself sinking down—and down—into the dark icy depths.

The shock was so severe that only his instinct for self-preservation made him struggle wildly to the surface—it seemed an eternity before he saw the bubbles breaking above his head and was able to fill his bursting lungs with air.

The disaster had happened so suddenly and unexpectedly that Tom was dazed. He could think of nothing—there was nothing in his mind but the determination to keep his head above water. He was a strong swimmer but his sodden clothes were dragging him down and fortunately he had enough sense to struggle out of them, kicking off his shoes and trousers and struggling out of his jacket. It was easier now to keep afloat—but how cold it was! How bitterly cold! Already his legs were beginning to feel paralysed.

The sea had looked calm from the bridge of the *Starfish* but it is never really calm in these uneasy waters and there was enough swell to make swimming extremely exhausting and to make it very difficult to see for more than a few yards. When he was on the crest of the waves he tried to look round for the ship, but he had no idea where to look—and the next moment he was down in the trough and could see nothing but dark green water.

(What on earth happened? he wondered, and what will happen now? How long will it be before they realise I was swept overboard? The ship will be in confusion. They may not notice that I've disappeared.)

A crate floated by. It was a big square crate which Tom remembered having seen on the upper deck of the ship.

It was empty, so it floated tipsily upon the rolling waves. Tom swam to it and got hold of the rough wooden side . . . if only he could get on to the crate, out of the ice-cold water! He tried to pull himself up but the crate rolled over and over . . . and then he found a rope-handle attached to the side of the crate and heaved himself up. His weight sank the crate so that it was barely above the level of the sea, but it still floated. Tom spread himself upon it face downwards gripping the sides with his hands.

He was safe—or at least temporarily safe—but the effort had been frightful and he was so exhausted that he was suddenly engulfed in a roaring cloud and lost consciousness.

It might have been a few minutes or it might have been an hour before the blackness lifted and Tom came to his senses. He sat up very carefully, balancing his crazy craft and looked round for the ship. There was no ship. There was nothing to be seen but the starry sky and the heaving waves. There was not even a piece of wreckage floating upon the water, not even a patch of oil. Could a ship go down and disappear completely? It was too ghastly to think of. It must have been a mine, thought Tom. One of those devilish mines that float beneath the surface—it couldn't have been anything else. The ship had run straight on to it and the thing had exploded . . . and then . . . and then the ship had either steamed on . . . or else . . . gone down.

Tom began to shout at the top of his voice, half in a sort of panic and half in the hope that somebody else might have survived the disaster. He shouted until he was hoarse but nobody answered. Then he lay back, cold and shivering, pounded by feelings of misery and despair. If the ship had gone down—if they had all gone—all those good fellows he had lived with for months and loved like brothers—he did not want to survive. Why should he, and he only, be saved?

The stars were paling now and the sky was filled with a grey ghostly light. Tom watched it spread and brighten. After what seemed years the sun rose out of the sea amidst grey and silvery clouds. The light was cheering after the long dark night and Tom's courage began to return; he even began to hope. Although he had declared to himself that he did not want to live the instinct to fight for life is strong and persistent. He knew nothing about the currents in these parts but there was a gentle breeze blowing from the east and the tide was making. The tide had been at its lowest ebb when he and Dennis had seen the Bell Rock. All this was in his favour. If he could just hold on he might be washed ashore. How long could he hold on? He tried to sit up again, for perhaps he might see the shore, but he was too weak and dizzy; he was so cold that his teeth were chattering and there was no feeling in his limbs. It's no good—I'm done, thought Tom.

2

There was a queer sort of rumbling in Tom's ears. It cleared gradually and became the sound of a deep voice talking.

"Dinna take on, Bob," the voice was saying. "The lad's no deid yet. See he's coming roond! We'll lift the blankets an' gi'e him a wee rub. The great thing is tae get the circulation gaein'. Mind that, Bob. It's a useful thing to ken. There's some folks would pour whusky doon his gullet—an' mebbe choke him. Niver dae that, Bob. It's a rideeculous thing tae dae."

The blankets were removed and Tom was rubbed and pomelled vigorously by hard, knotted hands. It was painful and unpleasant but he had enough sense to realise it was doing him good so he bore it without a murmur. When his attendants had finished the job they rolled him up again in the rough brown blankets.

By this time Tom was able to look about him and saw that he was lying in a wooden bunk in the small dirty cabin of a fishing-boat. His two companions were fishermen; one was old, with a brown wrinkled face and a grizzled beard, the other was a mere boy with a smooth brown face and dark hair. Tom tried to speak to them but he could not.

" He's better," declared the old man.

" Wull I gi'e him a drink noo, Granfer? " asked the boy.

" Aye, but mind an' raise him up a bit—here, lad, ye'd best let me help ye."

They raised Tom's head and held a mug of steaming liquid to his lips. It was strong tea and condensed milk, laced with whisky. The warmth flowed through his body and the fumes dulled his brain. He drifted off to sleep.

It was pitch dark when Tom woke and he could not think where he had got to. He was not in his cabin in the *Starfish*. The air was warm and stuffy and smelt of fish and tar and paraffin. The motion was unusual too, it was an unstable sort of pitch and roll; quite unlike the purposeful surge of the ship.

Where on earth, thought Tom—and then suddenly remembered. He remembered standing on the bridge of the *Starfish* with Dennis; he remembered the explosion; he remembered floundering in the sea; he remembered lying on the crate for hours and hours, shivering and hopeless. All this was quite clear in his mind, but at the same time far away as if it had happened months ago. The ghastly shock and the horror of his experience had faded.

Presently the boy came in with a lantern and hung it upon a hook in the beam.

" Are ye feeling a wee bit better? " he asked anxiously. " Granfer said ye could have a boiled egg."

" I just—want a drink," said Tom feebly. But when the boy had propped him up and brought him some food he found that he was hungry.

" That's grand," said the boy, watching every mouthful with delight. " That'll dae ye guid. D'ye ken this—I thocht ye was deid. It was me that saw ye. We was fishin' off the rocks. Granfer pit a rope roond ma waist an' I went over an' pulled ye in. I thocht ye was deid," repeated the boy earnestly.

" Did you see the ship? "

" There wus nae ship—just you, floatin' in the sea on a boax. It was lucky I saw ye."

The boy's eyes were very friendly, they surveyed Tom with a proprietory air—and Tom suddenly understood. He feels I belong to him, thought Tom, and so I do. If it hadn't been for Bob's sharp eyes I'd be dead by now.

Tom stretched out his hand and seizing Bob's hand shook it firmly. For a few moments the boy looked bewildered, and then he smiled shyly, showing a mouthful of strong white teeth.

" Could ye eat anither egg? " he asked eagerly. " I could get it in a minute, honestly I could. It would be nae bother."

Tom could not—not even to please Bob—but he accepted another cup of tea and drank it gratefully.

The old man came in while Tom was finishing his meal. He was so big and burly that he seemed to fill the little cabin to overflowing. He sat down at the little table and folding his arms upon it looked at Tom thoughtfully.

" Are ye feeling weel enough for a wee crack? " he inquired.

" I'm all right," said Tom hoarsely. " I just feel a bit—

done. I want to thank you and Bob. If it hadn't been for you——"

" Och away! We did naethin', naethin' at all."

" Saved my life—that's all."

" Hoots! We did naethin'. But I'll need tae ken whaur ye came frae, if ye're feelin' weel enough tae speak. Glaister's my name—Robert Glaister. The lad's my grandson."

Tom told Mr. Glaister his name and explained what had happened. He found it very difficult to talk for his throat was sore and he still felt weak and dizzy but as a matter of fact there was not much to tell.

" Could it have been a mine? " asked Tom. " And if it was do you think the ship could have sunk—with everybody on board? "

" It would be a mine," said Mr. Glaister. " But I canna' believe the ship would ha' gone doon sae quick an' left no wreckage."

" You're hopeful? " Tom asked.

Mr. Glaister nodded. He reminded Tom that it was not rough, so even if the ship had been damaged by the explosion she might not have sunk at all. If the worst came to the worst there would have been time to lower the boats. There were strong currents off the Bell Rock (explained Mr. Glaister in his slow deep voice) and Tom might have drifted some distance from the scene of disaster before he was missed. Mr. Glaister was so large and solid and so sure of his opinion that Tom was comforted.

" It's Leith we're makin' for," said Mr. Glaister at last. " We'll be in before dark gin the breeze haulds. I'll need tae report tae the authorities——"

" I'll have to do that," said Tom wearily.

" Ye'll dae nae sich thing," declared Mr. Glaister. " Ye'll gang straight tae the hoaspital, ma lad. If they're

wantin' tae see ye they'll need tae send some buddy doon
tae the hoaspital—but that's their beesness, no mine."

" I think I ought to——"

" There's tae be nae argument aboot it," said Mr.
Glaister firmly.

Tom was much too weak to argue with Mr. Glaister; he
decided that you might as well try to argue with a rock,
besides he had an uncomfortable feeling that he was going
to be ill.  His chest felt tight and talking to Mr. Glaister
had made him cough—and coughing was extremely painful.

" It's my belief ye're in for pew-monia," added Mr.
Glaister looking at him with a worried frown.  " The sooner
we can get ye tae hoaspital the better pleased I'll be."

Mr. Glaister was a man who knew his own mind and was
afraid of nobody (red tape had no terrors for him) and
having decided that Tom was to go to hospital he accom-
plished his purpose with the least possible delay.  He saw
his charge comfortably tucked up in bed and then went off
to make his report and to despatch a reassuring telegram
to Amberwell.

Tom made him promise to come back when he had
found out about the disaster to the *Starfish* and Mr. Glaister
fulfilled his promise, but by that time Tom was too ill to
be seen.  Mr. Glaister was sorry, but not surprised.  He
told the ward sister to tell Tom that the ship had sunk but
his friends had been saved.

" He's a fine lad.  See an' luik efter him weel," added
Mr. Glaister sternly, and the ward sister (who was an
absolute dragon) replied meekly that Surgeon Lieutenant
Ayrton was being moved to a private ward and would have
every care.

## 3

Tom was very ill; it was nearly a fortnight before he emerged from the no-man's-land of sickness and began to take an interest in the world. Even then it was a feeble sort of interest and the news that Mussolini had been murdered and Hitler had committed suicide seemed less important than the departure of his nurse, whom he had liked, and the arrival of her successor who was much less sympathetic and did not dry between his toes.

So far Tom had been allowed no visitors, but one afternoon he was awakened from a refreshing sleep and informed that his tea was ready and a friend had called to see him.

" I'm not allowed visitors," objected Tom.

" Oh, but you're much better now."

" I don't want to see anybody."

" What nonsense! " exclaimed the unsympathetic nurse in bracing tones. " It will do you good to have a visitor. Sit up and put on your bed-jacket."

Tom was sitting up arrayed in the bed-jacket when the door opened and Dennis Weatherby walked in.

" Hallo! " said Dennis. " You're a nice one! What d'you mean by deserting the ship like that? "

For a moment Tom could not speak. He was so pleased to see Dennis that tears of weakness pricked his eyes and there was a lump in his throat. He was obliged to swallow several times before he could find his voice, but at last he managed it. " Hallo," he said. " You're a nice one! Call yourself a sailor? What d'you mean by running the ship on to a blinking mine? "

Having greeted each other in this peculiar manner the two young men felt at liberty to show their feelings—or at least to hint at them.

" It's good to see you, old cock," declared Tom affection-
ately.

" It's good to see *you*," echoed his visitor, sitting down
on a chair beside Tom's bed and accepting a cup of tea.
" I got the wind up properly when I discovered you weren't
in the ship . . . but that was later, of course. At first
nobody knew what had happened and there was a certain
amount of confusion."

" She didn't go down at once? "

Dennis shook his head. " It was nearly an hour. Sparks
sent an S O S and we got the chaps into the boats. The sea
was reasonably calm so there wasn't much to worry about
really. The lifeboat came out from St. Andrews . . ."

Dennis went on talking cheerfully. He had been told
to talk cheerfully so he refrained from mentioning the fact
that not everybody had been saved. He also concealed
his distress at Tom's emaciated appearance.

" Why aren't you on leave? Or are you? " asked Tom.

" Oh, I've got to hang about here and answer a lot of
silly questions before I get my leave. I went and saw old
Glaister (what a grand chap he is!) and I thought I'd have
a look at you. By the way I was wondering if you'd like
me to ring up your people and tell them I've seen you.
They've been ringing up the hospital about you, but you
know what hospitals are."

" Oh—yes——" said Tom. " That would be Nell of
course. My stepmother wouldn't bother. Yes, you might
ring up Nellie and give her my love. Tell her I'll be coming
to Amberwell as soon as they'll let me out—probably next
week."

Dennis did not think it would be next week but he took
down the telephone number and promised to give the
message.

" And another thing," said Tom. " Look here, Dennis,

what could I do for that boy, Bob Glaister? If it hadn't been for him I'd be dead. Somehow I don't believe they'd like money."

"Money? No, I don't see old Glaister accepting money for pulling you out of the drink. He'd just say it was all in the day's work."

"I'd like to do something."

Dennis considered the matter. "I'll sound him for you if you like. It would be easier for me. I'm off home to-morrow night for a month."

"A month?"

"Well, we're almost out of the tunnel," said Dennis smiling. "There's not much more to do in this part of the world, but we've still got to beat the Japs. I expect I'll be going east." He rose as he spoke.

"Don't go yet," pleaded Tom. "I've been dead to the world, but I'm coming alive now. Do you really think the war is over?"

"It's just a matter of days," replied Dennis cheerfully. "Well, be good—if you can."

Dennis had been told not to stay more than ten minutes; he had exceeded the time limit, but his visit did Tom a lot of good. Seeing his friend had drawn Tom back to the world of men and had given him something to live for. Amberwell! thought Tom, lying and staring at the oddly-shaped cracks in the ceiling, which he had got to know so well. Amberwell—in May—with the wild hyacinths in the woods, the lily-of-the-valley in the shady corners, and the trees coming into leaf! That's what I need.

## CHAPTER NINETEEN

It was the middle of May—and the war was over—before Tom was well enough to leave hospital and travel home. He had been laid up for nearly six weeks but it seemed more like six months, and he felt like Rip Van Winkle. He felt as if everybody were staring at him, and quite possibly they were, for he was attired in garments borrowed from the doctor who was short and stout. Tom's lean lanky figure was lost in the folds of the borrowed jacket, and the trousers displayed his bony ankles. The noise and bustle of the station dazed him and the rattle of the train made his head ache; he was thankful when at last he arrived at Westkirk and saw Nell waiting for him on the platform.

" Oh Tom! " cried Nell, hugging him. " Oh darling, how thin you are! But never mind, the war is over—and you're alive—and Roger is alive—nothing else matters. We'll soon feed you up and make you nice and fat. Where's your suitcase? "

" My luggage is coming by special train," replied Tom, trying to smile and not succeeding very well. " There was too much to bring with me."

" That was silly of me, wasn't it? " murmured Nell, taking him by the arm, which felt exactly like a bare bone inside the sleeve of the ill-fitting jacket. " I'm rather a silly person——"

" Glad you're better, Mr. Tom," said the station-master. " If you wait a few moments till the train's away you can come across the line. It will save you the steps."

This was a great honour, so they waited and were conducted across the lines, and Tom had to shake hands with the station staff. He found it a little trying for he had had no idea that he was returning to Westkirk as a " hero " and did not feel entitled to play the rôle.

" Never mind," whispered Nell. " Your bed is all ready —and Nannie is all ready to put you into it."

" Don't worry, dear Nellie," replied Tom, hoisting himself into the car like a very old man. " I'm a bit tired, that's all—it's such a noisy world—but Amberwell will put me right. I want to lie on the ground in the woods and——"

" Not without a waterproof sheet," said Nell firmly as she leapt in beside him and drove off.

Tom laughed.

" Oh, I know you're Antæus, and all that, but you're not going to lie on the ground without a waterproof sheet . . . and you'll have to hurry up and get better because your friend is coming on Tuesday."

" My friend? Who on earth——"

" Dennis Weatherby of course. He said you'd asked him."

" Oh yes, of course," said Tom in bewildered tones.

" He rang up, you know. In fact he rang up twice. The first time was to say he had seen you, and the second time was about the boy."

" Bob Glaister? "

" Yes. He wants to be a gardener—so of course he can come to Amberwell," said Nell cheerfully. " He's only fifteen but Mr. Gray is delighted to have him and teach him everything. What could be better? We were only just waiting for you to come home before fixing things up. Commander Weatherby will tell you all about it when he comes."

" Lieutenant Commander——"

" No, Commander. He's been promoted; he told me that. And then he said you had invited him to stay at Amberwell and would it be all right if he came on Tuesday. We'll have to see what we can do about food," added Nell anxiously.

They were both silent after that. Nell presumably was thinking about food; Tom was wondering what had happened to make Dennis change his mind. Of course he had asked Dennis to come (he remembered mentioning it to Dennis that night on the bridge of the poor old *Starfish*) but Dennis had given him to understand that he preferred to spend his leave at home.

2

For a few days Tom led the life of an invalid, waited upon and cosseted by everybody in the house. Stephen was his devoted fag, running to fetch a paper for him to read, or a shawl to put round his shoulders, and sitting upon his bed and talking to him. Tom found it so pleasant that he might have remained an invalid for a good deal longer if it had not been for Dennis Weatherby's visit . . . but Dennis was arriving on Tuesday and it was essential to make an effort so that Dennis might be properly received.

By Tuesday Tom was so much better that he was able to take the car to the station to meet his friend. They had never seen each other out of uniform before so it was natural that they should be a little surprised at each other's appearance—and natural that they should comment upon the fact in uncomplimentary terms. Tom certainly looked queer for he had had no time to buy clothes and was wearing a very old suit of Roger's which had been discarded by its owner long ago and for some reason had escaped Nell's eagle eye when she was looking out garments for the Jumble Sale. Dennis, on the other hand, was arrayed in brand new grey flannel trousers and a lovat-tweed jacket of immaculate cut.

" Oh my dear paws! " exclaimed Tom. " The perfect little gentleman! "

" You're jealous of my nice new clothes," retorted Dennis. " I think it was pretty low of you to rob the Amberwell scarecrow, but perhaps he'd finished with those togs and was getting a new rig-out."

Having established relations as usual they both laughed cheerfully.

Dennis was carrying a suitcase and a large brown-paper parcel, curiously shaped, which he put very carefully into the back of the car.

" The body, I suppose? " inquired Tom—but Dennis did not reply.

They drove through the town and up the avenue.

" Great Scott, are those palm trees?" Dennis exclaimed.

" Yes," replied Tom. " My father put them in. He was very proud of them. I think they're ugly and out of place."

But Amberwell House was not ugly and Tom slowed down to give his passenger a good view of his home . . . and Nell and Stephen, who were waiting upon the doorstep were relations of whom Tom could be proud.

Tom was rather disappointed at the formal manner in which Dennis greeted Nellie, for he had hoped they would be friends—but of course Dennis had no use for girls. Tom liked girls, and girls usually liked Tom. Sometimes they liked him too much which was rather tiresome.

The large parcel was removed from the car and bestowed upon Stephen who fell upon it with cries of delight and tore off the paper.

" Oh, it's a teddy-bear! " exclaimed Stephen joyfully. " Look Aunt Nell! It's the biggest teddy in the world! "

Stephen's rapture broke the ice and they were all chatting and laughing in a friendly manner when they went into the morning-room where Mrs. Ayrton was sitting waiting for them to have tea.

" This is Tom's friend, Commander Weatherby," said Nell. She had explained about Commander Weatherby before so it was all right: Mrs. Ayrton greeted the guest graciously and congratulated him on his promotion.

After that the conversation did not thrive very well for although Tom had a great deal to say to his friend he could not talk naturally with his stepmother listening to every word he said—and Nell was always silent.

" I hear you want us to have a protégé of yours in the garden," said Mrs. Ayrton. " I hope he's a hard-working boy."

" He's nothing to do with Dennis," said Tom quickly. " Bob is my protégé—or rather I'm his. I thought you understood. Besides, it's not settled yet."

Mrs. Ayrton looked bewildered. She was apt to forget things nowadays and rapid conversation muddled her.

" It's almost settled," said Dennis. " Mr. Glaister is very pleased for Bob to come to Amberwell. He intends to sell his boat and retire. Bob doesn't want to be a fisherman, he's always wanted to work on the land, so it all fits in beautifully. I said you would write and fix it."

" I'll write," said Tom. " If he's not wanted at Amberwell I'll find him something else."

" Of course we want him at Amberwell," declared Nell.

" We will give him a trial," said Mrs. Ayrton. " If he's a suitable boy, and hard-working——"

" I've told you," Tom interrupted. " If you don't want Bob here I'll find him another job."

There was a slightly uncomfortable silence.

"I could call him Winnie, like Winnie the Pooh," said Stephen thoughtfully. "But I think perhaps he'd rather have a name of his very own. Don't you, Uncle Tom?"

This was a very welcome change of subject. Various names were suggested by Tom and Dennis and Nell but none of them met with approval.

"He's a very special bear," explained his owner. "It's very important to get a name to suit him. I think I'll wait and ask Mrs. Duff. She's *very* clever."

This statement, though uncomplimentary to the present company, was good for another laugh and for explanations about Mrs. Duff.

"Will you have some more tea, Commander Weatherby," asked Nell.

"Yes please, Miss Ayrton," he replied.

"Oh, for goodness' sake!" exclaimed Tom laughing. "You must call her Nell. Nobody calls her Miss Ayrton."

"I should like to, if I may—and if she will call me Dennis," said Dennis looking at her gravely.

"Why don't you call her Aunt Nell?" suggested Stephen, "that's what I call her, you know."

They all laughed again—and Nell felt relieved, for now she need not reply to the question. Tom's friend was nice but she did not know him well enough to call him Dennis. It took Nell some time to get used to strangers, and he was quite different from what she had expected. He was not like Tom, in fact he was Tom's opposite in every way. If he had been Roger's friend she could have understood it.

"Nell," said Mrs. Ayrton. "Stephen is talking too much. You had better send him up to the nursery."

Nobody agreed with this; they were all grateful to Stephen.

"Stephen's all right," declared Tom. "Dennis likes kids, don't you Dennis?"

Stephen had got down off his chair with a piece of bread and butter in his hand. He looked at Nell to see what she wanted him to do.

"It's all right," said Tom, picking him up and putting him back on his chair. "We like to hear you talking. You finish your tea, Stephen, and then we'll take the bear out for a walk in the garden."

Mrs. Ayrton was annoyed. "Really, Tom——" she began.

"Do you know Harrogate, Mrs. Ayrton?" asked Dennis, throwing himself into the fray.

"Harrogate?" echoed Mrs. Ayrton vaguely.

"My home is about three miles from Harrogate," explained Dennis. "I just wondered if you knew that part of the country at all."

Fortunately Mrs. Ayrton did—and when it was discovered that Dennis knew the house which had belonged to an aunt of Mrs. Ayrton's, and in which Mrs. Ayrton herself had stayed when she was a girl, the situation was saved and peace was established.

Nell was ashamed. It seemed dreadful that a guest should have to step in and save the situation; she herself ought to have been able to cope. Tom was naughty, of course. There was constant friction between him and his stepmother; he resented her dictatorial rule, and especially resented her attitude to Stephen. Tom saw no reason why he should be tactful; indeed it is doubtful whether he could have been tactful if he had tried. When they were alone the friction did not matter so much—Nell could bear it—but it was very uncomfortable when a stranger was present.

Oh dear, thought Nell in dismay. He is to be here for five whole days. We shall have to try to entertain him.

3

Nell need not have worried about their guest for he was a peaceful sort of person and, what was even better, he had a peaceful influence upon Tom. He made it clear that he did not want to be entertained but preferred to share the life of the household; he settled down comfortably into its ways. Fortunately the weather was fine so he and Tom were out most of the time, wandering round the gardens or playing with Stephen.

Dennis was particularly interested in the bowling-green and evinced a desire to play bowls. Neither of the young men had played the game before but that did not deter them, and after some search they found a box of bowls in the attic and carried it down to the green. Fortunately there was an ancient Book of Rules in the box and when this had been read and the green had been mown by Dennis they began to practise.

The game had been started in fun (" What's the good of having a first-class bowling-green if you don't play bowls? " Dennis had demanded); but soon they became enthralled and clamoured for Nell to join them. They also enlisted Mr. Gray. Neither Nell nor Mr. Gray was free to play during the day but after tea the four of them met and enjoyed a game. It was then discovered that Mr. Gray was an expert (or at least an expert compared with his fellow-players) so he was able to give them valuable instruction and improve their style.

Mr. Gray and Nell took on the Navy, and beat them, and were immediately challenged to a return match the following evening. After that it became a definite part of the day's routine. The bowling-green, which for so long had been merely a sheltered part of the garden for the children to play in, came into its own again and echoed to the click of " woods " and to shouts of joy and cries of dismay.

One morning Tom and Dennis went up to the woods taking with them a waterproof sheet, some writing materials and a flask of coffee. They settled down comfortably near the old mossy stone which was a favourite spot of Tom's. It was sheltered and peaceful, the grass was soft to lie upon and the view of Amberwell and its surrounding gardens was enchanting. Beneath the shade of the budding trees there was lily-of-the-valley, growing wild, and the scent of the tiny bell-like flowers filled the air with fragrance.

Tom lay spread out upon the waterproof sheet and Dennis sat beside him. They drank their coffee and chatted for a bit and then Dennis started to write.

" Letters are a bore, aren't they? " said Tom after a long silence. " I ought to write letters, but I'm too lazy."

" It isn't a letter," replied Dennis. " It's—well, it's a poem—or at least it's meant to be."

Tom was not unduly surprised for he was aware that his friend had cultivated a neat turn of verse. Dennis Weatherby's poems were valued by his brother officers; they were usually of a ribald nature and roused gales of laughter. The most popular of all was a parody of *Drink To Me Only With Thine Eyes* which was excruciatingly funny and quite unprintable. This being so Tom was eager to read his friend's latest composition.

" Let's see it," said Tom, holding out his hand.

Dennis hesitated for a moment. " You'll laugh at it," he declared.

" I bet I'll laugh," agreed Tom. " Come on old boy, hand it over."

" Oh well—it's one way of telling you," said Denni enigmatically and handed it over forthwith. Then h lighted a cigarette and waited somewhat nervously for Tom's reaction.

### LILY OF THE VALLEY

*The lovely lily of the dell,*
*With pale green leaves and pearly bell,*
*Grows in the woods of Amberwell*
 *When Spring is there.*
*Unlike the proud and gaudy flowers*
*Which glory in the sunny hours*
*It hides itself in woodland bowers*
 *And scents the air.*

*How like the lily of the dell*
*Is lovely Nell of Amberwell!*
*More beautiful than words can tell,*
 *More good and fair.*
*She's full of gentleness and grace;*
*The peace of God shines in her face;*
*She makes the world a sweeter place*
 *In which to dwell.*

Tom read the poem carefully: he had been prepared to laugh his head off so it was several minutes before he got the hang of it and realised that it was not intended to be funny at all.

" Gosh, it's a real poem ! " said Tom at last. " I say —look here—I suppose it's meant to be Nell? "

" Yes," replied the poet simply.

" She'll be awfully pleased——"

" You ass! I'm not going to show it to her! " cried Dennis, snatching it away and proceeding to tear it up into very small pieces.

H

" But it's good! Nell would like it! "

" It's rotten—the last line is all wrong—and Nell would hate it. Nell doesn't know me well enough to love me. Perhaps some day she will, and then I'll write a much better poem; the poem of my life."

Tom sat up and gazed at his friend in astonishment. " But I thought you didn't like girls! "

" I don't," agreed Dennis gravely. " I never could be bothered with the silly creatures, but Nell's different. I love Nell and I mean to marry her."

" Oh, my sainted aunt! " murmured Tom.

" You don't object, I hope."

" Object? Good lord no! There's nobody in the world that—that I'd rather. It's only——"

" Well, that's all right," said Dennis hastily. " I just thought I'd warn you. That's why I came to Amberwell. I shouldn't have come, really, because there's such a lot to do at home and I'm off to Burma next week."

" That's why you came to Amberwell? "

Dennis nodded. " I fell in love with her voice when I spoke to her on the phone, so I had to come and see whether she was—I mean whether she was like what I thought she was—if you see what I mean—and then, when I saw her, I realised that she was sweet and kind and good—and a million times more wonderful and beautiful than I had imagined."

Nell's brother was speechless. He was very fond of Nellie of course, but——

" I've thought about it a lot," continued Dennis, who had dug a little hole in the moss and was burying the fragments of his poem. " The trouble is there's no time to do anything about it before I go off to Burma. Nell isn't the sort of girl to be rushed."

" But you'll tell her——"

" Don't you understand? " asked Dennis impatiently. " I've got to go to Burma next week. I couldn't get out of it if I tried. There's no time to make friends with Nell."

" I think she likes you."

" She likes me because I'm your friend, that's all. She doesn't know me. It would be hopeless to try to rush her. If I said anything now she would be scared to death; it would spoil everything and I should never have another chance. Nell is perfectly happy here at Amberwell; she's got a full-time job looking after the place and bringing up Stephen. She wouldn't give up her job if I asked her—and I shouldn't dream of asking her. When I come back from Burma things may be different."

" You don't mean you're going off to Burma without a word to Nellie? "

" That's exactly what I mean."

For a few moments there was silence. Tom did not know what to say. It was all so utterly unexpected. To think that Dennis Weatherby, who had never looked at a girl in his life, should have fallen for Nellie!

" Nell is very shy," continued Dennis. " To me that's part of her charm, I wouldn't have her otherwise for the world, but it will take a long time to—to make friends with her and—and to win her trust."

This was true, thought Tom. He realised that Dennis knew quite a lot about Nell—which was odd considering he had only known her for three days. " Yes, but what are you going to do about it? " inquired Tom doubtfully.

" I shall write her long friendly letters and when I come home I shall ask her to marry me. That's what I'm going to do."

This plan of campaign seemed extraordinary to Tom. " I wouldn't if I were you," he declared. " Honestly, old

boy, it won't work. I mean I know much more about these
sort of things than you do, and——"

" You know nothing about these sort of things," exclaimed
Dennis with some heat. " You've never been in love with
a girl in your life. You've had lots of ' affaires '—kissing
and cuddling in corners—but that isn't the same sort of
thing at all. It's not only different in degree but different
in kind."

For once Tom was crushed. He was so crushed that he
could not even be angry: he could find nothing to say.

" Never mind," said Dennis smiling a little. " You
don't understand, that's all. Perhaps some day you'll
meet the right one—the girl you want to marry—and then
you'll understand. You'll love her so dearly that you'll be
willing to wait years, if need be, as long as you get her in
the end." He rose and added " Come on, it's getting a bit
cold. We'd better go in."

## CHAPTER TWENTY

NELL WAS sorry when Dennis Weatherby's visit was over, for he had been a delightful guest and his influence upon the mercurial Tom had been extremely good. It would be too much to say that she missed Dennis, but certainly she thought of him occasionally in a friendly way and she was quite pleased to listen when Tom sang his praises. Dennis had asked Nell to write to him, explaining that letters from home were very welcome to an exile, and Nell had promised to do so—she could not refuse—but she did not feel very happy about this new commitment, for it was one thing to write to Roger and tell him about Amberwell and quite another to write to a stranger who knew nothing about Amberwell at all. Nell's life was so busy, and yet so uneventful, that it would be difficult to find anything to say. For instance she knew Roger would be interested to hear that after six years of war she had at last been able to get a man from Westkirk to paint the outside woodwork of the greenhouses; that a recent storm had cast up a great deal of seaweed upon the shore, and that they had carted it up to the garden and used it for manure, and that Nannie's nephew was getting married and Nannie was going to Edinburgh for a week to stay with her sister and join in the jollifications. These were the sort of things she told Roger, but these were not the sort of things she could tell Dennis; they would not interest him in the least.

Soon after Dennis left Bob Glaister arrived at Amberwell. It had been arranged that he was to board with Mr. and

Mrs. Gray temporarily until they saw how he got on. At first poor Bob was rather homesick (Tom, who felt responsible for his welfare, was somewhat worried about him) but after a bit he settled down and began to take a real interest in his new job.

" He's a good lad," declared Mr. Gray when Tom inquired about his progress. " There's a deal for him to learn, of course. I couldn't have believed a lad could be so lamentably ignorant—he knows no difference between a weed and a flower—but it would be a funny thing if I couldn't have the patience to learn him, *considering*."

" I don't want him to be a burden," said Tom rather anxiously.

" Och, he'll not be a burden. He'll just need to be watched till he gets into the way of things. We'll keep him with us," added Mr. Gray. " He's nice and cheery in the house and Mrs. Gray likes him. We can see to it that he rises early and doesn't get into mischief."

So Bob was accepted at Amberwell, partly because he had been the means of saving Tom's life and partly on his own merits.

Bob would not have settled down so quickly if it had not been for Tom.

Bob still had the feeling that " Mr. Tom " belonged to him. He did not say anything about this feeling, nor did he bother " Mr. Tom," but he liked to see " Mr. Tom " walking in the gardens. It was wonderful to think that if it had not been for him " Mr. Tom " would not be here. Bob would stop digging for a few minutes (unless Mr. Gray happened to be about) and watch " Mr. Tom " walking across the grass . . . and he would think of the poor bedraggled creature that he had pulled out of the sea. Then he would spit on his hands—as Mr. Gray had told him— and continue his work cheerfully. " Mr. Tom " often spoke to him and had jokes with him . . . and one day they had a serious conversation: " If ever you're in a scrape," said " Mr. Tom " gravely: " If ever you get into any sort of mess you're to write and tell me. I'll pull you out—just as you pulled me out of the water. Don't forget that, Bob." It was not likely that Bob would forget.

By the middle of the summer Tom had recovered completely and was posted to a ship in the Mediterranean. Nell hated saying good-bye and she had done her best to persuade Tom to leave the Navy and to settle down ashore. She was sure he could easily get a post as assistant to a general practitioner, or in a civilian hospital, but Tom was a sailor at heart—and a nomad—so he smiled and said that he was not ready to settle down; now that the fighting was over he intended to enjoy himself and see a bit more of the world.

It was sad to say good-bye—but it was a very different good-bye from the last time Tom had left Amberwell, for there was now no need to worry unduly about his safety.

As a matter of fact Nell was very happy that summer —happier than she had ever been in her life—for the black cloud of anxiety had rolled away and the skies were clear. All sorts of small things gave her happiness: it was delightful to remove all the stuffy black-out curtains (this sign that peace had returned to the war-weary world was symbolic) and every night when darkness fell it gave Nell a quite ridiculous thrill of pleasure to switch on the lights of Amberwell and let them shine out bravely. Nell was happy because Stephen was growing and developing and becoming a real companion; wherever she went Stephen went too and they chatted together incessantly. Perhaps he was a little too old for his age but that was because there were no other children for him to play with and Nell had found that however hard you tried it was impossible to play with a child on his own level.

In September Nell had an even greater cause for happiness: she received a letter from Roger to say he was coming home.

2

The Amberwell gardens were in a terribly neglected condition for it was still impossible to get men to help Mr. Gray. Nell had become used to it by this time, and it did not distress her unduly, but now that Roger was coming home the scales fell from her eyes and she saw the place as Roger would see it; Roger who had not been home for nearly five years!

Nell took Stephen and went out to speak to Mr. Gray and as she went she looked around at the desolation—and wondered what Roger would think of her stewardship. The hedges were unclipped and straggling, the borders were choked with weeds and many of the paths were so overgrown that they had merged with the grass verges. Only in the walled garden was there anything like order and even here there were battalions of nettles growing in disused corners. The greenhouses were unheated for lack of fuel and most of the delicate plants had withered and died. The whole place was shabby; everything needed repairs.

Nell gazed about her. For a few moments she beheld, as if in a vision, the picture of Amberwell gardens as they had been before the war: Amberwell gardens, the show place of the county; its herbaceous borders banked up with gorgeous colours; its carefully-pruned roses; its shaven lawns, neatly trimmed edges and paths of smooth brown gravel. In those days it had been difficult to find a weed.

"Aunt Nell, you're not listening," complained Stephen. "And it's frightfully important."

"What is it, Stephen?"

"Can I tell Mr. Gray about Daddy coming?"

"Yes, of course. Look, there he is, planting out the cabbages!"

Stephen sped away, his feet beautiful with news. "Mr. Gray, my daddy is coming nex' week!" cried Stephen. "You know I haven't seen him since I was a baby."

"Well now, that's the best news I've heard for long enough," declared Mr. Gray rising from his knees and smiling. "He'll be getting leave, I suppose."

"Yes," said Nell. "It seems a lifetime since he went away, doesn't it?"

Mr. Gray did not answer. His smile had faded and he was looking round thoughtfully. "I'm wondering what he'll say about the gardens, Miss Nell."

"He won't say anything. It's what he'll think."

"Maybe that's what I was meaning," nodded Mr. Gray. "Next week, you said. That's not giving us much time— but there are one or two lads in the town that are home on leave. Maybe I could get them to come and do a day's work."

"Try," said Nell. "They might tidy up round the house. We're used to seeing the place in this condition but it really is frightful. Now what about manure, Mr. Gray? Are you getting it from Stark Farm as usual?"

3

Stephen was not interested in manure so he wandered off by himself and finding a russet apple lying upon the ground ate it with relish. It was funny how much nicer apples tasted when you found them yourself than when they appeared upon the table in a silver dish.

Stephen was musing about this curious fact when he heard a car drive up to the garage and being of an inquiring mind he went to investigate.

There was a small car standing in the yard; Stephen saw a tall thin figure in uniform climb out of the car and stand for a moment looking all round him.

"Hallo," said Stephen, advancing politely. "Would you like me to open the garage for you? I know where the key is."

The tall man did not reply. He gazed at Stephen as if he were bewildered.

"Have you come to lunch?" asked Stephen. "We're going to have mince to-day. I heard Mrs. Duff ord'ring mince—so I know. I expect Aunt Nell will ask you to stay if you're a friend of hers."

"Stephen!" exclaimed the tall man incredulously.

"Yes?" asked Stephen, answering to his name.

"I'm—I'm your father."

It was now Stephen's turn to gaze and be astonished. "You're—Daddy? But Daddy isn't coming till nex' week!"

"I got away sooner than I expected."

"You're Daddy—really and truly?"

"Really and truly," replied the tall man gravely.

For a few moments the two gazed at each other—the man and the child. To the man there was something rather embarrassing in the meeting; he did not know what to do or what to say. But to the child there was nothing embarrassing at all. Stephen knew that his Daddy was the most wonderful person in the world; his Daddy was a hero; his Daddy had saved his life when he was a tiny baby; his Daddy loved him dearly. Aunt Nell was never tired of

elling him stories about his wonderful, marvellous Daddy.
And now that Stephen looked at this man he saw that he
was exactly like the large photograph which stood upon the
table beside his bed.

"Oh Daddy, what fun!" cried Stephen joyfully and
with that he rushed at the tall man and leapt into his arms.

It was so sudden and unexpected that Roger was un-
prepared for the human bomb-shell, but he was used to
dealing with sudden emergencies and his reactions were
rapid. Somehow or other he managed to catch it and hold
it. Two thin arms wound themselves round his neck and
a soft pink cheek was pressed against his brown one.

"Daddy," murmured Stephen. "I didn't know it was
you. We thought it was nex' week. Aunt Nell *will* be
excited." He gasped and added, "Oo, you *are* squeezing
me hard."

"I'm sorry!"

"Oh it's all right. I like it really. It's because you're
so pleased to see me. I do that to Aunt Nell when she's
been away—I almost strangle her—and of course you
haven't seen me since I was a baby. That's a long time."

"A very long time."

Roger held his son away so that he could see him properly.
He had half hoped and half feared that he would see
Clare's face in the face of his son. There certainly was a
look of Clare, but for some reason it did not distress him.
Oddly enough Roger could see himself as well, and there
was a distant resemblance to the portrait of the first Stephen
Ayrton which hung upon the dining-room wall.

"Why are you looking at me?" asked Stephen. "Am I
like I was when I was a baby?"

"No, not a bit. You were a poor little scrap when you
were a baby."

"It must be funny to find I've grown up."

"It's lovely," declared Roger.

"But it must be funny."

"Very funny indeed. I never realised you would b
a—a person."

This was beyond Stephen's understanding. He struggle
and said, "Put me down, Daddy. Aunt Nell's in th
garden talking to Mr. Gray. They'll be so excited." H
took Roger's hand. "Come on quick," he urged. "I'
show you the way——" and then suddenly he began t
laugh.

It was a delightful chuckling laugh and it reminde
Roger of Anne. Anne used to laugh like that, doubled u
with uncontrollable mirth. It used to make you laugh jus
to see Anne laughing.

"What's the joke?" asked Roger.

"I said—I'd show you—the way," gasped Stephen
"Aren't I silly!"

Roger tried to laugh but it was not easy. He felt mo
like crying. This was his very own son—Clare's son—an
he was indeed "a person." He was real and beautiful an
he had a delightful sense of humour. He could laugh whole
heartedly at himself.

"Come on, Stephen," said Roger in a husky voic
"We'll go and find Aunt Nell."

4

Later when lunch was over Roger and Nell took a stro
round the gardens.

"It's dreadful, isn't it?" said Nell with a sigh. "
wish we could have had the gardens tidied up a little befo
you came."

"Don't worry," Roger replied, smiling a little at h

distress. " You've done a marvellous job, Nell, and I'm so grateful to you that I don't know what to say."

She looked at him in surprise for they were standing in front of the herbaceous border which had once been the pride of Mr. Gray's heart and was now a solid phalanx of nettles with a few miserable chrysanthemums struggling for life amongst them.

" You've looked after Stephen," explained Roger. " That's what I mean."

" Yes, people are more important than gardens," she agreed in a thoughtful voice.

" And Stephen is perfect," added his father with conviction.

Nell smiled; she thought Stephen was very nearly perfect —perhaps, if anything, too good. Sometimes she had a feeling that she had been too strict with Stephen, that she had taken the " object lesson " of Connie's children too much to heart. She would have liked to see Stephen a little bit naughty just occasionally. She explained the matter to Roger and asked him what he thought. " You and Tom were often naughty," said Nell. " Do you remember that day at the Fountain Party when Tom made his nose bleed and you both went off and bathed? And there were lots of other things too—even naughtier."

" I see what you mean," replied Roger with perfect gravity. " But Stephen isn't a poop. I think it's because he's sensible that he isn't naughty—and because he's treated sensibly. For instance Stephen wanted to come with us this afternoon and you said we were going a long way and he would be tired if he didn't have his usual rest, so he went off with Nannie as good as gold. We were never treated like that."

" ' Never explain,' " murmured Nell.

" Exactly," agreed Roger.

" You don't believe in Disraeli's maxim? "

" It's absurd! Why, goodness me, we don't expect disciplined troops to carry out orders without some sort of explanation. You get far better results if you can tell the chaps exactly what you want them to do—and why."

" ' Their's not to reason why. Their's but to do and die,' " quoted Nell, mischievously.

" Yes, and look what happened! They were all killed —and quite unnecessarily. They did no good except to provide a subject for a silly poem."

Nell was a trifle shocked for she had learned the poem when young and had frequently declaimed it with a fervour which brought tears to her own eyes—if to no one else's. However her admiration for her brother was such that she decided he must know best.

" About Stephen," said Nell, reverting to a subject upon which they were in absolute accord. " I wish I could find some other children for him to play with. You remember what fun we used to have. There are no children round here nowadays—I can't think why. Connie brings Gerry and Joan to stay in the holidays sometimes, but they're being brought up in the New Way."

Roger had not heard about the New Way so he inquired about it and was given an exposition of the method and its results. He roared with laughing.

" But it's not really funny," declared Nell smiling.

" Connie is an idiot," said Roger. " She wasn't so bad when she was a child but when she grew up she became unbearably smug."

" Not smug, exactly," objected Nell.

" She is," declared Roger. " She always says and does the right thing, but there's no warmth in her. She wrote me a letter when Tom's ship was sunk and he was missing; it was perfectly expressed and said all the right things but

I could have murdered her with the greatest of pleasure. She took it for granted he was drowned. I was certain old Tom was alive and kicking and thank heaven I was right."

Nell's thoughts went back to the dreadful day when the Admiralty telegram had arrived at Amberwell. She had not had much hope, but Roger and Tom had always been such close friends, sharing everything, just as she and Anne had shared everything, so perhaps that was why Roger had been certain that Tom was still alive. She remembered, too, the joyful day when they heard Tom had been picked up by the Glaister's fishing-boat and was safe and sound. If only they could hear the same sort of joyful news about Anne!

Roger must have sensed her thought, or perhaps his own thoughts had followed the same line. " No news of Anne, I suppose? " asked Roger.

Nell shook her head.

" Do you think she's—alive? "

" Yes," replied Nell slowly. " I have a sort of feeling— but perhaps it isn't worth much. Sometimes when I'm in the gardens by myself I feel as if we were all here, running about and playing as we used to do. And sometimes I feel as if there were other children too—children who played here long before we were born."

" Little ghosts? "

" Not frightening ghosts, just nice friendly children."

" I've been thinking," said Roger after a short silence. " I've been wondering what I should do to ' improve the amenities of Amberwell ' in the traditional way. Have you any bright ideas on the subject? "

Nell had not. She had been far too busy trying to hold the place together and to prevent it from slipping back into primeval jungle to think of anything else.

"I don't want a fountain—or anything like that," added Roger.

"The poor fountain!" said Nell with a sigh. "We never have it playing; Mother won't have it—not even to please Gerry and Joan. It seems such a waste, doesn't it? Mr. Gray keeps it oiled and turns it on sometimes to prevent it from getting rusty, but we have to do it when Mother isn't there."

"I wonder why."

Nell did not know. She had never understood her mother.

"I thought of trees," said Roger, returning to the previous subject. "Not very spectacular, of course."

"Oh yes—trees," agreed Nell. "Trees are much nicer than fountains, but even trees cost a good deal of money you know."

"Yes—well—I wanted to talk to you about that," said Roger a trifle diffidently. "There's quite a lot of money. Father left enough to keep things going comfortably and there's all Clare's money as well. Lord Richmore was a wealthy man and he left his money to Clare—who left it to me. Of course I look upon it as belonging to Stephen and I don't intend to splash it about, but there's plenty for everybody. You can easily have more to spend on the house and the gardens and get everything put right, and you ought to spend more on yourself."

"You give me a good allowance," said Nell quickly.

"Not nearly enough—considering all you do."

"More than enough, Roger. I mean what would I spend it on?"

"Well, we'll see. We'll talk it over later."

"If you have enough for your needs you don't need more," Nell told him.

"It's funny that you should say that," declared Roger.

" It's absolutely true, but very few people would agree with you. Money is a queer thing. If you haven't got enough it's terribly important, but if you have plenty you don't think about it at all, and what's even stranger you don't spend any more. I could live on my pay quite easily —in fact I do." He hesitated for a moment and then added thoughtfully : " Sometimes when I hear other fellows in the regiment talking about not being able to make ends meet I feel quite ashamed."

" Couldn't you help them? " asked Nell anxiously.

Roger smiled. He reflected that his little sister was very unworldly. " Not really," he said. " There are various snags. The people you would like to help won't accept it —or if they're in an awful mess they take it as a loan and come and pay you back a little at a time, which makes you feel quite sick and completely spoils your friendship. Then of course there are the other kind—the spongers—who approach with a Cheshire Cat grin and murmur, ' I say, old boy, could you possibly lend me five quid? ' They always give you a long explanation of how they happen to find themselves in Queer Street . . . and of course they'll pay it back at the end of the month . . . and of course they never do."

Nell could not help smiling for Roger's predicament reminded her of a picture entitled " The Boy with Many Friends " a print of which hung upon the wall of the upstairs landing. The Boy was engaged in unpacking a hamper of " goodies " while his schoolmates hung round him with affectionate smiles.

" I suppose it's funny—in a way," admitted Roger. " But it's rather horrid too. I wish I knew the right thing to do about it. It's all very well to say ' Neither a borrower nor a lender be ' but if you've got the money to lend the fellow you simply can't refuse—at least I can't—and is it right to let him get away with it (which is much the easiest) or should you remind him that he hasn't paid you back?"

Nell gazed at Roger. The matter was beyond her.

"Well never mind," said Roger. "Let's talk about trees."

They talked about trees as they walked on through the walled garden and into the bowling-green. Here they stopped and looked round. The other parts of the garden were bad enough but this was worst of all for Mr. Gray had given it up in despair. Bob Glaister cut the grass occasionally but his other duties left him no time to keep it trim and neat. The yew hedge had straggled wildly and the stone steps which led up to the stage were covered with green moss. Everywhere there were dead leaves, scattered upon the ground or blown into untidy heaps and mouldering where they lay.

"Oh dear!" exclaimed Nell. "It must be sad for you to come home to this changed place."

It was sad of course, but perhaps not as sad as Nell thought, for Roger had been about the world and had seen far worse sights than a neglected garden. His own perfect marriage and its tragic end had at least rendered him invulnerable to lesser sorrows; he had realised that life went on whatever happened and it was useless to grieve over the past. If something knocked you down you had to pick yourself up and go on as best you could. He had learned that much about life.

Certainly Amberwell was a " changed place." The house was very shabby after six years of war, carpets were worn and walls needed redecorating. The gardens were in a frightful condition, it would take years to get them right. Roger noticed a change in the people as well. His step-mother was autocratic and self-centred and she was still very

handsome, with her pretty complexion and her wavy silvery
hair, but she was definitely old; occasionally her mind
wandered a little and she was apt to tell you the same thing
twice over. Nannie was wrinkled and bent and moved
more slowly—she was very different from the trim bustling
Nannie of bygone days. Even Nell had changed, but in
Roger's opinion Nell had changed for the better; she was
very good-looking indeed, and there was more life about
her (more pep, thought Roger, glancing at her sideways) but all the same she was still unsure of herself
and still terrified of her mother . . . which was a pity.
Roger had a feeling that this little sister of his would
never grow up properly and be a whole person unless
she got right away from Amberwell and her mother's
influence.

" You ought to get away from here! " Roger said.

" Away—from here? " asked Nell in amazement. " What
*do* you mean? Who would look after Stephen—and
Amberwell—and everything? "

" Don't you ever want to get away? "

" Never. I should be lost if I had to go away."

" That's lucky for me," said Roger, smiling.

Roger had asked the question with a purpose, for Tom
had written and told him about Dennis Weatherby (it was
right that Roger should know for he was the head of the
family). According to Tom, Dennis Weatherby was the
best fellow in the world, a paragon of all the virtues, but with
somewhat peculiar views about girls . . . but Roger, when
he had read the letter carefully, decided that Dennis
Weatherby's views were sound. Nell was certainly not the
sort of girl to be rushed, and she might be wooed more
easily by " long friendly letters " than by word of mouth.
All the same it was sad, thought Roger. Nell ought to
have married and had children of her own instead of

spending all her mother-love upon Stephen. Probably, if it had not been for the war, she would have been happily married by this time; the war had broken and twisted a great many lives.

"Well, anyway we've got Stephen," said Roger after a long silence. It seemed to him that this was the one valuable possession which he and Nell between them had saved from the wreckage.

# PART FOUR

---

*For there is no friend like a sister*
*In calm or stormy weather.*

CHRISTINA GEORGINA ROSSETTI

# CHAPTER TWENTY-ONE

Mr. Orme had not been able to get in touch with the older Ayrtons, but he was friends with the youngest Ayrton from a very early age.

"Make Stephen feel safe," said Nell earnestly. She had said it for the first time at Stephen's christening and she continued to say it frequently; so one of the first faces in little Stephen's world was the gentle saintly face of the Rector . . . and later, when Stephen was able to run about the gardens, it never occurred to him for a moment to hide from Mr. Orme. Indeed it was Stephen's practice to lie in wait for him and to pounce out suddenly with a joyful cry. This was not particularly good for Mr. Orme's heart, but you can't have everything exactly right in this world . . . and Mr. Orme would have risked worse dangers for the pleasure of Stephen's friendship.

One afternoon when Stephen was six years old they met in the woods. It was early Spring; the trees were beginning to bud and the rooks were nesting. They had a long interesting chat, sitting upon the old mossy stone from which you could look down upon Amberwell House and the bowling-green and the walled garden. By this time Amberwell was beginning to look more like itself—less shabby and neglected—but there was still a long way to go before everything could be put into the apple-pie order so dear to Mr. Gray's heart.

Stephen told Mr. Orme all the Amberwell news: Daddy was in Germany, but might be coming home on leave before very long; Uncle Tom's ship was on its way to

Australia; Aunt Nell had gone to Glasgow for the day. Mr. Orme told Stephen about the birds that had come to his bird-table and, on being asked for a story, related the story of the Prodigal Son.

"What were the boys' names?" asked Stephen with interest.

This reaction surprised Mr. Orme considerably and he was obliged to admit that he did not know, and to explain that the story was just a story, and had been told to illustrate the enduring quality of the love of God.

"Yes, I see," nodded Stephen. "And it's very nice, but all the same I wish we knew their names. It makes a story much more real if you know the people's names."

As Mr. Orme walked home he reflected how very interesting it was to talk to somebody with a perfectly fresh mind; a mind which had not been cluttered up with too much study and which did not run in a groove. He knew the story of the Prodigal Son by heart—indeed he had repeated it to Stephen word for word as it was written in St. Luke's Gospel—but the mere fact of thinking that the "boys" might have names gave it added reality . . . and this was by no means the first time Stephen had given Mr. Orme a new angle upon an old story and jolted him out of a well-worn rut.

The Rectory was not as comfortable as it used to be, for Mrs. Green had been obliged to leave (not without tears and lamentations) and to go and look after an invalid sister whose husband had been killed in the war. Her place had been taken by a "daily woman" who did as little as possible and that with reluctance. Mr. Orme did not complain of her work (he had been far too comfortable when Mrs. Green held sway at the Rectory) but sometimes he wished that Mrs. Kenny were a little more willing and obliging, a little less grudging of her services.

As Mrs. Kenny did not "live in" it was the habit of the Rector to prepare his own supper. Sometimes Mrs. Kenny left him a dish of macaroni-cheese to warm up, and sometimes she did not. Quite often if Mr. Orme were reading or writing he forgot all about his supper, until the pangs of hunger reminded him that it was long past the proper hour, and as it was then too late for the warming-up process he would cut a slice of bread and make himself a cup of cocoa. If Mrs. Green had known of these goings on she would have been frantic—but of course she did not know.

Curiously enough in spite of the discomfort of his home, and in spite of his increasing age, Mr. Orme's heart had become less troublesome. It was seldom now that he experienced the uncomfortable sensation that everything was slipping sideways which was the warning signal that he was about to be attacked. The second phase of his illness was even more uncomfortable: a violent battering as if his heart had become a mad bird trying to escape from its cage. The third phase was black oblivion and the fourth an uncontrollable trembling in all his limbs which sometimes lasted for an hour and then gradually died away leaving him exhausted. Dr. Maddon had a string of long words to describe these attacks but Mr. Orme preferred to think (like St. Paul) that the messenger of Satan had come to buffet him lest he should be exalted beyond measure. It certainly kept one humble to be laid out in this ignominious manner ... and quite apart from being laid out it was humbling to have to be careful; to pause with one's hands upon the cords of a window and to decide that it would be wiser—and in the long run much less bother—to go and get somebody else to shut the window. It was humbling to start out to visit a friend who was in trouble and to realise suddenly that one felt a little tired and had better go home unless one wanted to add to the trouble by collapsing on his doorstep.

Naturally Mr. Orme was very glad that Satan's messenger came less often. Dr. Maddon was both glad and surprised for he had expected Mr. Orme's heart attacks to become worse rather than better as the years went by. However, after some thought, Dr. Maddon found a reason for the improvement and explained it to his old friend; it was a very ingenious reason and his old friend listened to it indulgently but did not believe a word. Mr. Orme's explanation was very simple: as he grew older the consciousness of his Master's presence came to him more often and more easily, it warmed him and comforted him and shielded him from harm.

2

To-night was one of the nights when Mr. Orme's supper was forgotten for his talk with Stephen had given him material for a sermon. It was nearly eleven o'clock and he was still hard at work when he heard a tap on the window. This was not a very unusual occurrence at the Rectory for sometimes people found their troubles worse at night and wanted to share them, to pour them into a sympathetic ear.

Mr. Orme rose and, pulling aside the curtain, looked out. The window was open at the bottom and the garden was bright with moonlight; a slim figure in a dark cloak was standing on the path below. She pushed back her hood and he saw that it was Nell Ayrton.

" Mr. Orme," she said in a breathless voice. " I'm so sorry to disturb you—I meant to come earlier but I couldn't get away—and I saw your light through the chinks——"

" There's nothing wrong with Stephen! " cried Mr. Orme in alarm.

" No—not Stephen——"

"Come in, my dear child. Come round to the front door."

As he went to open it for her he conquered all feelings of surprise, for it did not help people who needed help if they realised you were surprised to see them.

"You'll think I am mad to come at this hour," said Nell. "It is mad, of course, but I didn't want Mother to know——"

"Come in and tell me about it." He took her arm and put her into the chair by the fire. The fire was low—nearly dead—but he piled on some dry wood and it began to burn up briskly. "That's better, isn't it?" he said. "Now we can talk comfortably."

Nell did not speak and when he looked at her he saw that her lips were trembling and her eyes were full of tears.

"Nell!" he said gently. "What is it, my dear? What has happened? You can tell me about it, can't you?"

For a few moments she hesitated and then she took a little book out of her pocket and handed it to him, still without speaking.

Mr. Orme took it and looked at it in bewilderment—it was a child's book, a little story-book with coloured pictures—the dreadful thought crossed his mind that Nell had gone mad.

"Anne," said Nell in a trembling voice.

"Anne?"

She nodded. "I bought the book to-day—when I was in Glasgow—for Stephen—and I looked at it coming home in the train. When I looked at it—I knew."

"You mean——"

"Anne wrote it—and—and drew the pictures. Pictures of the garden——" Her voice broke and she could not go on.

"Are you sure?" asked Mr. Orme incredulously.

"Yes, it's Anne. I'm sorry to—to be so silly, but—but it upset me—frightfully—reading all about what we used to do. It brought Anne back—all her funny little ways. I must find her! Oh, Mr. Orme I must find Anne!"

"Perhaps we could find her," said Mr. Orme thoughtfully. "I mean we could certainly find the author of the book. The publishers are bound to know where she lives."

He spoke in a quiet matter-of-fact voice which had the effect of calming Nell and helping her to control herself.

"It's Anne," she said with conviction. "I know Anne so well. It was the garden pictures that first caught my eye. Then I read it carefully—every word. I made myself read it carefully."

"And you were sure?"

"Absolutely certain. There are things in it—all sorts of things which nobody else could possibly know—things that we did and said. There was one thing for instance: the two little girls' cots were close together and they put their heads through the bars and touched noses—with their eyes shut—and then they said, 'Owls!' and opened their eyes wide. Quite silly," said Nell in a shaky voice. "Quite silly—I expect you'll laugh."

He did not laugh.

"We did that every night. Then one night I couldn't get my head back—I forgot you had to twist your head sideways to get it through the bars—and it was dark and I panicked—and Anne put out her two little hands and twisted my head and pushed it back. Anne never panicked. Anne! Oh Mr. Orme, perhaps she's poor and lonely!" Nell was crying now—but very quietly.

"We'll find her, my dear. I'll find her for you."

"You?"

"Yes, of course."

"How kind you are!" Nell exclaimed.

Mr. Orme was leaning forward in his chair. The firelight shone upon his thin face and silver hair and his hands with their long sensitive fingers were lightly clasped between his knees. " What shall I tell Anne? " he asked.

" I could go and see her! She could come home! "

" Would your mother welcome her? "

Nell made a helpless gesture. " I don't know," she said. " Sometimes I feel as if I didn't know Mother at all—what she's thinking or feeling."

" Well, never mind," said Mr. Orme with a sigh. " The first thing is to find Anne. Then we can see what to do."

Nell gave a little sob of relief. " Oh dear," she said. " I feel—I feel like Christian when the burden fell off his back. I've carried the burden for years. I've wondered and wondered where she was—and how she was. Of course I haven't thought about it all the time—when I was busy— but the burden was always there. Sometimes I've had a horrible feeling that she was in trouble and needed help —a feeling that she was lonely and miserable. You see she depended upon me so much. I could always comfort her."

Nell was silent for a few moments, remembering, and then she continued, " I've lain awake at night for hours wondering about Anne, wondering why she didn't write. They must have told her not to write to me, I suppose . . . but even so . . . I mean if she had just written one little line to say she was well and—and happy. I've tried *willing* her to write. I've tried saying over and over, ' Anne where are you? Please write to me.' Then sometimes I've felt she must be dead . . . and yet I couldn't believe it." Nell sighed and added, " Now we shall find her and I can help her—if she needs help."

" We'll find her," agreed Mr. Orme.

Nell rose. She said, " It's frightfully late and I expect

you're tired. I'm sorry for—for bothering you and giving you so much trouble."

Mr. Orme rose too. He took her hand and held it firmly. " Listen, Nell," he said. " You haven't bothered me. I like to help when I can; it's a privilege I value very highly. Besides I'm very fond of Anne. I want to find her, and I shall find her if it is humanly possible. Do nothing and say nothing until you hear from me."

" Thank you," murmured Nell. " I don't know how to thank you, but——"

" Go home and sleep soundly," said Mr. Orme.

When Nell had gone Mr. Orme took up the little book and read it . . . and having been told that Anne had written it he found it very interesting indeed. It was a delightful little book, very simply phrased, and the children in it were real and human. The names were different, of course, but through the slight disguise it was easy to recognise the Ayrtons. The little pictures were quite definitely pictures of Amberwell gardens by somebody who knew them well. Reading the little book brought Anne before his eyes very clearly and his memory went back to the day when he had seen her dancing in the early morning sunshine on the bowling-green. She had been so beautiful in her youth and innocence, and so pathetic in her ignorance, that he had wanted to pick her up in his arms and take her home.

His mind was full of Anne as he went upstairs to bed, and full of plans for finding her. It was not until he had undressed and was getting into bed that a curious sort of feeling halted him. There's something I've left undone, he thought. I've bolted the door and snibbed the windows and put the guard on the fire . . . but there's something.

Mr. Orme stood there for a few moments, thinking, and then he remembered that he had had no supper. He smiled at his foolishness and got into bed.

# CHAPTER TWENTY-TWO

NELL TRUSTED Mr. Orme, so she did exactly as he told her; she went home to bed and slept soundly, and the next day she got up and went about her usual avocations and said nothing to anybody about the little book. She thought about Anne of course—sometimes with pure joy at the idea of seeing her again, and sometimes with a feeling of unease. She had said to Mr. Orme that Anne could come home but now that the thing seemed possible the difficulties loomed larger. Anne was married to Martin Selby and naturally she would not want to leave him ... and what about Mother? thought Nell. Roger had said that Anne could come home but it would be utterly impossible to have her at Amberwell unless Mrs. Ayrton approved; it would be very difficult indeed for Nell to go and see Anne, wherever she might be, without Mrs. Ayrton's approval.

The little household found Nell very *distrait* and at one time or another they all asked in their different ways what was the matter.

" Nell, you're wool-gathering," said her mother. " It was my reading spectacles I wanted. These are the tinted ones that I wear out of doors ... and I've asked you twice to shut the window. I don't know why you're so strange."

" Did you ring up the butcher, Miss Nell? " asked Mrs. Duff. " No, I thought not. Maybe I'd better go and ring him up myself and then I'll know it's done."

" What's wrong with you, Nell? " demanded Nannie. " You seem far away. Are you feeling well enough, this morning? "

" Aunt Nell, you're not listening! " cried Stephen.

Nell tried to pull herself together but it was not easy.

There was no news from Mr. Orme for several days, nor did she see him. On Thursday Nell could bear the suspense no longer and on her way back from her usual shopping expedition she called at the Rectory. There was nobody about and the door was locked but she rang the bell and waited.

After some moments there was a shuffling sound in the hall and the door was opened by Mrs. Kenny looking even more drab than usual in a dirty overall and with curlers in her hair.

" He's away," said Mrs. Kenny and shut the door in her face.

Nell did not mind the rude reception—if reception it could be called—for if Mr. Orme were away it meant that he had discovered Anne's whereabouts. Or at least Nell hoped it meant that. She walked home on air and meeting Stephen in the drive had a boisterous game with him, chasing him round and round the palm trees and eventually catching him and kissing him and tickling him and behaving in a perfectly ridiculous manner . . . and then they went up to the house hand in hand and arrived there late for lunch, breathless and dishevelled.

Mrs. Duff met them at the door with an anxious face. " It was the butter I was wanting, Miss Nell. We haven't a bit in the house."

" Oh goodness! " cried Nell. " I've lost the basket! I must have put it down somewhere."

" When you were tickling me," suggested Stephen. " I'll get it, Aunt Nell."

" Do you know the time? " inquired Mrs. Ayrton emerging from the dining-room.

" I'm sorry," said Nell.

Nell had been saying she was sorry all week.

There was no news from Mr. Orme on Friday, nor on Saturday, and Nell could not ring him up because the Rectory was not on the telephone, but surely he would be back on Sunday.

Nell decided to go to church early; she enjoyed the quiet peaceful service at eight o'clock and often went to it, slipping out of the nursery door and going down to St. Stephen's through the gardens. This morning was beautiful; the sun was shining, the hills were swathed in a pearly mist and there were tiny green leaves on the hedges. Browning must have been thinking of a morning like this when he wrote Pippa's song:

> *The year's at the Spring,*
> *The day's at the morn;*
> *Morning's at seven;*
> *The hill-side's dew-pearled;*
> *The lark's on the wing;*
> *The snail's on the thorn;*
> *God's in His heaven—*
> *All's right with the world!*

The lark was singing—Nell could hear him—but the dew was more like diamonds than pearls. As she pushed open the wicket-gate into the little churchyard she tried to make herself believe that all was right with the world. Perhaps Browning had meant the natural world of hills and trees and flowers; he could not have meant that all was right with the world of human beings. So many things were wrong—people were unkind and unforgiving—but God was in His Heaven. Nell believed that.

The church was empty when Nell got there (for she was early) so she went to one of the front pews and kneeled

I

down. She prayed for Anne and for her mother—that they might be reconciled—and she prayed for wisdom so that she might know what she ought to do and how she could unravel all the tangles.

Presently Nell heard other people come in and take their places in the pews behind her with the usual quiet scufflings; then Mr. Orme appeared and the service began.

Nell could not help wondering as she looked at Mr. Orme whether he had been able to do anything about Anne . . . and then with an effort she controlled her thoughts and fixed them on the service. She had found, as most people do, that sometimes this service meant a great deal and sometimes not. One always hoped to be caught up out of the world and all its problems and sorrows and to lose oneself completely. This morning the little miracle happened and a beautiful feeling of peace filled the little church.

Nell waited for a few minutes after the service was over (she always waited so that she should not be brought down to earth too quickly by meeting people and having to talk) and then she rose and came out into the sunshine, feeling a little dazed but happy and at peace.

Everybody had hurried home to breakfast except one woman—a slender woman in a shabby grey coat and skirt —and as Nell came down the path the woman turned and smiled at her.

It was Anne.

Nell had often imagined a meeting with Anne but she had never imagined it would be like this—alone, quiet and peaceful in the early morning sunshine. She had sometimes feared that her first meeting with Anne might be a little—difficult—a trifle embarrassing, but here and now there was no embarrassment at all. It was not even exciting, nor strange; it was perfectly natural; it was almost as if they had parted only yesterday.

Nell held out her hands and said, " Anne."

Anne said nothing; she took Nell's hands in hers and they stood there looking at each other for what seemed quite a long time.

" You haven't changed a bit," said Anne at last.

Nell wished she could say the same. This was her own dear Anne but how thin she had become, how worn and tired she looked!

" He found you," said Nell in a low voice.

Anne nodded. " Yes, he found us. Dear kind Mr. Orme, how glad I was to see him! He brought us back to his own house——"

" Do you mean you're staying with him? "

" Yes."

" But, Anne——"

" Darling, I've no time to tell you anything now, and there's so much to tell that I don't know where to begin. I must hurry back and get the breakfast. When can I see you? "

Nell tried to think. Sunday was a difficult day to escape from everybody.

" Come to-night," said Anne urgently. " Promise me you'll come."

" Yes, of course," said Nell. " But Anne, tell me——"

" Not now—it's no good beginning—I must go, honestly." She gave Nell's hands a little squeeze and turned and ran down the path. She ran lightly, as if she were used to running, and when she reached the little gate which led into the Rectory garden she turned and waved. Then she was gone.

For a minute or two Nell stood there, dazed. It had been so unexpected; it had happened so suddenly, and was so quickly over, that she could hardly believe it was real. Had she really and truly seen Anne—and held her hands?

Then she came to earth with a bump and glancing at

her watch realised that if she did not hurry home she would be late for breakfast—in fact she was already late for breakfast—so she hurried home.

2

" You didn't tell me you were going to church early," said Mrs. Ayrton fretfully. " I wish you would tell me the night before. Mrs. Duff has boiled my egg hard—I can't think why she does it. She knows I don't like hard-boiled eggs."

Nell heard herself commiserating with her mother over the hard-boiled egg but the real part of her mind was thinking of Anne, wondering about her. What had Anne been doing all these years? Why was she so thin and worn? Where had Mr. Orme found her? Anne had said, " He brought us back to his own house." Did that mean Martin Selby was there too, staying in the Rectory? Would they come to Amberwell and try to make up the quarrel? Perhaps that was Mr. Orme's idea. Perhaps that was why he had brought them . . . and if so what would happen?

It seemed strange to Nell that her mother could not see all these thoughts chasing each other through her head, but went on talking about how long an egg should be boiled and complaining that the tea was too strong.

" Mrs. Duff always makes it far too strong," said Mrs. Ayrton. " And why don't you sit down and eat your breakfast? Your egg will be like a stone and the tea is getting cold. Mrs. Duff has forgotten the tea-cosy."

Nell went to the drawer of the sideboard and took out the tea-cosy. It struck her as she did so that her mother might have done this herself. There was nothing to prevent her—except that she had never done such a thing in her life. Mrs. Ayrton had never done anything in her life, she had never boiled a kettle or fried a rasher of bacon, she was as help-

less as an infant and, left to herself, she would have starved.
It was dreadful to be as helpless as that, thought Nell,
looking at her mother pityingly . . . and then her thoughts
swung back to Anne. She would see Anne to-night!

"You look a little feverish, Nell," said Mrs. Ayrton.
"I hope you haven't caught a chill. Sometimes it's very
cold in St. Stephen's."

"No, I'm quite well, Mother."

"Your eyes look feverish."

"I'm perfectly all right—honestly."

"Why haven't you eaten your breakfast? You haven't
eaten anything."

"Haven't I?" said Nell in surprise.

It was not easy for Nell to go out after dinner for the
simple reason that she never did—except occasionally to
the Lamberts' or to the Women's Rural Institute. Mrs.
Ayrton disliked anything unusual; she liked Nell to sit
with her in the evenings, sewing or knitting and listening
to the wireless. All day as Nell went about the house,
doing the hundred and one things that had to be done, she
tried to think of some way in which she could escape without
telling an actual lie. Unless she could think of a reasonable
excuse for going out there would be endless arguments. It
even occurred to her to tell the truth, to say quite simply
that Anne was at the Rectory and she was going there to
see her—but of course that was impossible because she did
not know Anne's plans. She might wreck everything by
telling her mother the amazing news.

Nell always prepared supper on Sundays when Mrs. Duff
was out, and as they ate their simple meal she suddenly
decided to take a firm line. Never explain, thought Nell
smiling a little to herself. She cleared the dishes and washed
them up and then looked into the cosy little morning-room
where her mother was settled by the fire reading the papers.

" Listen to this, Nell," said Mrs. Ayrton. " It's perfectly frightful. I don't know what the world's coming to——"

" Not now," said Nell. " You must tell me about it to-morrow. I'm going out."

" Going out! " exclaimed Mrs. Ayrton in amazement. " Where are you going? "

" Just—out," replied Nell. " You'll be all right, won't you? If you want anything you can ask Nannie. Don't wait up for me."

" Nell, where are you going? "

" Out," repeated Nell smiling cheerfully. " Why shouldn't I go out? It's a lovely evening."

" But you can't! " cried Mrs. Ayrton. " I mean you can't go out—at night—for a walk—by yourself. Are you going to the Lamberts'? "

" No," said Nell. " Don't wait up for me; I may be late. I'm taking the key."

" Nell—— "

" Good night, Mother! " She kissed her mother and ran.

As she went out of the front door she heard her mother calling but she took no notice. I'm not a prisoner, she thought. There's no earthly reason why I shouldn't go out. Nannie and Mrs. Duff go out, so why shouldn't I? It's ridiculous to feel guilty . . . but she felt guilty all the same.

The feeling of guilt persisted uncomfortably as she ran down the path through the gardens and did not vanish until she got to the Rectory and rang the bell. The door opened almost immediately and Anne was there and the next moment they were in each other's arms.

" Oh Nell," whispered Anne. " I was beginning to think you weren't coming."

" I couldn't get away before," explained Nell. " Mother wanted to know where I was going—and of course I couldn't tell her. Anne, you must tell me everything."

" It would take days and days! "

" But you're here—and well. That's the main thing. I was so terribly worried about you—so miserable. Why didn't you write? "

" I did write—and then I got your letter saying that you hadn't heard—and a letter from Father to say I was not to write to you again; saying that my own foolishness had cut me off; saying . . . Oh well, never mind. What he said was true. I was terribly foolish."

" But you've been happy? " asked Nell, drawing back and looking at her. " You married him because you loved him. It isn't foolish to marry somebody you love."

Anne did not answer directly. She said, " Oh I don't regret what I did, because it's given me the most valuable thing in all the world."

" You're talking in riddles! "

" I know, but I can't help it. How can I begin to tell you everything that's happened to me in all these years. I *will* tell you some of it if you give me time."

" All of it," urged Nell.

" No, darling, just some of it. Come into Mr. Orme's study. He was tired so he went to bed early. He gets tired very easily you know. He's so kind and good and never thinks of himself; he really needs somebody to look after him."

They went into the study and the first thing Nell saw was a large doll with flaxen hair lying upon a chair. It was such an unexpected sight and seemed so out of place that she gave a gasp of amazement.

" This is Jenny," said Anne smiling and picking it up. " Isn't she lovely? Mr. Orme bought her and gave her to Emmie . . . but of course you don't know about Emmie—I keep on forgetting that you don't know anything about us —Emmie is my most valuable possession."

## CHAPTER TWENTY-THREE

NELL HAD said she wanted to hear " all of it " but of course that was impossible. Anne knew before she began her story that she could never make Nell understand. Anne herself did not understand how it had happened. When she looked back and thought about her visit to Edinburgh (when she had stayed with Aunt Beatrice and met Martin Selby) the whole thing seemed crazy.

Why had she married Martin? She had never loved him —that was very certain. Of course she had been flattered and thrilled at Martin's attentions; Martin was so much older than herself and so clever. He had been to Rome and Florence and could talk about all sorts of interesting things.

Martin enjoyed talking and Anne enjoyed listening to him; usually she listened without comment but one evening when Martin came to dinner at the flat he began to tell Anne about a friend of his who had an apiary.

" Oh, monkeys! " cried Anne. " What fun to keep monkeys! Aunt Beatrice and I saw some at the Zoo."

" One keeps bees in an apiary, not monkeys," said Martin without a smile. " The word is derived from the latin— apis, a bee. An apiarist is a man who studies the habits of bees."

" Oh, I thought——"

" You thought the word was derived from ape," said Martin.

Anne felt slightly annoyed; but of course it was very

silly and Martin was so clever. It was ridiculous to feel annoyed.

Apart from that somewhat unfortunate contretemps everything went well and Martin's visits became more frequent and prolonged. Aunt Beatrice was very excited about it.

"Martin is devoted to you," she declared. "He's so tall and handsome and so romantic! It's wonderful to see him look at you with his heart in his eyes."

It *was* rather wonderful, thought Anne. Nobody had ever looked at her like that before. Nobody had ever sprung to his feet to open doors for her; nobody had ever given her roses. All the same when she discovered that Martin wanted to marry her she was a little frightened.

Aunt Beatrice soothed Anne's fears and pushed her very gently into Martin's arms.

It was all settled and everybody was happy and excited. Anne lost her head completely; she was swept away. It was delightful to be the principal person in the affair, to be praised and cherished and to have all her wishes consulted. That night they had a celebration—a little dinner for three in Aunt Beatrice's flat—Anne wore her new pink frock and looked enchanting; her eyes shone like stars and her cheeks were rosy. They drank each other's healths.

"I wish Nell were here," said Anne at last. "That would make it quite perfect."

"Yes," agreed Aunt Beatrice. "But things can't be absolutely perfect in this world."

"I suppose it will be all right," said Martin. "I suppose Anne's father won't object. You haven't told him yet, have you?"

"No, we must talk about that," replied Aunt Beatrice. "As I said before things can't be absolutely perfect—and I know my brother so well. He's very unreasonable."

" But, Miss Ayrton! " exclaimed Martin in alarm. " You said——"

" It will be all right, I promise you," declared Aunt Beatrice and forthwith revealed her plan that they should marry without the consent of Anne's parents.

" But why? " asked Martin. " Surely it would be better to ask them."

" They wouldn't give their consent."

" Good heavens! " Martin exclaimed. " You don't mean——"

" I know my brother," repeated Aunt Beatrice. " He's very unreasonable indeed. He would absolutely refuse to allow you to be married. If you go and ask Anne's parents you may as well give up the idea of getting married altogether. They would send Martin away and you would never see each other again. My parents did that to me. If you wait and talk and argue it will all fall through. That's what happened to me. I shall never forget how dreadful it was—all the talk and the arguments—all the unkind things that were said to poor Harry! Eventually he went away and I never saw him again."

There was a horrified silence.

" Then you think——" began Martin.

" I know," said Aunt Beatrice firmly. " The only thing to do is to get married and then tell them. They can't part you once you're married."

Anne had said nothing. She had a feeling that Aunt Beatrice was right; her father would not like Martin. Martin was wonderful of course, but he liked his own way —so did her father. The idea of talk and arguments between them was appalling. It would end in a row, thought Anne. Martin would be sent away and she would never see him again . . . and she would be like Aunt Beatrice, unloved and unwanted.

" What do you think about it, Anne? " asked Martin.

" Well, Aunt Beatrice knows better than I do," said Anne doubtfully.

" Of course I do," agreed Aunt Beatrice. " You leave it all to me. I'll arrange everything."

Aunt Beatrice was as good as her word, and for the next few days she was extremely busy. Minors can be married in Scotland without their parents' consent so there was no trouble on that score. She bought Anne's small trousseau out of her own pocket.

" I'll get the money back from your father afterwards," she said.

" Do you think he'll give it to you? " asked Anne.

" Of course he will! And even if I don't get it back from him it won't matter. I'll give it to you as a wedding present . . . or you can pay me out of your allowance if you would rather. Your father will give you an allowance when you're married. He gives Connie a very generous allowance and of course you'll get the same."

" You're quite sure they'll be pleased? " asked Martin.

" Of course they'll be pleased."

" Then why not tell them? "

" Because they won't be pleased at first," replied Aunt Beatrice. " I've told you before. They'll say Anne is too young, and they'll put all sorts of obstacles in the way, but once they realise that it is a *fait accompli* they'll come round and everything will be all right. I know what I'm talking about." She sighed and added, " If only I could have my life over again! I had nobody to help and advise me. When I was Anne's age . . ."

Martin had listened so often to the story of Miss Ayrton's romance that he was heartily sick of it. He glanced at the clock and said he had no idea it was so late; he must go at once . . . and Anne as usual went with him to the door.

"I don't know why you love me," said Anne. "I'm not clever or—or anything."

"You're sweet," declared Martin kissing her. "You're innocent and sweet. That's why I love you."

2

It was all very thrilling. Anne longed to write to Nell and tell her what was happening but Aunt Beatrice explained that it would not be fair to Nell—and of course Aunt Beatrice was right. It would put Nell in a very difficult position if she were told before her parents. Once it was all over and everything was smoothed out Nell could be told . . . and perhaps Nell could come and stay in London and they could go about together. What fun that would be!

Martin had a flat in London, quite near the school, so the problem of where they were going to live did not arise. It was a very small flat, said Martin, but that would not matter. Anne agreed that it would not matter at all. There would be no time for a honeymoon, because Martin had to go back to the school, his holiday was over, but that did not matter either.

Anne and Martin were married quietly; it was very different from Connie's wedding with all the fuss and excitement, but Anne was so excited about all the wonderful things that were happening to her, about her new clothes and the prospect of going to London with Martin that she did not mind. She was on top of the world. She had been nowhere and seen nothing so the journey to London was marvellous and she was interested in everything and delighted with all she saw and made Martin laugh with her naïve comments.

It was very late when they arrived at Martin's flat. He opened the door with his key and ushered her in.

"It's very small," said Martin. "I told you that, didn't I?"

Anne said nothing. She was absolutely horrified at the sight of Martin's flat. It brought her down to earth with a bump. Martin had told her it was small but she had imagined it to be a sort of doll's house; she had imagined a tiny bright sitting-room and a kitchen with a glittering array of pots and pans on the shelves. This place was dark and squalid and dirty, it was the dirtiest place Anne had ever seen. Her first thought on seeing Martin's flat was that she could not live here—it was impossible.

"It's a little dirty, I'm afraid," said Martin cheerfully. "Of course it's been shut up for some time, but perhaps we can get a woman to come and help you to clean it up. Then, once it's nice and clean, you can look after it yourself."

"I can't cook," said Anne. "I told you——"

"I know, but you'll soon learn. Every woman knows how to keep house and cook—it's an instinct. Birds don't have to be taught how to make nests. But there's no need to worry because it will only be temporary; your father will give you an allowance—Miss Ayrton said so—and then we can move to a larger flat and have a daily maid. You must write to your father to-morrow."

"Yes, I suppose so," said Anne.

The next morning Martin went off early to his work and left Anne alone in the flat. She had thought last night that the flat was horrible and it seemed even more horrible in the light of day, it seemed dirtier and more dingy. It was terribly cramped and inconvenient—the meanest cottage on the Amberwell estate was a palace compared with Martin's flat. The worst part of it was that Martin did not seem to notice the dirt and discomfort (or at least he did not seem to mind) and the discovery that his standards were so different from her own alarmed and depressed her. However it was no use giving way to despondency, Anne had promised to write the all-important letter and to have it ready when Martin returned so she sat down at the battered old desk which stood near the window and began her task.

The letter took hours. She had known it would be difficult but it was far more difficult than she had expected. With the paper before her and the pen in her hand, she found she had not the slightest idea what to say. She had felt depressed and discouraged before she started and she became more so. A dozen times she began the letter and a dozen times she tore it up . . . but at last in sheer desperation she finished it and when Martin came in she showed it to him.

" My dear girl! " exclaimed Martin. " This letter is supposed to be to your father. It reads like a letter to a total stranger—and incidentally there are two spelling mistakes."

" I'm not very good at spelling," said Anne meekly.

" Well, never mind the spelling. The whole thing is wrong."

Anne had felt the same herself. She sighed and said, " I don't know what to say. Perhaps it will be better if you write it out and then I can copy it."

" Good heavens! " exclaimed Martin. " Can't you write a letter to your own father? How can I tell you what to say? I don't know him."

Anne realised that she did not know him either.

" Look here," said Martin. " You said it would be all right. You said you would write to him and explain everything and he would understand."

" I don't think he *will* understand," said Anne miserably. " I think he'll be very angry."

" Why have you changed your mind? "

She found this difficult to explain. The truth was she had been so buoyed up with excitement that she had not really thought about her father at all. It was not until she had sat down to write to him that his personality took shape before her eyes. She envisaged her letter arriving at breakfast-time and her father receiving it, opening it and reading it. The vision was horrifying in the extreme. Nell would have understood Anne's somewhat lame explanation of this curious phenomenon, but Martin did not, and what was worse he did not believe in it. He did not believe what she said.

" It's absolute nonsense," he declared. " Either you knew all the time that your father would be angry or else something has happened to change your mind. What is it? "

" Nothing," said Anne with a sob. " I never thought about it properly. Aunt Beatrice said——"

" For heaven's sake don't cry," said Martin in exasperation. " Sit down and write your letter. I'll tell you what to say."

Somehow or other the letter got written and Martin took it to the post.

### 3

When the letter had been despatched they settled down to wait for an answer and Anne did her best to cope with household affairs. She tried to clean the flat but as fast as she cleaned it the smuts drifted in at the windows; she tried to cook but the meals she produced were practically uneatable. She toiled all day at her unaccustomed tasks and by the time Martin returned she was always tired.

Martin was quite patient with her, he gave her money and told her what food to buy and how to cook it. " You'll learn," he kept saying. " It isn't difficult once you get into the way of it . . . and of course it will be much easier when we get our new flat."

Anne was not quite so confident as Martin; she had her doubts about her father's reaction to the news of her marriage (and as the days went by her doubts became increasingly oppressive) but when at last the letter from her father arrived it was worse than even Anne had expected. It forbade her to write or to hold any communication with her family. Anne's eyes saw the sentences written in her father's neat and slightly old-fashioned copperplate hand but her brain could hardly take them in:

Your mother and I were horrified to hear of your outrageous behaviour . . . I have made inquiries concerning the man you have married and discovered he has nothing to recommend him . . if our consent had been asked we should most certainly have refused it, but now that you have married this undesirable person we can do nothing and you must abide by your rash act . . . your letter seems to suggest that I am under an obligation to help you financially but you are mistaken. I have no intention of doing so either now or in the future . . . you have disgraced yourself by your ill-considered marriage and what is a great deal worse you have disgraced your family . . .

Anne would have kept the letter from Martin but he came in while she was still reading it and took it out of her hand.

"Don't!" Anne cried. "Don't read it!"

But already Martin was reading it—at first with incredulity and then with rage. Martin's fury knew no bounds. He was furious with the Ayrtons and furious with Anne, he was even furious with himself. He tore the letter into shreds and stamped round the tiny flat cursing and swearing. He had been tricked; tricked into marrying a penniless girl, a useless girl who could not boil a potato, a girl who went about with a miserable face!

Anne, cowering in a chair, asked him most unwisely if he had married her for her money.

"No!" shouted Martin. "Of course not."

"Then why——"

"Because I couldn't afford to marry anyone unless she had a little money to help out."

"It's the same," said Anne.

"It's utterly different," stormed Martin. "Don't you understand plain English? I asked you to marry me because I loved you, but I wouldn't have dreamt of asking you to marry me if I had known your parents would cast you off."

"Neither would I," declared Anne weeping bitterly.

This brought Martin to his senses. "It was your aunt," he said more quietly. "It was all her doing. It was she who—who——"

"Who told you to marry me," suggested Anne.

"Well—yes—if you want the truth," said Martin. "And I suppose she pushed you into it too?"

Anne nodded.

"Why?" asked Martin savagely. "Why the hell! The woman is crazy. I shall write and tell her exactly what I think of her."

He sat down at the desk and took out a sheet of paper.

"Oh don't!" cried Anne. "It isn't really her fault. It

was our fault for listening to her. She really thought it would be all right."

" How do you know? "

" Because—don't you see?—she's cut off too. Father is furious with her. She'll never be able to go to Amberwell again. She's cut off from Amberwell—and so am I! " sobbed Anne.

" Amberwell! " exclaimed Martin. " I hate the sound of the name! If you were so enamoured of the place why did you leave it? "

Why indeed?

In spite of this quarrel, when both had said words which were hard to forgive, Martin and Anne managed to settle down and arrange their lives together. There was nothing else to do. Anne learnt to shop economically and to cook reasonably well, and somehow or other they managed to make ends meet on Martin's meagre salary. Anne did not mind pinching and scraping, or at least she would not have minded if Martin had been kind and friendly—but he was not. Any love he had had for her seemed to have vanished and had been swallowed up in bitterness. Martin felt he had been tricked and cheated. His resentment turned inwards and poisoned his whole life, it poisoned his relations with Anne. Sometimes when Anne looked at his sulky face she wondered what had happened to the Martin who had kissed her so fondly and had given her roses. This Martin was like a different person.

Anne was different too, for she was no longer gay and happy and she was not experienced enough to hide her misery and put on a cheerful face. It was dreadful to be tied to a man who had a grudge against you; it was dreadful to have to share his life. It was dreadful to have to eat food bought with his money. Lack of money was one of the hardest things to bear . . . Anne was obliged to ask Martin for money to pay for every small necessity, for money to have her shoes mended or to replace a worn-out toothbrush.

The misery of her life and the worry of cooking and trying to keep things clean wore her out and detracted from her appearance. When she looked at herself in the damp-spotted mirror she saw a white peaky face, two large grey eyes and lank dejected hair . . . I'm definitely ugly now, she thought. No wonder Martin doesn't love me . . .

Tears came very easily. They ran down her cheeks suddenly and for the silliest reasons. Anne wept when the milk boiled over and the flat was filled with a greasy smell and she had to clean the gas-stove; she wept when she found that one of the eggs she had bought was bad; she wept over the holes in Martin's socks—which she had to darn.

Sometimes Anne tried to look into the future; she wondered what would happen, how long could she go on bearing this life? It was so loveless, it was so frightening. She was literally frightened of Martin now. He did not ill-treat her physically but he ill-treated her with words and looks which played havoc with her nerves. When the time drew near for Martin to return from school she would find herself holding her breath—and listening. His key would scrape in the lock as he turned it and he would throw down his satchel of papers with a bang. Anne, struggling with the supper in the kitchen, would feel her heart begin to thump in a suffocating manner and her hands would tremble so that she could scarcely lift the pan from the stove.

Then Martin would appear in the doorway. " Well, what sort of muck have you got for supper to-night? " he would inquire.

Perhaps if Anne had been able to stand up to Martin things might have been better, but she was too nervous and frightened to hold her own. Hitherto the companion of her life had been a gentle and beloved sister who shared all her thoughts and understood them. She had had no experience of men. Once or twice she decided to make an effort to talk to Martin, to tell him about things she had seen when she was out shopping, but it was not a success.

" Is that supposed to be amusing? " Martin would ask. " Am I supposed to laugh? "

### 4

The school where Martin taught was very draughty and he was scarcely ever without a cold. Anne worried about this and one day she bought a bottle of cough-mixture at the chemists and put it on the table.

" What's this rubbish? " asked Martin.

" For your cold. You've had that cough for weeks and——"

" What d'you mean by wasting money on rubbish? "

" But it isn't rubbish. It's good. It says so on the bottle——"

" It says on the bottle! " jeered Martin. " Well of course it says on the bottle . . . The people who make the filthy brew want to sell it. That's how they make their money—by taking in fools with a lot of flap-doodle."

" I thought—it might—do you good," said Anne shakily.

" So you spent half a crown on the stuff! If you had spent the money on a decent piece of steak and taken the trouble to cook it properly it would have been more sensible. Heavens, why did I have to marry a fool! "

Anne said nothing. She had been told so often that she was a fool that she had come to believe it . . . and it was true that she said and did foolish things especially when she was scared. Certainly by Martin's standards she was uneducated and by any standard she was ignorant of the world and its affairs. Her *naïveté* which had seemed to Martin so sweet and innocent now exasperated him and he made no secret of the fact. Sometimes he sneered at her openly and at other times he showed his disapproval without words—and Anne had become so sensitive to his moods that her heart fluttered at the curl of his lip or the scornful glance of his eye. So many things annoyed him and so many subjects were taboo that she was obliged to think carefully before she opened her mouth . . . usually she decided to remain silent. But this was not right either.

" Chatty, aren't you? " asked Martin.

" I was just—thinking—— "

" Thinking about Amberwell, I suppose? "

Quite often it was true. Anne thought about Amberwell constantly, she dreamt about Amberwell and awoke thinking she was there (in her own little bed with Nell beside her) she would turn and stretch out her hand for comfort and assurance . . . and then she would remember. It was not Nell who lay beside her in the other bed. It was not a loving friend. There was no comfort to be found in her companion.

The home-sickness which Anne suffered was almost unbearable. As she went about her daily work trying to clean the little flat—so stuffy and airless in the hot summer months—she saw visions of Amberwell with its wide spaces, its trees and flowers and emerald-green lawns. She could smell the clean cool air and hear the sea splashing upon the sandy beach. The visions tore her heart so that part of the time she scarcely knew what she was doing. It was only now when Amberwell was lost to her for ever that she realised to the full its sweet enchantment and understood what Aunt Beatrice must have felt when she was exiled. Aunt Beatrice had thought marriage would break the spell and perhaps a happy marriage might have broken it—but not this marriage. Amberwell held Anne spellbound.

The little flat was horrible but it was almost more horrible to venture forth into the streets that surrounded it. Anne had never lived in a town before and the noise and the crowds of jostling people alarmed her. It seemed to her that the very air of London was tainted and unfit to breathe. She knew nobody of course and she dared not spend money upon bus fares (it was Martin's money and she was obliged to account to him for every penny) so she saw nothing of London except the dreary streets where she shopped. It never occurred to Martin to take her to see the sights of London and she was far too frightened of him to suggest it. Martin spent his Sundays lying in bed and reading the papers. Sundays were even more unbearable to Anne than the other days of the week.

The shadow of approaching war loomed darker and darker during that summer of 1939. In the shops and in the streets people were talking about Hitler. What would he do next? What would happen to London if there was another war?

One evening in July Martin returned from school in unusually good spirits.

" I'm giving up my job," he said. " I'm going to enlist." Anne gazed at him in surprise.

" Why not? " asked Martin. " I'm sick to death of teaching snotty little boys. It's much better to enlist now than to wait until I'm called up. Have you any objection "

Anne still said nothing. She was aware that Martin's question was merely rhetorical, he did not care whether or not she objected.

" You'll have to get a job," Martin continued. " You'd

better look about for something. Even a nit-wit can get some sort of a job nowadays.

" I suppose I could . . ." said Anne thoughtfully. The idea was completely new but it was not unpleasant. Her life was so miserable that any change would be for the better. Perhaps she could get into one of the women's services if she tried.

" Well, you aren't saying very much," declared Martin. " Most wives would be upset at the idea of their husband joining the Army. You'll be glad to see the last of me I suppose."

" I shall be glad to leave this flat! " exclaimed Anne impulsively.

Anne so seldom answered back that Martin was taken by surprise. " It's not a bad little flat——" he began.

" It's dreadful! " cried Anne wildly. " It's the most horrible place I've ever seen! It's dark and dingy and depressing! It's driving me mad! If you were mewed up in it all day long—if you had to try and keep it clean—you would hate it as much as I do."

" All right, don't lose your hair," muttered Martin. " Everyone knows you're used to a palace and to being waited on, hand and foot. If that's the sort of life you want you shouldn't have married a schoolmaster. A duke would be more in your line."

# CHAPTER TWENTY-FOUR

MARTIN SELBY was not accepted for the Army. When he went up for his Medical Examination the doctor told him he had tuberculosis in the lung. The doctor was efficient and kind; he assured Martin that the disease was in its early stages and could be cured by proper treatment in a Sanatorium; he told Martin to see his own doctor without delay. Instead of taking this sensible advice Martin decided that it was all nonsense, he could cure himself; hospitals were no good at all; what he needed was an open-air life. Nothing that Anne could say had any effect upon him except to make him angry and to confirm his intention.

It was not difficult to get a job; so many young men were being called up for the Services that farmers were only too glad to get anybody to work for them however inexperienced he might be. Martin had the offer of several jobs and eventually settled to go to Mr. Steele who ran a big market-garden about forty miles from London and grew fruit and vegetables. There was a tiny cottage on the estate, a mean little place consisting of two rooms and a lean-to shed which could be used for washing. There was no gas and no electricity and no facilities for heating water. The little cottage had been empty for years and was in very bad repair but Mr. Steele patched it up for the Selbys and they moved in. Martin grumbled about it continuously but Anne was so thankful to leave the flat that she would have consented to live in any sort of hovel. At least the little cottage was bright and airy and could be kept clean. There were no smuts to drift in at the windows and spread their oily film over everything . . . and although the place was very small one did not feel shut in, for one had only to open the door and step out into the garden.

They had brought the furniture from the flat—the old pieces of ragged carpet and the ramshackle chairs and cupboards—and Anne managed to pick up a wooden settle at a sale for a few shillings. She put it in the window of the sitting-room so that she could sit there in her scanty leisure moments and look out at the trees and the sky and see the birds hopping about the garden. Martin did not approve of the settle, of course, he said it had probably come out of a public-house and made fun of its battered appearance, but for once Anne stood up to him.

" I like it," she said. " It's very old. I expect it has an interesting history. If it could talk——"

" If it could talk it would tell you about a lot of drunken yokels," jeered Martin . . . but he said no more and the settle remained where Anne had put it.

There was no more talk of Anne finding a job. Martin was ill and needed her. She blamed herself for not noticing before that Martin was ill. Why had she not realised that he was losing weight and looking more haggard every day? Now that her eyes were opened she saw that he looked ghastly. She decided that she must try to be more patient with Martin's moods and more cheerful—and this was easier because she felt more cheerful herself. Life was not such a struggle and was not so dreary.

Although Martin was getting less pay for his work in Harestone Gardens they were really much better off than they had been in London for they could have vegetables whenever they liked and Mr. Steele gave them free milk from his own cows. The people who lived in the other cottages on the estate were friendly and pleasant—it was delightful to have people to talk to. None of his fellow-workers liked Martin, they found him stuck-up and intolerant, but it was agreed that " young Mrs. Selby didn't give 'erself no airs " and she was accepted as one of the community.

Several of Anne's neighbours made a habit of dropping in to see her and staying for a cup of tea and a chat. They discovered that she was willing to " mind the baby " while they went to the village to do their shopping. Old Mrs. Wight, who lived next door and kept house for her son, was a help to Anne in many ways and gave her hints about cooking. Mrs. Wight was apt to borrow things and forget to return them, for she was very old and her mind was not very clear, but all the same she was a kind neighbour and a useful friend.

In September, when war was declared, Anne and Martin were so dug in, so settled in their new life, that they were not very much affected by the news. Anne thought of Roger and wondered where he was. She thought of Amberwell and wondered who was looking after the gardens . . . but the spell of Amberwell was fading and although she often dreamt about the place she seldom thought of it in the daytime. Only occasionally was she gripped suddenly by a longing to see her home . . . to see Nell. It was unbearable while it lasted and could only be banished by seizing a spade and digging in the little cottage garden or by a visit to old Mrs. Wight.

All this time Anne had heard nothing from her family nor had she expected to hear. She had been half crazy with misery in London but now she was sane and she began to wonder whether it would be any use writing home. Perhaps she should write to her mother and say she was sorry for the foolish way she had behaved. In a few months Anne had grown up, she was no longer a silly ignorant girl, she was a serious-minded woman. The change had taken place so quickly that she was able to measure her growth. She saw her foolishness so clearly that she could not understand why she had not seen it before. She could not understand why she had allowed herself to be pushed into Martin's arms by Aunt Beatrice. There was no sense in it. She must have been mad!

One day she sat down with pen and paper and began a letter to her mother—but she did not get far. She realised that the whole thing was hopeless. She could say she was sorry and ask for forgiveness but what was the use of that? Even if they forgave her and asked her to go home she could not go. Martin was ill and needed her, she could not go without Martin, and the idea of taking Martin to Amberwell was out of the question . . . Martin at Amberwell!

Anne rose and put away her writing materials and went in to see Mrs. Wight.

" Come in, dearie," said Mrs. Wight. " I wis jist goin' to make a cuppa. Did I ever tell you about when I wis kitching-maid at the big 'ouse? "

Anne had heard about it half a dozen times but she sat down and listened to it again.

The Selbys had been at Harestone for nearly a year when Anne's baby was born. Anne would have liked to call the baby Elinor, but Martin would not hear of this, so she was christened Emmeline after Martin's mother.

The baby made a great deal of difference to Anne. Martin's habit of finding fault with everything she did ceased to depress her. Martin might think her useless and foolish, but little Emmie depended upon her for everything and repaid all her care. Little Emmie was a model baby; she was out all day lying in her pram, sleeping peacefully or watching the trees and the birds.

By this time Martin was very much better; his cough

had practically gone and in spite of the long hours of physical work he had put on weight. His spirits were better too and scarcely a day passed without his pointing out to Anne that he had been right and the doctor completely wrong.

"Doctors don't know anything," declared Martin. "Their one idea is to cart you off to a hospital. If I had taken that doctor's advice I should be dead by now."

His moods were still uncertain. Sometimes he was very difficult; he resented the baby as an added expense. It irritated him to come in and find her clothes airing in front of the fire, it enraged him if she cried—fortunately she did not often cry. At other times he would be quite amiable in his own peculiar way and would ask Anne what she had been doing. This was the old, old question but Anne had found that it must not be answered in the traditional way; when Martin asked what she had been doing he expected a detailed answer. She had to think quickly and choose out those details of her day's activities which would be least likely to annoy him. For instance it was out of the question to mention that she had been in to see Mrs. Wight, ("That dreadful, common old woman!" Martin would exclaim. "What on earth did you go in there for!") but it was fairly safe to tell him she had been in the garden or washing the clothes.

"Is that all you did?" he would say. "Well, you seem to have had an easy day. I've been working like a black— but I managed to score off old Steele."

The pleasure which Martin took in "scoring off" his employer worried Anne considerably for if Martin really spoke to Mr. Steele as he reported it was a wonder that Mr. Steele did not sack him then and there . . . but Mr. Steele did not sack him and Anne concluded that the clever repartee could not have been uttered aloud; possibly it had only been thought of afterwards when the conversation was over.

2

One afternoon in May when Emmie was two years old Martin returned from his work early complaining of feeling shivery. The rubber boots which he always wore were leaking and his feet were soaking wet. Anne helped him to bed, filled hot-water bottles and made him a hot drink—and for once he seemed grateful for her ministrations.

His gratitude worried Anne. It was so unlike Martin. She had a feeling that he must be ill. She worried about Martin all night and by the next morning it was obvious that her fears were justified and that he was very ill indeed: he was burning and shivering by turns and coughing continuously.

"It's just a little cold, that's all," said Martin hoarsely. "It's nothing. I'll be better to-morrow. Don't let them take me to the hospital."

"We had better get the doctor," said Anne in anxious tones.

"All right, perhaps you'd better, but I won't go to the hospital."

Dr. Frome had attended Anne when her baby was born so she knew him well, and liked him. He came in the afternoon and examined his patient carefully. Then he looked round the miserable little cottage.

"We'll get you into hospital," he said.

"No, you won't," said Martin in his husky whisper. "I won't go to the hospital. I shall be all right in a day or two——"

"He doesn't like hospitals," explained Anne.

" Mrs. Selby, he must go to hospital," said Dr. Frome earnestly. " You can't possibly nurse him here."

Anne did not know what to do; she was only too well aware of the inconveniences of the little house and of her own shortcomings as a nurse, but she was also aware of Martin's dread of hospitals.

" I don't want to go to the hospital," croaked Martin. " I can't stand hospitals. All I ask is to be allowed to lie here on my own bed until I'm better. I suppose it would be too much bother to make me a hot drink now and then and fill a hot-water bottle. That's all the nursing I want."

" It isn't a question of bother," said Dr. Frome. " I'm quite sure Mrs. Selby is willing to do everything she can, but this house is unsuitable for illness and you'll get better much more quickly in hospital. I'll send the ambulance for you."

" I shall die if you send me to the hospital," declared Martin.

They argued with him kindly but it was useless and after a few minutes Dr. Frome took his leave.

Anne followed the doctor into the garden. " What are we to do? " she asked in despair.

" He must be moved to hospital," replied Dr. Frome. " He's very ill and he needs skilled nursing and proper treatment. It would be madness to keep him here."

" But, Dr. Frome——"

" Don't worry too much, Mrs. Selby. Quite a lot of my patients say they'll die if I send them to hospital and when they get there they settle down comfortably and decide to get better." He smiled at her kindly and went away.

Martin was moved into hospital that evening (by which time he was too ill to care) but he did not get better; he died of pneumonia three days later.

3

Anne had found it impossible to love Martin but she had not known her real feelings about him until now. She could grieve for Martin, of course—poor Martin had had a wretched life—but she could not grieve on her own account however hard she tried. It distressed her to discover that instead of feeling miserable without his companionship she felt as if a cloud had vanished from the sky. She ought to feel miserable, she ought to be lonely and unhappy, but she was not. Her neighbours were very kind. Mrs. Wight came in with a pathetic little gift of butter and a few spoonfuls of tea from her own meagre rations and besought Anne to " bear up."

" We all 'ave our troubles," said Mrs. Wight sympathetically. " I bin through a lot meself, so I knows. But you must bear up, dearie. You've got Emmie to think of, 'aven't you ? "

Anne could do nothing but accept the butter and the tea and the sympathy, all of which made her feel very uncomfortable indeed.

At half-past five in the afternoon (the hour when Martin usually returned from his work) Anne suddenly found herself singing cheerfully as she prepared Emmie's bath . . . and realised with a shock of horror what she was doing. The cheerful song broke off in the middle of a bar and Anne stood aghast, gazing before her unseeingly. She had been singing . . . because she was happy . . . because there was no chance of Martin appearing suddenly at the door and asking what there was to sing about in this miserable hole; asking why the baby was not in bed and what sort of muck she had got for supper and why the lamp was making such a confounded stink.

Oh, poor Martin, thought Anne. She sat down and cried.

This was bad enough but there was another feature of Martin's death which distressed Anne even more; she could not help wondering if she had done wrong in following the doctor's advice and allowing them to take Martin to hospital. Perhaps if she had kept him at home and done her best to nurse him he would have recovered. This was a dreadful thought. If this were true she was little better than a murderer.

Fortunately Dr. Frome seemed to understand exactly what she felt about it. He came to see her after the funeral and sitting down upon the settle by the window he explained the whole matter in simple words. He explained that Martin ought to have gone to a sanatorium at the very beginning and that if he had been properly treated the disease would have been cleared up in a few months.

" But he was so much better," said Anne. " He was almost well."

" No doubt he was better, but he wasn't cured," replied Dr. Frome. " The disease was there, ready to flare up on the slightest provocation. That was the trouble."

Anne nodded thoughtfully.

" That was the trouble," repeated Dr. Frome. " When I saw him on Tuesday I realised that there was very little hope; but there was just a chance that if we got him into hospital where he could be properly treated and skilfully nursed he might pull through . . . just the barest chance," said Dr. Frome earnestly. " If he had remained here there would have been no chance at all. Do you believe me, Mrs. Selby ? "

" Yes," said Anne with a sigh of relief.

Dr. Frome's visit relieved Anne of another secret fear, the fear that Emmie might have inherited her father's dread disease and that later on, when she was older, it might develop and cause trouble.

" Nonsense," said Dr. Frome. " That child is as fit as a fiddle; you have only to look at her."

They looked at her. She was playing in the little garden outside the window, running to and fro and picking daisies and laughing with sheer joy of life. Emmie was all Anne's. She had Anne's rounded limbs and clear complexion and soft dark hair, she had Anne's happy nature.

" Yes," said Anne, smiling at the sight of her darling. " Yes, it does seem silly to worry about Emmie."

" It's quite absurd," agreed Dr. Frome.

When Anne had recovered a little from the shock of Martin's death she began to realise her own predicament. She was penniless and very soon she would be homeless. Mr. Steele would want the cottage for another man to take Martin's place and work in the gardens. But Mr. Steele had other ideas; he came to see her and after offering her his sympathy he asked somewhat diffidently if she would care to take Martin's place herself.

" Me! " exclaimed Anne in surprise.

" Well, I just thought—— " said Mr. Steele. " I mean of course it's pretty hard work for a lady, but you could stay in the cottage and the little girl could run about the place—— "

" It would be splendid," declared Anne. " It's very good of you—very kind indeed. I expect you'll find me rather slow and stupid but I'll do my best."

Mr. Steele was pleased. It was almost impossible to get a man; any man he was likely to get would be old or unfit, a strong young woman was infinitely better value. Mr. Steele had not liked Martin Selby, who was a trouble-maker and extremely difficult to deal with, but he liked

K

young Mrs. Selby immensely. He thought it unlikely that he would find her slow and stupid.

" Well, that's all right," said Mr. Steele. " You start as soon as you feel inclined—the sooner the better as far as I'm concerned."

" I'll start to-morrow," said Anne.

4

Working in the gardens was tiring at first but quite soon Anne got used to it and her back ceased to ache. She had always loved flowers and it was fun learning how to grow them; vegetables were interesting too and how satisfactory it was to see them coming up in orderly rows and to know that one had helped to produce them! Emmie was very happy, she ran about the gardens all day long and made friends with everybody, for although Emmie was like her mother in most ways the shyness which had afflicted little Anne was completely absent in little Emmie.

The war went on but there was peace at Harestone, even the bombs did not bother them very much. Occasionally when there was a big raid on London the planes would come over the gardens and they would hear the guns firing but that was all.

Anne's only worry was money: she had got a fright, for she had realised that she had nothing behind her, nothing to fall back upon if she became ill. She saved money carefully and put aside a little every week; she saved upon everything except food—good food was necessary. Their clothes became more and more shabby—carefully patched and mended until there was little of the original garment left—and the furniture in the little cottage became more and more ramshackle.

Emmie had no toys (except what Anne could make from scraps of cloth and empty reels of cotton) but Emmie did not need toys when she could go out and play. In winter when the darkness came early Anne got out her mending and lighted the lamp and told Emmie stories. She retold all the old nursery favourites: Cinderella and Goldilocks and Jack the Giant Killer: and when these came to an end she told Emmie stories about Amberwell. Anne could talk about Amberwell for hours and Emmie never seemed to grow tired of listening.

" Tell me more about Ponticum," she would say. " Tell me about when you danced on the bowling-green; tell me about the mermaid fountain."

Soon after this Anne began to notice something a little odd in Emmie's manner. She had always watched over the child very carefully for in spite of Dr. Frome's assurance there was still a lurking dread at the back of her mind. If Emmie so much as sneezed she would look at her anxiously; if Emmie coughed she was nearly beside herself with terror. But this was not a cold, this was something different and in its own way equally alarming; Emmie had begun to talk to herself—or, if not to herself, to some invisible companion. The more Anne watched Emmie the more frightened she became. When Emmie went out of a door she would wait for a moment, as if there were somebody following her, before she shut it. When Emmie was called in to bed she would wave cheerfully and kiss her hand— to nobody.

One day when Anne was busy she asked Emmie to lay the tea and when she came in there were three places laid on the table.

" Is somebody coming," asked Anne in surprise.

" It's for Nell," explained Emmie.

" For Nell! "

" Yes, she said she'd like to come. You see she plays with me in the garden like she played with you at Amberwell when you were little." Emmie hesitated and then added in a lower tone: " Of course she's not really real, but I like having her for a little sister and playing with her. You don't mind, do you Mummy? "

Anne did not mind. It was all right as long as Emmie realised that it was make-believe. She looked at Emmie's round chubby face and her calm, widely-spaced eyes and realised she had been worrying herself unnecessarily. Emmie was as sane as a judge and as wholesome as an apple.

" You don't mind, do you? " repeated Emmie.

" Of course not," replied Anne. " It will be lovely to have Nell to tea. You can give her half your chocolate biscuit."

Emmie's chocolate biscuit was the one luxury allowed in that frugal household.

After that Nell often came to tea and sometimes stayed and went to bed with Emmie; they played "owls" together and talked themselves to sleep. Anne could hear them as she sat sewing in the other room and she had an odd feeling that it really was Nell—the Nell of long ago—who came and played with Emmie in Harestone Gardens.

Now, once again, Anne began to wonder if she should write to her parents . . . but although Martin was dead he still prevented her. Somehow she felt it would be a betrayal of Martin—he had hated Amberwell and all it stood for. That was one reason why she did not write; but there was another reason as well, far stronger and more practical. All her life Anne had been in subjection to other people and now, for the first time, she was free. She was independent, earning her weekly wage and spending it as she pleased. Nobody had any right to order her about or to disapprove of what she did. It was wonderful to be free. Anne knew very well that she would be free no longer if she crawled back to Amberwell as a humble suppliant.

So the days and months passed and Anne did not write.

5

When Emmie was five she went to the school in the village with several other children whose parents worked in Harestone Gardens. She liked school and learnt very quickly and soon she was clamouring for picture-books. The other children had books about rabbits and squirrels and Emmie wanted some too. It was natural of course but Anne grudged the money to buy picture-books; she had made toys for Emmie so why not a book? She bought a large exercise-book with firm cardboard covers and a child's paint-box and began her task.

At first Emmie was not very interested (she was a trifle disappointed, for this would not be a " proper " book) but quite soon she changed her mind and decided that it was much more fun to make your own book than to buy one in a shop. Miss Clarke had taught Anne the rudiments of water-colour painting and now, with a brush in her hand, Anne discovered that she had not forgotten the art.

Of course the book was all about Amberwell; it was all about Roger and Tom and Connie and Nell and Anne. It was all about what they had said and done and the fun they had had in the gardens. Anne and Emmie worked at the book every evening all that winter, Anne painting industriously and Emmie sitting beside her offering encouragement and advice.

" You must put in about finding the little saucer," said Emmie. " I like that story best of all . . . and you must put in about the mermaid. D'you think we could have a little picture of the mermaid?"

Anne thought they could.

It was fascinating to watch the book grow and take shape. The coloured pictures were very simple but Emmie was delighted with them. It was all such fun that they were both quite sorry when their task was finished.

The little book was so enchanting that Emmie could not part with it; she took it into the garden and showed it to Nell and one morning she took it to school with her. At lunch-time she returned home bursting with pride and importance.

"Mummy!" she cried, rushing in like a whirlwind. "Mummy, where are you? Mummy, listen, I showed it to Miss Haines and she says it ought to be made into a real book to sell in a shop so that lots of other children can read it."

"But that's nonsense, Emmie!"

"It isn't nonsense. Miss Haines really means it. She says she knows a man in London who makes real books. She says you're to let her know and she can arrange it."

"But we can't!" cried Anne. "It's Amberwell. They're real people."

"We'd get money for it," declared Emmie. "We want money, don't we?"

Most certainly they wanted money. Anne's life was a constant struggle to make one shilling do the work of two. "Perhaps if we changed all the names——" she began doubtfully.

"That's what she said!" cried Emmie, hopping from one foot to the other in her excitement. "Miss Haines guessed it was all real but she said we could change the names. Oh Mummy, do let's! Think what fun it would be if it was made into a real book! Oh Mummy, please!"

It was the money that tempted Anne. What a relief it would be to have a few pounds in the bank, to have something to fall back on if anything went wrong!

"You will, won't you?" cried Emmie who had been watching her face. "I'll tell Miss Haines."

"Well, we can try," said Anne reluctantly.

Miss Haines was extremely helpful. She helped Anne to alter the names, and showed her how to prepare the manuscript, and she took it to her friend in London who happened to be a well-known publisher.

Anne had heard about the wicked ways of publishers and expected to hear no more of the little book for months (and then possibly have it returned) but her experience was different, for in ten days' time the book was accepted and six months later it appeared upon the bookstalls. It did not make Anne's fortune by any means, but it sold reasonably well, and continued to go on selling, for a great many people (who were sick to death of books about piggies and pussies and darling little mousies) were only too glad to get hold of a sensible book about real children to read to their offspring. Anne was able to buy some new clothes for herself and Emmie and to put some money in the bank as well . . . and that Christmas they had a feast of chicken and plum pudding and a small Christmas Tree and there were real presents in Emmie's stocking.

# CHAPTER TWENTY-FIVE

THE WAR was over now, it had been over for eighteen months and the men who had fought in it were being demobilised and were coming home to the jobs they had held before being called up. Several men who had worked in Harestone Gardens were returning and Mr. Steele was obliged to take them back. He explained this to young Mrs. Selby and said regretfully that he was afraid he would need the cottage; he was afraid he must ask her to leave. Mr. Steele was unaware of Anne's circumstances; she was obviously " a lady " and therefore (in Mr. Steele's opinion) she must be quite well-off. He thought she had been working in the gardens as a war job, as an alternative to joining one of the Services, and now of course she would go home—to wherever her home might be. It never struck Mr. Steele for a moment that young Mrs. Selby was homeless and completely dependent upon her weekly pay.

" Yes, of course," said Anne, trying her best to smile. " Of course you must take back your men—that's only right. When would you like me to go? "

" Oh, perhaps in May if that would suit you," muttered Mr. Steele. The fact was he did not want young Mrs. Selby to go at all; it had suddenly occurred to him that he would miss her dreadfully.

Anne was to leave in May—and it was now the end of February—so she had three months to find another job. What could she do? Where could she go? If she had been alone it would not have mattered—any sort of job would have done—but there was Emmie.

Anne tried to get a post as housekeeper in a place where she could have her child; she answered advertisements until she was sick and tired of answering advertisements but nothing seemed to suit. Some people offered her a home without pay—or with so little pay that she knew it was hopeless—other people suggested that she should come to them herself and put her child into a home. There was one place which sounded as if it might suit her until she discovered that she and her child were expected to live in a basement. This would not do for Emmie. There were several posts in London—quite well-paid posts—but she was determined that Emmie must have country air.

The three months were passing and Anne had begun to feel quite desperate, so desperate that she was considering the possibility of swallowing her pride and asking Mr. Steele if he could let her stay on a little longer. She had a feeling he would. She had a feeling that he did not want her to go. Sometimes Mr. Steele looked at her in an odd sort of way which made her feel uncomfortable. Mr. Steele was very kind . . . he was rather too kind. She decided that whatever happened she would not ask Mr. Steele to allow her to stay on . . . but if she left the cottage where was she to go?

These thoughts went round and round in Anne's head. She lay awake at night, frightened and miserable.

2

One afternoon Anne was working in the garden of the cottage waiting for Emmie to come home to tea. She was planting out lettuces, a job which she usually enjoyed (for it was delightful to pick out the tender seedlings and tuck them up securely in their bed) but to-day she was not enjoying it for she would not be here to watch them grow. Where would she and Emmie be when the lettuces were ready to eat?

Anne had planted one line and had started another when she heard the squeak of the gate and Emmie's voice prattling gaily. Emmie was talking to Nell. Emmie was bringing Nell to tea, thought Anne smiling indulgently.

"Mummy is digging in the garden, I expect," Emmie was saying. "Mummy will be awfully pleased to see you."

The child's shrill excited voice carried very clearly in the still air . . . and then, as Anne listened, she heard the rumble of a man's voice in reply. It was not Emmie's invisible companion. It was somebody real—a man! Who on earth could it be? Anne's smile faded; she rose from her knees and as she did so Emmie came round the corner of the cottage dragging her visitor by the hand. He was a big man, tall and thin, with a head of silvery hair which shone in the afternoon sunshine.

"Here she is!" cried Emmie. "Here's Mummy, come and talk to her!"

Anne's heart gave an odd sort of leap; it was Mr. Orme.

"Anne, my dear child!" cried Mr. Orme, stretching out his hands.

"My hands—are dirty——" began Anne in a choked voice.

Mr. Orme took no notice, he strode across the lettuce-bed and seized both her hands in his. "I've found you," he said. "Thank God I've found you!"

Anne was speechless. Tears were pricking behind her eyes.

"Isn't it lovely!" cried Emmie, almost delirious with excitement. "Isn't it marvellous! He can stay to tea, can't he, Mummy? We've still got some of that lovely goodgy ginger-bread you made yesterday and there's one chocolate biscuit. He can have that, can't he? Shall I go and put on the kettle? Shall I, Mummy?"

"Yes," said Mr. Orme. "You go and put on the kettle. It will do us all good to have a cup of tea."

Emmie sped off, bounding like a ball.

"Oh dear," said Anne, trying to control her tears. "This is a funny way to—to welcome you. It's just that —I'm so—glad."

"I know," said Mr. Orme. "Perhaps I should have warned you I was coming, but I was afraid you might run away."

"Run away?"

"Well, I didn't know whether you would be pleased to see me—or not."

"Did they send you," asked Anne in a trembling voice. "Did Father—has Father—forgiven me?"

"Your father died," said Mr. Orme. "He died some time ago. It was Nell who sent me to you. Nell saw your little book and knew it was yours and brought it to me."

"Nell," said Anne in a low voice. "Yes, of course Nell would know."

"Nell loves you dearly, she has been very unhappy about you."

"Oh poor Nell—all these years——"

"All these years. We tried to find you before, but you seemed to have vanished. Why didn't you write?"

"How could I?" she asked, looking up at him with brimming eyes. "I had been told not to write—and I had been so—so foolish—and—and——"

"But I've found you," said Mr. Orme.

"How?" asked Anne. "How did you know——"

"Through your publishers," he replied. "I went to see them and got your address. It wasn't very difficult."

They talked for a few moments longer and then he put his arm through hers and they went in to tea. Mr. Orme did not bother her with questions for he realised that his sudden appearance had been a shock; later, when she had recovered a little, they would talk and he would hear Anne's story. He noted the poverty of the cottage; the mean little room, the threadbare piece of carpet on the floor, the poor shabby clothes which had been darned and mended so carefully—all these things told a story—but he noted too that everything was spotlessly clean and there was a little bowl of primroses on the well-scrubbed table. Anne looked thin and worn but the child was plump and bonny. She was so like the little Anne of long ago that he had picked her out from the other children as they crowded out of the school, and had asked her name. What other child except Anne's could have looked so like the " fairy " who had danced on the bowling-green in the thin grey overall? There was a difference of course. Anne had always been shy and silent (he had tried so hard to make friends with her and to win her confidence, but without success) but little Emmie was not frightened of him and certainly was not silent. It was Emmie's gay excited chatter that gave him an insight into their life.

" Wasn't it funny that you knew me? " said Emmie. " Fancy knowing me amongst all the others because I was like Mummy when she was little and lived at Amberwell! We talk about Amberwell a lot, you know. We wrote a book about it and drew pictures—at least Mummy did. I just helped. It was made into a real book that you can buy in the shops. We got money for it. So I could have a new dress for school and new shoes as well—and we had a Christmas Tree for Christmas. You see Mummy only gets just enough money to buy food—she gets it from Mr. Steele for working in the gardens—so it was very useful to have a little extra, wasn't it? "

" Mr. Orme doesn't want to hear about that," said Anne, trying to quell her excited little daughter.

" Doesn't he? " asked Emmie, quite undaunted. " Well

p'raps it's not very interesting. P'raps he'd rather hear about Nell. That's my little sister, you know."

" Oh, you've got a sister," said Mr. Orme smiling and looking round the room for evidence of another little girl.

Emmie laughed delightedly. " You can't see her, I'm afraid. She isn't real. At least she isn't real to other people—only to me and Mummy. You see I haven't got a real little sister to play with, like Mummy had, and it isn't much fun playing by yourself."

" I see," said Mr. Orme nodding. He was seeing a good many things and taking them all in.

" Do have some more ginger-bread, Mr. Orme," said Anne.

" Or a chocolate biscuit," suggested Emmie, handing it to him. " There's only one, because I ate the other one yesterday. I wouldn't have if I'd known you were coming."

" You eat it," said Mr. Orme.

" No," said Emmie earnestly. " No, I'd like you to eat it—honestly, I would."

" We'll cut it into three pieces and then we can each have a piece. How would that do? " asked Mr. Orme.

Emmie was delighted with the idea. She watched eagerly while Mr. Orme unwrapped the chocolate biscuit and cut it carefully into three equal portions. Anne watched too and again she was nearly in tears. How good he was—how understanding! She was glad he had come—and yet she was sorry. He will go away again, thought Anne. He will say good-bye—and go. It would have been better if he hadn't come!

" Isn't this a dear little cottage? " asked Emmie, taking her piece of biscuit and eating it with enjoyment. " Mummy and I like it awfully and we don't want to go away; besides we've got nowhere to go."

" We'll find somewhere to go," said Anne hastily.

" But there isn't much time, is there? "

"Go on with your tea, Emmie. Finish up your milk," said her mother. "You're talking too much."

### 3

Mr. Orme said nothing, but the little exchange of words was by no means lost upon him, and later when Emmie had run out to play in the garden he sat down upon the old wooden settle by the window and tried to make Anne talk. This was not very easy, for Anne was reserved and there was a pride in her which was hard to overcome, but Mr. Orme was patient.

"I don't want to interfere in your affairs, my dear," said Mr. Orme gently. "But you see I'm Nell's messenger and she'll think me a very poor sort of messenger if I go back to Westkirk without finding out all about you."

"It would take a long time to tell," replied Anne with a wan smile.

"Yes, of course," he agreed. "But perhaps you could tell me a little; at any rate you could try."

Anne looked at him sitting upon the settle with his silvery hair framed in the dark oak of the carved back. His fine old face was full of interest and sympathy.

"I'm not very good at telling people things," she said doubtfully. "And I don't know where to begin . . ." But all the same she managed to tell him something of what she had come through and Mr. Orme listened and nodded and occasionally prompted her with a question.

"Well, that's all, really," said Anne at last.

It was not all by any means (Mr. Orme was aware that there were big gaps in the story which Anne did not want to fill) but it was quite enough to show that her path had not been easy.

"That's all," repeated Anne. "The last few years have

been happy; I've enjoyed working in the garden and of course it suits Emmie to be here. I know this little cottage must seem very primitive to you, but it has been our home."

" Why are you leaving? " asked Mr. Orme. " Where are you going? "

Anne explained. She added, " One thing I'm determined upon, I'm not going back to London. Emmie must have plenty of fresh air."

" Emmie looks the picture of health."

Anne smiled. " Yes I know, but I want her to go on looking the picture of health. I must get some job which will suit Emmie."

" What sort of a job? "

" Oh, a housekeeper's job—I'm not fitted for anything else. I've answered dozens of advertisements for housekeepers but there's always some snag. Usually a child is an objection," added Anne, trying hard to smile. " Usually people prefer housekeepers without encumbrances."

Mr. Orme was silent for a few moments and then he said, " I need a housekeeper and a child would not be an objection."

Anne stared at him in amazement.

" Perhaps you'll think I'm mad," continued Mr. Orme with a helpless gesture of his hands. " I haven't thought it out properly—it's just a wild idea—but if you're really at a loose end and have nowhere to go——" he looked at her but she said nothing. She was speechless.

" It's just—a wild idea," repeated Mr. Orme. " You would have to think it over very seriously. It might be very uncomfortable for you—to come back to Westkirk—and of course there's your mother to consider. I can't tell you what she would feel about it. I simply don't know. She might be very angry and refuse to see you, or she might be glad."

" But you—if she were angry——" gasped Anne.

"It doesn't matter about me," Mr. Orme replied. "I'll risk it willingly. The whole thing has been so wrong—so dreadful—and this may be a way of putting it right. But if she refuses to see you I shall tell her what I think." As he spoke he threw back his head and his face grew stern. "I tried before," he continued. "I spoke to your parents several times but they wouldn't listen and it seemed to me that I was doing more harm than good so I was obliged to let it alone. It's different now that I've found you. There's more hope of bringing about a reconciliation."

"If Mother was very angry——"

"Well, what of it!" exclaimed Mr. Orme—and oddly enough there was a twinkle of humour in his eyes. "Listen, Anne. Seven years ago I was told, very politely of course, that the domestic affairs of the Ayrton family were none of my business. Needless to say I disagreed, for a shepherd's duty is to look after his flock . . . but it certainly is none of Mrs. Ayrton's business to interfere with my domestic affairs and if I choose to engage a housekeeper to look after——"

"Mr. Orme!" said Anne, trying to speak calmly. "Do you really mean it? Would you really have Emmie and me? She's a good little girl, and she—she wouldn't—bother you—and I'm quite a good cook—honestly—and—and——" suddenly she bowed her head to her hands and burst into tears. "Don't—say it—if you don't—mean it——" she sobbed.

"My dear child, I mean every word!" exclaimed Mr. Orme in distress. He rose and went over to her and patted her shoulder. "You shall come home with me," he said. "Now that I've found you I'm not going to lose sight of you for a moment. I shall take you home—both of you——"

"Kind——" murmured Anne brokenly. "So—kind ——"

"Not kind at all," declared Mr. Orme, running along at

a great rate and hardly knowing what he was saying in his desire to comfort her. " Not kind at all, just a selfish old man. I've been miserable ever since Mrs. Green left; I'm at the mercy of a daily help who comes in ' to oblige ' and is anything but obliging. You've no idea how dreary she is, poor soul; you've no idea how grudgingly she makes my bed and how reluctantly she cooks my porridge and how unappetising it is when she has cooked it—full of lumps— and sort of gritty, like sand. And the house is not as clean as I should wish. A little dust is nothing—I don't mind a little dust—and I used to think Mrs. Green was a trifle too particular—she was always polishing things and moving my papers so that I couldn't find them—but now things are positively dirty—and sad to say Mrs. Kenny herself is not very—er—particular about her own—er—personal hygiene —so you see, my dear, if you and Emmie will come and look after me I shall be the happiest man alive."

Anne had recovered a little. She looked up and smiled through her tears.

" That's right," said Mr. Orme. " That's splendid! It's all settled isn't it? I shall give you the same—er—salary that I gave Mrs. Green."

" But that would be—too much," said Anne. " You'll have to feed Emmie, and—and housekeepers with encumbrances always get less."

" Nonsense! "

" It isn't nonsense! Oh dear, I wish I could come for nothing, but of course I can't because clothes wear out— and shoes."

" I shall give you what I gave Mrs. Green—no more and no less," said Mr. Orme firmly. He smiled and added, " We shall be happy together—you and I and Emmie— and I know another person who will be happy too."

" Nell," whispered Anne.

# CHAPTER TWENTY-SIX

ANNE HAD told some of her long and complicated story to Mr. Orme, and now she told some of it to Nell—just the bare outline with all the miseries and agonies left out. They sat in Mr. Orme's study and talked, and all the time the flaxen-haired doll lay upon Anne's knee with its blue eyes staring at the ceiling. Anne had forgotten it (she did not seem to notice it at all) but Nell could not take her eyes off the doll; there was something almost horrible about it. The doll with its pink cheeks and staring eyes seemed part of the incredible story.

Every now and then Anne would break off in the middle of her narrative to ask about some member of her own family. Mr. Orme had given her most of the news but there were all sorts of things which Mr. Orme had not been able to tell her. Was Tom really happy in the Navy? How was Mr. Gray? Did Nannie still hold sway in the nursery?

Nell answered the questions of course. She answered them fully, and from various matters which cropped up in her replies she was led into further explanations. She found herself telling Anne about the night when she had gone to Carlisle to meet the unknown woman and little Stephen . . . and broke off to say " But I want to hear about you. It must have been dreadful when Martin died and you were left all alone with the baby. Weren't you terrified? "

" Terrified? " echoed Anne in surprise.

" Terrified of being alone—and dreadfully miserable! Oh poor darling, how miserable you must have been! "

Anne gazed into the fire. It was impossible to reply.

"Well, never mind," said Nell, misreading the cause for her silence. "It's over now. You're coming home to Amberwell."

"To Amberwell? Oh no! I'm staying here with Mr. Orme as his housekeeper."

"Anne!"

"Why not?"

"You can't! It's ridiculous! Of course you're coming home."

Anne shook her head.

"You *must* come home," declared Nell. "Roger said we were all to look upon Amberwell as our home. He mentioned you especially; he said if you could be found you were to come home."

"It was very kind of Roger but I'm staying here," said Anne smiling. "Mr. Orme needs me. The house is in an awful mess and the kitchen is absolutely filthy. It's a wonder the poor darling hasn't been poisoned! I'm starting to clean the whole place to-morrow morning, and I must wash all the blankets. You needn't look so surprised, I'm quite a good housekeeper."

Nell smiled too; she said, "I'm not as useless as I was in the old days. The war taught me a lot . . . but that isn't the point. Amberwell is your home, so——"

"No, it isn't any more. Besides you haven't told Mother about me, have you?"

"It's Roger's house."

"But Mother lives in it. No, Nell, you can't persuade me. I've taken on this job—it's a worth-while job to look after the dear old man—and I'm going to stick to it."

"But Anne——"

"And there's another thing; what should I do about money?"

"About money?" asked Nell blankly.

Anne could not help smiling. "Money to buy clothes," she explained. "Money to buy shoes and to have them mended; money to buy a toothbrush."

"Oh but—but you could——" She hesitated.

"You've never had to think about money—to buy a toothbrush," said Anne with just the slightest hint of bitterness in her tone.

Nell was silent for a moment and then she said, "But Anne, people will think it so funny."

This aspect of the matter had not occurred to Anne. It was years and years since she had worried about *what people thought*. Life had been much too grim and bare for her to bother about the opinion of her neighbours . . . but of course it was different here. She saw that quite clearly now that Nell had mentioned it.

"Will it matter very much?" she asked. "I mean people are doing all sorts of jobs nowadays, aren't they? Of course if it's going to make things uncomfortable for you Emmie and I must go away. I'll try to find another job."

"Oh no!"

"Well what? Look here, Nell," said Anne earnestly. "I've been on my own for years. I've been independent——"

"You could be independent."

"Not if I lived at Amberwell. You aren't independent, are you? You can't go out in the evening without a fuss. That's not being independent."

"Oh dear, I don't know what Mother will say," declared Nell. "She's getting old—and sometimes she gets muddled. I wish I knew what to do."

Anne hesitated, she saw that Nell was upset. "You can ask her," said Anne in a gentler tone. "If Mother wants to see me I'll come—and I'll be as nice as I possibly can—but nothing will persuade me to come back and live at Amberwell—nothing."

Nell gave it up. She saw how firm Anne was and how clearly she knew her own mind and she was obliged to admit that it might not work. People might think it a little odd for Anne to go to Mr. Orme as his housekeeper instead of coming home, but they would get used to it—and it was true that nowadays everybody was doing a job of some sort.

Nell's one object now was to reconcile Anne and her mother; if they could be " friends " everything would be smooth and pleasant. Anne could come to Amberwell when she liked; she could come and spend the day and bring the child—perhaps little Emmie would get on well with Stephen. On the other hand, if the feud continued, there would be constant friction, and everything would be very unpleasant indeed. It would be an impossible situation to have Anne living so near and not be able to see her without a fuss. She explained all this to Anne.

" I'll do what you think best," said Anne. " I'll come and see Mother to-morrow if you like. You had better tell her I'm coming."

" Come to-morrow afternoon, I'll meet you at the wicket-gate," said Nell.

It was late when Nell went home; they had talked for hours, but as she walked up through the gardens she remembered all sorts of things she wanted to ask . . . and somehow she did not feel very happy. It was strange that she did not feel happy (for she had seen Anne, her beloved sister, who had been lost to her for years) but the truth was she could not envisage the future. If only . . . thought Nell . . . if only I could persuade Mother . . . if only they could be reconciled . . . if only they would both be sensible!

2

The next day was fine and sunny. Nell set out for the wicket-gate soon after two o'clock taking Stephen with her. She had not said anything to Mrs. Ayrton. She had not mentioned Anne's name. Several times she had tried to broach the subject but her heart had failed her. Now, when it was too late, she realised how foolish she had been. She ought to have been brave, she ought to have spoken to her mother and prepared her. I've muddled the whole thing, thought Nell miserably. I'm just a coward, that's all. I'm no good to anybody.

As they walked down through the gardens she explained matters to Stephen.

" We're going to meet Aunt Anne," said Nell. " She's very nice. You'll like her."

" Aunt Anne? " asked Stephen.

" Yes, she's my sister. I know you haven't heard about her before but she's been away, you see."

The explanation seemed very weak but children accept things easily.

" Is she like you? " inquired Stephen.

" No, not very. She's more like Uncle Tom. She has a little girl called Emmie."

" It's a pity she hasn't a boy for me to play with. Are they coming to stay? "

Nell explained that they were staying with Mr. Orme and Stephen accepted that too—without the slightest sign of surprise.

" They can come to tea sometimes," he said. " We might go for picnics. It's a great pity Emmie isn't a boy, but even a girl might be better than nothing. Can we ask them to tea this afternoon, Aunt Nell? "

Nell did not reply to this. It was no use raising false hopes—perhaps she had done so already. "Look, Stephen, there's a spotted flycatcher!" she exclaimed.

Anne and Emmie were already at the gate waiting for them and after greeting each other and introducing the children they stood and talked. The meeting was slightly constrained for it was difficult to talk naturally with Stephen and Emmie standing by, listening to every word.

"Emmie is just like you," said Nell.

"Yes, I know. Everybody says so. Who is Stephen like?" said Anne, looking at him thoughtfully.

"Like his mother, I think. But he has a look of Roger, too. Don't you think so?"

This sort of talk did not get them very far when they were both thinking hard of something else and after a few minutes they began to walk up to the house through the gardens and the children ran on ahead.

Anne would have liked to walk in silence, and to look about her at the well-beloved scene, but she realised that plans must be formed and arrangements made before she met her mother. She had talked to Mr. Orme about this all-important meeting and had decided to be humble and ask forgiveness for her foolish behaviour. She felt it was right and Mr. Orme agreed. If her mother refused to forgive her she could do no more. She explained this to Nell.

"Yes," said Nell. "It's the only possible way. It wasn't your fault, of course (I never blamed you because I understood) but I'm sure it's the right thing to do." She hesitated for a moment and then continued in anxious tones, "I haven't told Mother. I ought to have prepared her but I was so afraid of saying the wrong thing. It was very cowardly of me, but I just couldn't. Mother is sitting in the lily-pool garden this afternoon, it's nice and sheltered for her, and I think perhaps the best plan would be for you to wait until I go ahead and tell her. Then I can call you, and you can come."

Anne sighed, she was being drawn back into the atmosphere of deception and fear. " You do understand definitely that I'm not coming to live at home? " she said firmly.

" Yes, but you will try to—to be nice to her, won't you? It will be so dreadfully difficult for everybody if she—if you can't——"

" I'll try," said Anne. She had said this before and she continued to say it quite patiently for she was very sorry for Nell and understood exactly what Nell was feeling. It was not so very long ago since she herself had been in thrall, terrified to open her mouth, practising all sorts of silly little deceptions to keep things running smoothly ... but now she had tasted freedom and found it sweet.

### 3

The two children had run on. Stephen was a little shy at first (he was not used to other children, in fact he knew no children except his Glasgow cousins whom he did not like at all) but Emmie was not shy and it was she who did most of the talking.

" It's frightfully exciting seeing Amberwell," she said. " Of course I know all about it. We made a book about it—Mummy and I—a real book that you can buy in a shop."

" About Amberwell? "

" Yes, and about the children: Roger and Tom and Connie and Nell and Anne."

" Roger is my Daddy."

" Yes, I know—and Anne is my Mummy so we're cousins. My Mummy is wonderful," added Emmie proudly.

" So is my Daddy," declared Stephen, not to be outdone. " My Daddy won the M.C. in the war. He's terribly brave. When I was a baby he saved my life. We were in London, you see, and there was a bomb, and the house was blown to bits and Daddy crept into the ruins and found me. What d'you think of that? "

Emmie thought it was marvellous and said so without reserve; even Stephen was completely satisfied with her reaction.

" Oh! " exclaimed Emmie, stopping suddenly and looking round. " Oh, this is the bowling-green! I didn't know it would be so big. It's simply huge, isn't it? And there's the stage where the children used to have tea—and the steps and everything."

" Yes, it's nice, isn't it? " agreed Stephen. " I can show you lots of other things too. I'll show you everything —I'll even show you Ponticum."

Emmie was aware that this was friendship indeed, and she was suitably grateful.

" Perhaps you'd like to see the lily-pool first," suggested Stephen.

" Oh yes—and the mermaid! " cried Emmie. " The dear little mermaid sitting on the rock. Will you turn on the fountain for me? "

Stephen was not allowed to turn on the fountain. Nobody was allowed to turn it on except occasionally Mr. Gray. " Well, I don't know," he said doubtfully. " The fountain is rather special." He hesitated for a moment—he was very anxious to please his new cousin—" But we'll see," he added. " P'raps if there's nobody about I might turn it on—just for a minute."

He led Emmie through the walled garden, pointing out

the potting-shed and the greenhouses and other objects of interest, and then they came to the sheltered garden, surrounded by trees, where the lily-pool lay asleep in the sunshine in the middle of its emerald-green lawn. It was even more beautiful than Emmie had expected. She stood quite still and clasped her hands in delight.

" We can't turn it on," said Stephen.

" Oh Stephen, why not? "

" Because that's Grannie, sitting on the seat."

He spoke in hushed tones for, like everybody else in Amberwell, he was frightened of his grandmother (Stephen was aware that you had to be very quiet when Grannie was present . . . and as a matter of fact it never occurred to you to be anything else. She did not talk to you of course but sometimes she pointed at you with her stick and said, " That child ought to have his hair cut " or, even worse, " That child's hands are dirty." Certainly Grannie was not a person to be trifled with.) This being so, Stephen was more than a little alarmed when his newly-found cousin suddenly came to life and darted off like a rocket and did not stop until she was standing in front of the seat where the old lady was sitting.

Emmie had known several old ladies at Harestone. There was old Mrs. Wight, who lived in the cottage next door. Mrs. Wight was a little queer in the head, but very kind and full of interesting stories about the time when she was young and had been scullery-maid in " The big 'ouse." Emmie was not frightened of old ladies, in fact she liked them.

" Hallo! " said Emmie cheerfully.

The old lady had been asleep but now she opened her eyes and looked at Emmie in surprise. " Anne! " she exclaimed.

Emmie was too intent upon her project to notice.

" Please," she said breathlessly. " Please could we turn on the fountain? "

" You are Anne, aren't you? " asked Mrs. Ayrton in a dazed sort of voice.

" I'm Emmie."

" Emmie? None of them were called Emmie. I thought you were Anne—but Anne went away years ago——"

" Anne is my Mummy," said Emmie smiling. " Lots of people think I'm just like her when she was a little girl— and of course you were asleep, weren't you? I often get muddled when I wake up suddenly."

" Do you? " asked Mrs. Ayrton vaguely. " I thought it was just being old."

" Oh no, everybody's like that. You're not *very* old, are you? You're not nearly as old as Mrs. Wight. Her face is wrinkled and she walks with two sticks."

Mrs. Ayrton was not really listening. The mists of sleep were beginning to recede from her brain. " Are you really Anne's daughter? " she asked doubtfully.

" Yes," said Emmie nodding. " Yes, and you're her Mummy aren't you? So Mummy belongs to us both."

The wide eyes, innocent and trusting and friendly, looked straight at Mrs. Ayrton; and Mrs. Ayrton, who had now remembered everything, was at a loss how to reply.

" Your mother——" she began sternly and then stopped.

" My mother is your little girl," said Emmie (who had often had to explain things very clearly to Mrs. Wight). " Of course she isn't a little girl now—she's grown-up—but she was your little girl long ago."

Mrs. Ayrton was silent. Emmie puzzled her for she was not used to this sort of child. Stephen was completely dumb in her presence and she had formed the opinion that he was stupid; Connie's children were noisy and ill-behaved.

" She *was* your little girl, wasn't she? " asked Emmie with a shade of anxiety.

" Yes," replied Mrs. Ayrton. What else could she say?

Emmie smiled in relief. " You aren't a bit like Mrs. Wight," she declared.

" Mrs. Wight? " asked Mrs. Ayrton vaguely. It seemed to her that she had heard the name before—but where? Names were very muddling.

" Oh, you don't know her," explained Emmie. " She lived next door to us at Harestone. She was much older than you and not nearly so pretty."

Mrs. Ayrton had always liked compliments and she had not had any for years. Nobody bothered to pay her compliments nowadays. " Pretty? " she said with a little smile.

" I think you're pretty," said Emmie frankly. " Very few people are pretty when they get old—Mrs. Wight was rather ugly—but you've got pink cheeks and silver hair, haven't you? "

" I suppose I have," agreed Mrs. Ayrton laughing.

The conversation had been so interesting that Emmie had forgotten about the fountain, but now she remembered it and drawing a little nearer laid her small brown hand upon Mrs. Ayrton's knee. " Please," she said wheedlingly. " Please may I see the fountain."

Mrs. Ayrton hesitated. It upset her to see the fountain playing, for William had always turned it on. It was William's prerogative to turn it on and off and somehow Mrs. Ayrton could not bear to see other people " fiddling with it."

" Please," repeated Emmie. " I do want to see it so terribly much. She's such a darling little mermaid, isn't she? "

They both looked at the mermaid.

" Yes," said Mrs. Ayrton, whose mind had wandered

back down the years. " Yes, she's rather sweet. I made a little sketch for them to copy—in fact I made several sketches."

" You drew her out of your head? "

" It wasn't difficult. I knew just how I wanted her to look; sitting with her tail coiled round the rock, and a shell in her hand."

" Does the water come out of the shell? "

Mrs. Ayrton nodded.

" I *would* like to see it! "

" But I don't know how to turn it on," said Mrs. Ayrton. Emmie recognised the signs of weakening. " Stephen knows," she said eagerly. " Stephen could do it."

During this extraordinary conversation Stephen had been standing some distance away. His instinct had been to fly and leave Emmie to her fate but somehow he felt it would be cowardly: so he had remained where he was, neither approaching nor retreating. His grandmother had not noticed him before, but now she looked up and saw him and beckoned to him.

" Turn on the fountain, Stephen," said Mrs. Ayrton. She rose as she spoke and walked over to the edge of the grass where the drops would not fall; Emmie followed her and they stood there together waiting.

Stephen hesitated. It was difficult to believe that Grannie really wanted him to turn on the fountain, but obviously she did or she would not have moved from the seat. He came forward and began to roll up his sleeves.

4

It was at this moment that Nell and Anne came round the corner of the house and stood at the top of the steps which led down to the lily-pool. They paused there in astonishment (the little group below them was quite unconscious of their presence). They saw their mother and Emmie standing together at the edge of the grass and Stephen kneeling beside the pool, searching for the handle.

" Can't you do it, Stephen? " asked Mrs. Ayrton impatiently. " If you can't do it yourself you must run and find Mr. Gray. Your cousin wants to see it playing."

" I've found the handle," replied Stephen. " It's rather stiff—that's all—but I think I can do it with both hands——"

Suddenly the water began to flow. At first it was no more than a trickle which spilled out of the shell and ran down the mermaid's arm; and then the water leapt up bravely, a column of silver glistening in the sunshine; the drops pattered into the pool and the mermaid was veiled in the shower. To-day there was a fitful breeze, so that at one moment the fountain was as round and smooth as an upturned wine-glass and the next moment the drops were wafted across the garden like a gauzy scarf of rainbows. As always there was enchantment in the sight and the audience of five watched it for some time without speaking.

Mrs. Ayrton tired of it first and signalled to Stephen to turn it off which he did without any trouble.

" Oh, thank you—— " said Emmie with a sigh. " It was just beautiful—— "

Anne had been waiting for this moment. She ran down the steps and across the grass. " Mother," she said breathlessly. " I've come to say I'm sorry—I was terribly silly—I think I must have been mad—— " She hesitated, for she was not sure whether her mother knew her or knew what she meant.

" I think we'll have tea," said Mrs. Ayrton. " It's been—rather a tiring afternoon and—and I feel a little—upset."

"Mother, this is Anne," said Nell who had followed Anne more slowly.

"We'll have tea," repeated Mrs. Ayrton. "It would be nice to have it on the terrace—the children would like that—but we shall need the larger table. You had better see to it, Nell." She turned to Anne and added, "Mrs. Duff always makes the tea too strong."

"Mother, listen——" began Nell in anxious tones, but a look from Anne stopped her.

"Run along, Nell," said Mrs. Ayrton.

Nell obeyed. She collected the children and went in to give the necessary instructions and to make the tea herself. It was a strange way to welcome the prodigal but Nell had never understood her mother.

Anne understood. She realised that her mother had become a very old woman (it was pathetic to see her so small and frail); she realised that her mother did not want to rake up the past and have a reconciliation scene —she was too tired. All she wanted was a cup of tea made as she liked it, hot but not too strong, with a little sugar in it.

"I expect you notice a sad change in the gardens," said Mrs. Ayrton, taking Anne's arm to help her up the steps. "Gray is doing his best to get everything put right but it will take a long time."

"I'd like to see Mr. Gray," said Anne.

"You can see him to-morrow. I wonder where Nell is putting you. Perhaps the blue room would be best."

It was now or never, thought Anne. "It's very kind of you, but we're not going to stay here," she said. "You see my husband died and I haven't any money so I have to work. I was working in a nursery-garden for a time, after Martin died, but that came to an end."

"Oh well," said Mrs. Ayrton doubtfully. "I suppose

perhaps . . . quite a lot of girls are taking jobs now. Mary Findlater was in the Wrens. It seems funny, but——"

" I'm going to Mr. Orme as his housekeeper."

Mrs. Ayrton stopped and gazed at Anne incredulously. " To Mr. Orme—as his housekeeper! "

" He needs a housekeeper and I need a job," said Anne with the utmost simplicity.

" Oh dear! " said Mrs. Ayrton in a trembling voice. " Oh dear, I don't understand things very well—the world seems to have got so topsy-turvy—sometimes I feel it was a good thing that your father died. He wouldn't have liked the world nowadays."

" There's Nell waving to tell us tea is ready," said Anne gently. " It will be nice to have tea, won't it? "